Half A Wo

Tom Bromley was born in 1972 and
grew up in York. He currently lives in London,
where he works as a copywriter for a publishing house.
His first novel, *Crazy Little Thing Called Love*, was
published by Pan in 2002. *Half A World Away*
is his second novel.

'Bromley's Coe-like confection . . . has
bags of charm, some neat ideas and a refreshingly
emotional candour'
Time Out London

Also by Tom Bromley

Crazy Little Thing Called Love

tom bromley

Half A World Away

PAN BOOKS

First published 2003 by Macmillan

This edition published 2005 by Pan Books
an imprint of Pan Macmillan Ltd
Pan Macmillan, 20 New Wharf Road, London NI 9RR
Basingstoke and Oxford
Associated companies throughout the world
www.panmacmillan.com

ISBN 0 330 48986 0

1 3 5 7 9 8 6 4 2

A CIP catalogue record for this book is available from
the British Library.

Typeset by SetSystems Ltd, Saffron Walden, Essex
Printed and bound in Great Britain by
Mackays of Chatham plc, Chatham, Kent

For Elizabeth Bromley

Acknowledgements

I would like to thank
Imogen Taylor, Simon Trewin, Andrew Gordon,
Kris Kenway, Tim Whiting, Louise Davies,
Jonathan Coe and Joanna Thurman.

Richard Madeley: According to the proverb, what makes the heart grow fonder?
Contestant: Love . . . booze, er . . . I don't know.

Midday Money, quoted in *Private Eye*

August 1996

1

Above the crowd, above the noise, above the hands with their waves and their claps and their V-signs, above the shouts and the screams and the heat and humidity, above the hardcore fans and the fair-weather day trippers, the touts and the dealers and the liggers and the bootleggers, above the burgers and the hot dogs and the chips and the onion rings, the tabs and the wraps and the cigarettes and alcohol, above it all, above all the mad-for-it melee floats a single solitary condom; colourless, translucent, inflated like a balloon.

It's almost slow motion the way it moves. Serene. Otherworldly. Out of time. It's the contrast, I think, that makes it so captivating: the singularity compared with the carpet of people below. That and the way it effortlessly sways from stage left to stage right, as though it couldn't care less about the concert we are all pushing and straining and stretching to see. The condom banks up with a burst, pauses, then skips and slides gracefully downwards, down and down and down until a hand reaches out and punches it skywards again, a small cheer echoing in its wake.

Condoms were called toggies where I grew up, though I never knew that at the time. If I close my eyes, I can still picture that fateful lunchtime, and the clumsy, cumbersome, out of control figure of Stuart Rugby running towards me in breathless excitement.

'Ben! Ben! Oh, you'll never guess what I've found.'

What Stuart had spotted in the corner of the playing fields was a 'used toggy'. The way he told it, you'd have thought he'd discovered America. Stuart, blessed with that keen teenage eye for ridicule and humiliation, was going to show his find to Vicky. 'Thickie' Vicky, as our class had christened her. With a tone bordering on disgust, he told me how not only had Vicky never seen a toggy, she *didn't even know what one was.*

'Are you going to come and laugh?'

I'd like to say I didn't go out of compassion for Vicky, that somewhere in my heart I felt a shred of sympathy for her plight as cast out, left out, underdog. The truth is that I would have been happy to put the boot in as much as anyone else; not because I didn't like Vicky, but because I didn't want the boot put into me. More than that, though, I didn't want my toggy ignorance to be found out. I had to decline.

'You show her,' I said. 'You discovered it, after all.'

'Don't you want to see the toggy?'

'It's all right,' I bluffed. 'I, er, saw three the other night.'

'Three?' Stuart was half-disgusted, half-impressed. Then he called me. 'Where was that?'

I thought hard about where one might find whatever a used toggy was, apart from in the corner of a playing field. 'Er, on a bus?'

'Eeeurgh.' Stuart pulled a face. 'Can you imagine?'

4

'I know,' I said.

I don't, I thought.

'I mean,' Stuart laughed, 'what about the conductor?'

What *about* the conductor? I laughed too, a little too late, a little too loud. If Stuart had thought about it, he'd have realised how full of it I was. Instead he slapped me on the back and said, 'You're some kind of toggy king, aren't you?'

Never was there a ruler with less claim to his crown than King Benjamin the First.

As the condom floats its zigzag way towards me, my thoughts turn from school to music, from toggy monarchs to former kings of rock and roll. In its small, strange, rubbery way, the condom reminds me of Led Zeppelin, an echo of the airship that gave them their name, the airship that adorns their debut album cover. Led Zeppelin, who defined the word debauchery, notorious for doing unspeakable things with fish and young females, Great Danes and groupies, who once sat down with their manager and road manager and sank 280 drinks between them. Led Zeppelin who headlined here seventeen years ago, at the last of the great rock shows of the seventies.

When Blur taunted that 'only wankers play Wembley', Oasis went one better and booked Knebworth. It was a smart move: Wembley's so eighties, so, well, *Live Aid*. This place is much, much more impressive – there's 125,000 people here today, the equivalent of Wembley *and* Old Trafford combined. Then there's the scenery: Knebworth House behind us, the stateliest of stately homes with turrets and spires and flagpoles and battlements;

country not industrial estate around us – sky and trees and fields and space – the sort of vista you don't get in the concrete wasteland of north-west London.

And then, *then*, then there's the history. Playing here is more than a gig. It's a statement. In the seventies, Knebworth played host to the very biggest and the very best. Pink Floyd headlined here in 1975, did 'Dark Side of the Moon' with a Spitfire flypast. Then came the Stones, Mick Jagger losing his pants in Queen Elizabeth the First's four-poster bed. When Genesis performed in 1978, someone gave birth. And finally, in 1979, Led Zeppelin blew in and topped the lot. Two nights, 400,000 fans. The biggest stage ever constructed. Amps turned so far up to eleven that there were noise complaints from seven – seven – miles away.

As the condom reaches me, a plane flies over. 'Who threw that?' someone shouts to much laughter, laughter that drowns out the companionable cheer that should have been mine. Almost anonymously I give the condom a prod, and watch as the wind catches it, watch as it floats further and further away. And as I watch it slowly slipping from view, I have a third and final thought. Sarah. Sarah my girlfriend. Sarah my girlfriend who is going away next week. Sarah my girlfriend who is going away next week to the other side of the world. Sarah my girlfriend who is going away next week to the other side of the world for a year. Sarah who is somewhere in this vast mass of people, who I can't see now, but I will shortly, Sarah who will light up with a smile when I see her, Sarah who'll soon be long, long gone. And just as I helped the condom on its way, so Sarah followed my advice that she should 'go for it'. Like the condom working its way across the heads of the crowd, she'll soon be drifting away from me, slowly, silently out of sight.

The queues at Knebworth have to be seen to be believed. The queue for the bar – I am not joking, I wish I was – is hundreds of metres long. I'm just glad that Oasis have suitably scored the undercard. Kula Shaker went on first, so you didn't mind too much whilst you searched and searched and searched for a parking space. Dreadzone coincide with the queue to get in. And when Cast come on, Sarah's reaction is to head for the toilets. Mine is to make for the bar.

'This is mental,' says the girl in front of me.

'Crazy,' I agree.

The girl is pale, with thick black eyeliner and thick black hair tied in girlie grrl-ie bunches. I would have guessed she was a Manic Street Preachers fan even without her bright orange Manic Street Preachers T-shirt. She just has that look, the look of a person who writes long, scrawly letters in green fountain pen.

'You must be glad you're here though,' I say.

'I'll be glad when I get to the front of the queue,' the girl smiles. 'I'm Jenna, by the way.'

'Ben.' I look at the queue snaking its way ahead. 'They should put signs up, shouldn't they? "Fifteen minutes wait from this point", that sort of thing.'

'As long as I get served before the Manics come on, I don't mind.'

'You're a bit of a fan, then?'

'You could say that.'

'The proper sort? The in-from-the-start fan, not one of the Post-Richey-I-quite-like-"A-Design-For-Life"-we-only-want-to-get-drunk hangers-on?'

'Absolutely. Don't you just hate it when people you don't like catch on to your favourite band?'

I smile. 'What are you doing coming to see Oasis then?'

'Well,' Jenna smiles back. 'They're a different category, aren't they?' She looks around. 'Look at this place. This is something else. Something special.'

I nod. 'I know. I feel really lucky to be here. I mean, I'm sure Loch Lomond was great, and seeing them at Maine Road would have been fantastic, but let's face it, this is the one, isn't it? The gig that people are going to remember.'

I'm certainly going to remember it, I think. My last day out with Sarah. Sarah, I think. She hasn't gone, and already I'm missing her.

'It's one of those defining moments, isn't it?' Jenna agrees. 'Like Jarvis Cocker mooning at Michael Jackson at the Brits. Like Blur and Oasis releasing singles on the same day . . .'

Blur versus Oasis. 'Country House' versus 'Roll With It'. The high noon of Britpop was the event that catapulted the scene from the *NME* to the tabloids and the *Six O'Clock News*. The moment when my music, our music, became important again, the moment when our bands became the brands of a generation, household names that even the oldest and squarest members of the household had heard of.

Blur versus Oasis. The event that started me and Sarah.

'I probably shouldn't be admitting this here,' I say, 'but I bought "Country House".'

Jenna pulls a face.

'I know, that's what my girlfriend thought. Well, she wasn't my girlfriend at the time, but she was soon afterwards . . .'

I'd bumped into Sarah in a record shop. She was brandishing a CD of 'Roll With It', I had a copy of 'Country House' in my hand. Sarah said she'd have to ask me to step outside. I said she was going to have to get her ears washed out. Sarah asked if the B-side of 'Country House' was 'Knees Up Mother Brown'. I wondered if the B-side of 'Roll With It' was 'Rocking Around the World'. Sarah said that at least Oasis don't put on a pseudo-cockney accent. I reminded her that Blur didn't describe daylight as 'sunshee-yine'. Sarah pointed out that Oasis don't sing about feeding the pigeons. I offered that Blur didn't sing about lasagne-yerr. Sarah said that at least Oasis weren't a bunch of soft-southern art school drop-outs. I proffered that Blur had a brain cell to rub between them. Sarah wondered if 'Country House' was about Daddy's little weekend retreat. I asked if 'Roll With It' was how Liam liked his saveloy and chips. Sarah said that at least Oasis weren't pony and trap. I replied that at least Blur weren't a load of number two. I added, rather cleverly I thought, that this was where Oasis were going to be on Sunday night. Sarah asked if I wanted a bet on that. I suggested that she really was a mad ferret, wasn't she? So we bet two pints, which Sarah bought on Sunday evening after the charts were announced. Sunday evening that turned into our first date.

'So I take it Sarah's here today,' Jenna says.

'Queuing for the toilets. I got her the tickets as a present,' I say. 'A going-away present.'

'Anywhere nice?'

'Japan,' I reply. 'On Tuesday. To teach.'

'Like you do.'

'Yeah, like you do,' I echo quietly.

'So how long is she going for?' Jenna asks.

'A year,' I say.

A year. It sounds so short when you put it like that. But when you convert it into months, into weeks, into days, into conversations, into editions of *Top of the Pops* and episodes of *EastEnders*, into evenings out and quiet nights in, into Sunday mornings and lazy afternoons, into rows and arguments and kisses and make-ups and birthdays and celebrations and job interviews and leaving-dos, into going out with her friends and my friends, seeing her family and my family, into breakfasts in bed and post-pub takeaways, into coffees to go and cups of tea, cups and mugs and pots of tea, if your mind begins to unravel the minutiae that makes up a relationship, then short is the last thing a year seems.

'And you're still going out?' Jenna asks. 'You're not splitting up or anything?'

'Why would we be splitting up?'

'I don't know. Some people do, don't they? A year's a long time to wait.'

I find myself taken aback a little. I hear myself saying, 'Maybe some things are worth waiting for.'

'Like the beer?' Jenna laughs.

'Exactly. Like the beer.'

The conversation is unsettling me somewhat. I look away and say, 'We haven't even thought about splitting up.'

Should we have thought about splitting up?

'That's *good*,' Jenna says. 'You don't have to explain yourself to me. Hey, I don't even know you.'

'So why are you asking if we're splitting up?'

'You're getting wound up over nothing,' Jenna says. 'All I meant was—'

'What?' This sounds more aggressive than it's meant to be.

'I didn't mean *anything*. I've had friends in similar situations, and some of them split up. That's all.'

'Well, every relationship is different.'

'Yes,' says Jenna. 'Every relationship is different.'

I don't like this exchange. It's one I don't want to have. Especially not forty-eight hours before Sarah leaves the country.

'These other friends,' I say. 'The ones who didn't split up.'

'Ye-es.' Jenna sounds uneasy.

'What happened to them?'

I want reassurance now. I want to hear stories of people who lived apart and got back together again, whose relationship survived and flourished and who got married and ended up living happily ever after. The end.

Jenna smiles, a little sadly. 'It's like you say, Ben. Every relationship is different.'

I swallow hard. I'd really like a drink, but it's going to be halfway through the next band before I get served. I don't want to deal with this right now. Today's meant to be about me and Sarah, about sowing seeds of love, not doubt. I look at Jenna, I look at the queue, and I turn around and walk away.

'What about the beer?' Jenna's voice follows me.

Every relationship is different. I hope mine is. I hope mine is.

Later, after the Charlatans and the Manic Street Preachers, after the crowd has played its long, long waiting game of Mexican waves and throwing rubbish around, after the sky has dipped from day to dusk to dark, the sun lighting up the low ceiling of cloud as it disappears behind the horizon, after the screens have flickered into life and teased us with ten long minutes of logos and video, after a countdown sequence that came and went, adding to the excitement, after Noel has appeared on stage and declared, 'This is history!', after his brother has replied, 'No it's not. It's Knebworth', after the exhilarating rush of the opening bars of 'Columbia', after 'Acquiesce' and 'Supersonic', 'Some Might Say' and 'Morning Glory', after a string-laden 'Whatever' and an acoustic 'Cast No Shadow', after 'Wonderwall', 'The Masterplan' and 'Don't Look Back in Anger', after an hour and a half of the most extraordinary concert I have ever seen, Oasis plays the opening bars of 'Live Forever' and it starts to rain.

It streams down, the stage lights and the spotlights lighting up the downpour's descent. Steam rises from the roar of the crowd, drowned and drenched and soaked to the bone. And as I hug Sarah from behind, my arms around her waist like a seat belt, I find myself thinking about my conversation with Jenna, and about the year ahead. Is it going to work? Are we going to stay together? Questions that Sarah and I have spent the last few weeks tiptoeing around, parcelled up like her boxes of books and clothes and belongings.

Sarah is swaying gently to the music, and I move too, echoing her movements. I hug her closer, press my head into her soft, warm hair, hair that's damp with drizzle and sweat, and I try to soak up the feel of her body against mine, trying to remember her smell for the days and weeks and months ahead. I'm misted up with the moment and the emotion, swept along with the sound of 125,000 people singing along to Liam fucking Gallagher singing just the best fucking love song. And I can't tell if it's rain or tears that are running down my face, but every time Liam hits his high note and Noel strikes that killer fucking chord the lump in my throat just gets bigger and bigger and bigger.

Ben Lawrence
Goodricke College
University of York
York YO10 5DD

Mr Gareth Marks
Labour Party Head Office
John Smith House
150 Walworth Road
London SE17 1JT

21 May 1995

Dear Mr Marks,

I am currently conducting some research for a dissertation I am writing for my politics degree, and am trying to set up a series of interviews with various informed people. I was given your name by my politics tutor, Stefan Svensson, who thought you might be able to help.

My dissertation is looking at the link between politics and the media, and how much the latter bears an influence on the former. I am particularly interested in hearing an 'insider's view' about the whole process and, considering your several years' experience working within the Labour Party, you would be perfect. The interview would only take an hour or so, and I am more than happy to do it on the record, off the record, in person, on the telephone, whatever you would prefer. I am planning to come down to London towards the end of

June, so if you are available then, that would be particularly useful.

I look forward to hearing from you soon,

Yours sincerely

Ben Lawrence

2

I got the call from Gareth three months ago, a month before my university finals.

I'd liked Gareth immediately; in his mid to late thirties, he was a sharp, solid, northerner, with a worn-in face and a stomach full of years of drinking his way from the local Labour clubs to the parliamentary bars. His eyes were small and deep-set, their mischievous twinkle belying his harder edge. He helped me enormously with my dissertation, introduced me to various people, pointed me in various right directions, was my quote for everything from my 'Labour source' and 'party spokesman' to my 'senior party aide'.

'Favour for a favour,' he explained. 'I want you to come and work for me at Millbank.'

In 1992, the Labour general election campaign was run and lost in the party headquarters on the Walworth Road, south London. This time, the party has rented out a mass of floor space in Millbank Tower from which to run the campaign. Millbank Tower is a monstrous sixties office block ten minutes walk upriver from Westminster, next door to the Tate Gallery, overlooking the Thames and the MI6 building opposite. It is built on the site of the house Tony Benn was born in ('Who'd have thought it?' Gareth sighed. 'Mandelson Tower has political roots.').

'We're putting together the team,' Gareth continued. 'All the bright young things we can find. When you interviewed me for your doodah, I thought you were sharp and on the ball. And now's your chance to make a difference.'

'How do you know I vote Labour?' I asked.

'It's an instinctual thing,' Gareth said. 'There was something about your tone of voice. The way you framed your analysis could only have come from a left-thinking mind.'

'Really?'

'Really. That and the fact you called Thatcher a cunt in the pub afterwards.'

I laughed.

'Ben, if you come on board, it's going to be bloody hard work. I know you're busting a gut for your finals, but that's nothing to how much effort you'd put in for me. But what's the point of spending three years studying politics if you're not going to do anything with it?'

I paused. 'Gareth, I understand everything that you're saying, but I've already got plans.'

'Cancel them.'

'I can't. Sarah, that's my girlfriend, she's got a job teaching English in Japan. And I've agreed to go out with her.'

'I see,' Gareth said.

'I'm sorry,' I said.

'No, no. Don't be,' Gareth said. 'It's your conscience, not mine.'

'What's my conscience?'

'Your conscience that if you arrive back in Britain next summer and the Tories are still in power, you don't have a problem with having done nothing about it.'

'Now hang on. That sounds like blackmail.'

'Only if you've guilty feelings about it.'

I didn't like this conversation.

'Ben, look, obviously it's up to you. But can I ask you one question?'

'OK.'

'Do you love Sarah?'

I paused. This wasn't the question I'd been expecting.

'Well, er, yeah. She's my girlfriend, isn't she? That's why I'm going to Japan with her.'

'Is it?' Gareth paused. 'None of this is my business, so if you want to tell me to bugger off at any point, please do so. I don't really know you and I've never even met Sarah so I can't really comment, but for what it's worth, what I reckon is this. I think you shouldn't go for your relationship because if your relationship is a good one, it'll survive the year apart. And if you're going to Japan because you want to go to Japan, then all I can say is that you can go and teach English there any time, but you can only work on a historic election campaign once in a blue moon and this is it, Ben. This is your chance at a little piece of history, and I think if you don't go for it, you'll always regret it.'

'Um,' I said. I felt confused, cross, excited; lots of nerves touched, competing for my attention. 'Um, what's the, er, pay?'

'You *are* a New Labourite,' Gareth laughed. 'Not much, I'm afraid.'

'How much is not much?' I asked.

'Well. Sod all actually.'

'And how am I meant to live in London for a year on sod all?'

'Are your principles not enough to keep you sated?' Gareth asked. 'I'm sure we can sort something out.'

'Great,' I said. 'You're really selling it to me now.'

'All right,' Gareth said. 'Listen, I know your mind's on other things right now, so why don't you tell me you'll think about it, and I'll leave you alone.'

'Well, I can go away and chew it over, but I still don't think I'll change my mind.'

'That's fine. Just tell me you'll go away and think about it.'

'Whatever,' I said, a little sarcastically. 'I'll go away and think about it.'

'Brilliant,' Gareth said. 'It's great to have you on board.'

'Hang on, I never said yes.'

'No,' Gareth said. 'Not yet.'

It's interesting, but when I put the phone down and Sarah appeared and asked me who I'd been talking to, I found myself lying and saying my mum. And then we went off to the library and I realised I was behind on my work and got stuck into revising my revision timetable for the nth time that week. And by the time I got down to the serious business of reducing my A4 notes onto small white pieces of card, I'd forgotten all about it.

In fact, Gareth went clean out of my mind until halfway through my second exam.

The paper was one of my stronger ones, Modern British Politics, and in that traditional four essays in three hours format that had served me so well over the years. My tactics, which an English teacher had taught me to follow for my A level mocks, was to do your second best question first, as a warm-up, a loosener, then your best, then your third best, and then your worst. Two, one, three, four. I'd started with question six about privatisation, cruised through question nineteen about the rise and fall of the SDP, and was halfway though question four – How similar are John Major's ongoing struggles with the Eurosceptics to Neil Kinnock's problems with Militant in the 1980s? – when it happened.

Neil Kinnock's speech to the 1985 Labour Party Conference was my political awakening. I was off school sick with flu and watched it wrapped in a duvet on the sofa. I've always liked Neil Kinnock. I know he can be naff – falling into the sea on Brighton beach when he was elected Labour leader, punching the air and yelling, 'We're all right' ten disastrous years later, but as a speaker he has a fire and a passion that given the right circumstances, can just ignite. On this particular afternoon in 1985, Kinnock's fur was up. His target was the Militants, the hard left of the party who were running councils so dogmatically that they were putting principles before people. The Militants saw Kinnock as sacrificing ideology in the hope of electoral success. Kinnock saw them as latter-day public schoolboys, who believed it was more important to play than to win.

'I'll tell you what happens with impossible promises,' Kinnock growled above the walkouts and the boos and the heckles of 'lies' from the back, 'you start with far-fetched resolutions. They are then pickled into a rigid dogma, a code, and you go through the years sticking to that: outdated, misplaced, irrelevant to the real needs.' By now the atmosphere was electric. The catcalls were continuing and getting louder but Kinnock was in full flight. 'And you end in the grotesque chaos of a Labour council – a *Labour* council – hiring taxis to scuttle round a city handing out redundancy notices to its own workers. I am telling you, no matter how entertaining, how fulfilling to short-term egos – I'll tell you and you'll listen – I'm telling you, I'm telling you – you can't play politics with people's jobs and with people's services or with their homes.'

And the hall erupts.

As I recall this halfway through answering question four, exactly the same as all those years earlier, I could feel the hairs on the back of my neck rise up, a shiver of cold flick up and down my spine.

It was then that I realised that I wasn't going to Japan.

It's the Monday morning after Knebworth. I'm sitting alone in Sarah's parents' kitchen in Cambridge. Sarah's gone to say goodbye to her aunt and uncle. I've feigned a hangover, so I can write her a farewell letter, slip it into her suitcase as a surprise for when she arrives.

It's a nice, solid, traditional English kitchen, with a large pine table and six wooden chairs as the centrepiece. Dried flowers hang from the ceiling in bunches. In the opposite corner to the door sits a green Aga. I'm writing but I'm distracted by the newspaper, yesterday's *Sunday Times*, left out, I'll bet, by Sarah's dad to wind me up. The paper's folded open to an inside page, to a full-page advert by the Conservative Party. NEW LABOUR NEW DANGER it reads. The picture is a photo of Tony Blair, but with a 'rip' across the page at eye level, a black strip punctuated by two red, demonic eyes.

Every time you think election material can't descend any lower, somehow it finds a way of doing so. The 1979 'Labour Isn't Working' poster, complete with its long snaking queue of unemployed people outside the dole office – 'unemployed' people who were in fact a small group of Young Conservatives photographed over and over again – looks now like the model of subtlety. By 1992, the standard had dropped to 'Labour's Tax Bombshell' that, just in case you didn't get the message, showed a picture of a big black bomb. And now there's this. The press ad with its sinister eyes, the suggestion that there is something *evil* about Blair, about Labour, is cold, clinical, cynical. As I sit there, the steam from my coffee spiralling towards the ceiling, the half-finished letter to Sarah lying accusingly across the table, all I can think is, What on earth am I letting myself in for? I've given up a year abroad with my girlfriend for this. I'm not sure I'm up for months of muckraking and mudslinging. That's not me. What the hell am I thinking?

'What the hell are you thinking?' That was Sarah's initial response when I told her about Gareth's offer.

'I know it's out the blue . . .'

Blue/red, red/blue.

'. . . but it's something I think I should do. I think if I don't do it, I'll regret it later. I mean, I can go and teach English in Japan any time, but I can only do this now.'

'You can't teach English in Japan with *me* any time,' Sarah said.

I hadn't thought of that.

'What about us?' Sarah continued. 'I won't see you.'

'I think it'll be good for us,' I said. 'It'll be a test.'

'A test?'

'Yes, to find out if we're meant to be together or not. Think about it. If we can survive a year apart, then we can survive anything. By not coming with you—'

'You're what? Showing how much you care for me?'

'I'm showing how much faith I've got in the relationship. If we're going to be together for years and years, then what difference is a few months going to make?'

Sarah pulled a face.

'Sarah,' I said. I thought this might happen. Which is why I said what I said next. 'What if we got engaged? Would that make you feel more secure? Would that make you more comfortable about being apart?'

Sarah's face was difficult to read. Then, gradually there was a glimmer of a smile from the right side of her mouth.

'It might,' she said.

I reread the letter that I'm meant to be writing. *I think it's important to remember that this year's going to be different for*

you than for me, I've written. *You're off to the other side of the world to do new and exciting things. I'm the one left behind. We're going to be approaching this from different angles, and it's good to lodge that thought from the start. If we both remember where the other is coming from, then I think we're going to have a far better understanding of where we're going.*

It sounds, I think, more confident than I'm feeling. If only I was that together. *A far better understanding of where we're going?* A modicum of understanding of where we're going would be a start. The more I think about it, the more uncertain I feel. My mind echoes with the conversation I had with that girl at the Oasis concert: a year's a long time to wait, she said. Sitting here, in Sarah's kitchen, for the first time it hits me just what a long time it is.

I notice a picture on the kitchen wall. A family photo of Sarah, her parents, her elder brother, Jeb, hugging and smiling at some family wedding. It's from a few years ago, before I knew Sarah, but all the things that attracted me to her – the scraped-back explosion of hair, her huge welcoming grin, her long, elegant neck – all are captured perfectly. She's leaning forwards towards the camera: her eyes are alive, she's laughing. I'm going to miss you, I think, and pick up my pen.

The reason for writing, I continue, *is to tell you how much I'm going to miss you over the next twelve months, whether you (and I) like it or not. Not*, I think, *on the whole*, I pause, smile, then add, *(though I can appreciate you might get some sort of twisted comfort from the fact that I'm back here pining for you). You're very special to me, Sarah, otherwise I would never have undertaken to put myself through this. I wouldn't have done so without the highest of expectations that our relationship is . . .*

I hear a key scratch in the lock. The door opens and I hear a question.

'Ben?'

Sarah?

'In here,' I say. What are you doing back? I think. I've only just got time to slide the letter into the newspaper before Sarah appears.

'Hey there,' she says. 'What are you up to?'

'Nothing,' I smile, a smile that freezes as I see Sarah glance down at the newspaper. 'What?' My eyes dart round frantically. Is the letter sticking out?

'*One of Labour's leaders Clare Short says dark forces behind Tony Blair manipulate policy in a sinister way,*' Sarah reads the small print out loud. 'Quote. "*I sometimes call them the people who live in the dark.*" Is that you, Ben? Are you a dark force?'

'Grr,' I say.

Sarah laughs, unzips her coat. 'Can I have a cup of tea?'

'Would you like me to make it in a sinister way?'

'Just with milk will be fine,' she says, kisses me on the forehead and disappears to hang her coat up.

Dear Sarah,

Sarah? Sarah, is that you? What the devil . . . what are you doing here? Oh, it's your new home, is it? Right, right. Well, welcome. Yes, no I do like it. Very much so. You've got a good choice of colours going on, haven't you? Bags of natural light, buckets of space. There is something missing though, don't you think? One of those, oh what do you call them, they're kind of 5 foot 10 (when they stand up straight), with scruffy hair, bad breath and a penchant for belching. What's that? You've left yours behind? Probably wise, they do tend to start smelling the place out after a while.

Fancy finding you here. Sorry, that's a bit verbose, isn't it? Fancy finding you. No, that's still too long. Fancy finding. That doesn't seem quite right either. Hmmm . . . but wait . . . what if I . . . oh yes, of course! Got it now.

Fancy you.

I have, I have to confess, a confession to make. Do you remember the Monday morning before you set off for Japan? The morning after Knebworth, when we woke up after four hours' sleep with the sound of 'Champagne Supernova' still ringing in our ears? The morning after getting in at three thirty on account of the tens of thousands of cars attempting to get out of the concert car park at the same time. The morning when I suggested that maybe I wouldn't be having coffee with your Aunt Thing and Uncle Whatsistod on account of my exhaustion and migraine and the hangover I had hanging over me. And

26

after a short and perhaps not entirely sympathetic response from your good self, during which the words 'bed', 'made', 'lie' and 'it' were used, you stormed off alone, leaving me, somewhat ironically, to lie in the bed that you'd made up for me.

That morning is in fact this morning. Hi there! I am tired and I think I may well have got tinnitus, but I'm not half as bad as you may have been led to believe. You see, it was all an act, a pretty paltry one maybe but an act nonetheless, an exaggeration to carve out a couple of hours to write you a letter – this letter – and thence to secrete it cunningly in your suitcase, a surprise for when you arrive and unpack.

Anyway. Here I am, sat at your kitchen table. The sun is streaming in, making an elongated rectangle of light on the floor. It's odd, I have to say, being in your home without you. Just as it's odd seeing all your things pre-packed and sorted into piles in your bedroom. I went up and had a look just now, at the stuff you're taking to Japan, at the second selection of belongings, the collection of records and novels and pictures and posters and odds and sods for me to look after. There's not much between the two piles, a carpet strip all of a foot or so, but already the dividing line is being drawn between you and me. The separation of the clean from the unclean (I'll have a shower later, promise). It's only a matter of inches now, but by the time you read this letter the gap will have grown into thousands and thousands of miles, as our relationship is stretched to include the words 'long' and 'distance' in its definition.

I'll look after your stuff, of course I will, but I should warn you that they're liable to become as much longings as belongings to me. They're only a few of your favourite things, after all, and their presence may only remind me where the rest of your possessions are. What's the best thing to do with them, I wonder? Is it better to have them around or hide them away? I know it would probably be a bad idea to play your records – that's what I normally tell you, after all – but the topsy-turvy truth is that I'm likely to end up listening to the very albums I frequently implore you to turn off.

I've never been in a long-distance relationship before, Sarah, as you might be picking up. And, as you might also be deducing, I'm not too sure how to behave. The only time I've come close to being in a similar situation was my pre-university pas de deux with Gemma, but we – OK, she – decided that short term was preferable to long distance, and sent me packing before I could get value for money out of my Young Person's Railcard. As dumpings go, it was cloud-shaped with a delicate lining of silver – it meant I was single when I met you. But had Gemma put up with me for a couple more months, however messy things might have got, at least I'd have lost my long-distance virginity, and I'd know what to expect in the coming weeks.

I think it's important to remember that this year's going to be different for you than for me. You're off to the other side of the world to do new and exciting things. I'm the one left behind. My point is that we're going to be approaching this from different angles, and it's good to lodge that thought from the start. If we both remember where the other is coming from, then I think we're going to have a far better understanding of where we're going.

The reason for writing is to tell you I love you and how much I'm going to miss you over the next twelve months whether you (and I) like it or not. Not, I think, on the whole (though I can appreciate you might get some sort of twisted comfort from the fact that I'm back here pining for you). You're very special to me, Sarah, otherwise I would never have undertaken to put myself through this. Likewise, I wouldn't have done so without the highest of expectations that our relationship is . . . built to last. Which is why I'd like to propose the following. However we end up keeping up with each other, I think we should both put aside a couple of hours a week to write a proper letter, a love letter if you like. Cost aside, you know what I'm like on the phone after all; this way, we can really compose and contemplate and try to communicate with each other. Emails are fine and everything, but they kind of put the funk into functional, if you know what I mean. Letters are romantic – we get to see each other's handwriting rather than some badly typed Times New Roman derivative. And I don't know about you, but when it comes to fonts, that Sarah Brown one, point size fourteen and two thirds, has always been my favourite.

And here comes the clincher. When we're old, we'll be able to show our letters to our grandchildren, to explain how we stayed together. Actually, bugger the grandchildren – the letters can go in my literary archive. They'll be screaming out for a nice slim Faber and Faber paperback: *Over Here and Over There – The Love Letters of Ben Lawrence and Sarah Brown.* OK, I'll tell you what – we'll dedicate them to our grandchildren, how's that for a compromise? I don't know about you, but I like the idea of creating a testament to our love.

Do you know what I think about long-distance relationships? I think it's all in the name. If things go pear-shaped, then the buzzword becomes 'distance', as the physical gap stretches into an emotional one as well. However many thousands of miles away you are, Sarah, it's vital that that's as far as it goes. Because if we achieve that, then in a year's time the key word becomes 'long'. In fact, the 'distance' part disappears completely, as our long-distance relationship progresses into a long relationship instead.

Fancy finding you here. Fancy finding you. Fancy finding. Fancy you.

I'll be missing you and thinking of you.

All – and I mean all – my love, Ben x

PS Blue. The ones with the button.

3

On the Saturday after I've waved Sarah goodbye, watched her plane rear upwards and then away, slicing through the sky at forty-five degrees, ratcheting up the altitude, banking right for a hole in the clouds, on the Saturday after I've seen Sarah's plane disappear into the horizon I find myself staring at the sky again, at the clouds and the sun and the planes overhead. But this time, the rooftops of London are from a different angle. This time I'm in Greenwich Park with Sarah's best friend, Bex, looking out across London from the Royal Observatory, past the railings, the park dropping away below, scooping down to the precise perpendiculars of the naval college, the rich curve of the Thames and the Isle of Dogs beyond it, the Docklands and the shining tower of Canary Wharf, the white light winking from its pyramid top, to the familiar fuzzy skyline of the capital beyond.

I'd like to be looking at other things from a different angle too. But I'm not. Not yet. It's been five long, slow days since Sarah left, five days without a letter or a postcard or an email or a phone call, just a message from her mother saying she's arrived safely and she'll write soon. I've felt numb, sure, but above all I've been bored, frustrated, listless. I guess it's because our lives were so intertwined that I've been feeling at such a loose end. What's that line from 'Big Yellow Taxi', the one about not knowing what you've got until it's gone? Right now, I reckon Joni Mitchell's got it just about spot on.

'Careful.' Bex nudges me from behind. 'You're about to reach the end of the line.'

Bex and I are on the meridian line, the thick strip of brass embedded in the cobblestones that stretches from north to south, the line that marks nought degrees longitude, the precise point where east meets west. We're tiptoeing along it, one foot in front of the other as though it is a tightrope, hands out to balance ourselves. I look down at my feet. She's right. Delicately, and with the poise that would wring a round of applause from a circus audience, I spin round on the spot, one foot in the air, one hundred and eighty degrees, until I'm facing Bex.

'Almost balletic,' she laughs.

Bex, as ever, looks in the full flush of health. Whereas Sarah and I look white and pale even in the midst of summer, Bex's skin is soft and tanned and rich and radiant. Her swishy black bob is tucked in behind her ears, she is smiling in the sunshine, her pale pink polo shirt accentuating her small, curvy, gym-toned figure, a figure which she is constant need of reassurance about despite the fact she looks great. 'Scrumptious' is how Sarah describes her. 'Baptastic' is how her boyfriend Si puts it. Indeed, on his first attempt to chat her up, he suggested they got married, if only so the readers of *Readers' Wives* could see what they were missing. 'One wanker is more than enough for me,' was Bex's response.

Bex and I are living out here in a beautiful three-

bedroom flat overlooking Blackheath Common, fortui-
tously owned by Bex's absent aunt, away doing diplomatic
duties at the British Embassy in Brazil. Bex, after months
of indecision, and toying with doing a PGCE, finally opted
for the law conversion course at City University. 'Do you
want to see my briefs?' Si tried again. 'Shall we strike that
last comment from the record?' Bex replied.

Si is a good friend of mine from uni, a fact he also
tried to use. 'Two best mates with two best mates,' he
argued. 'Just think of the foursome we could have.' Bex
gave him two fingers, twice, but eventually, I think it
was his persistence more than anything, she stopped
finding his charm offensive offensive and, despite everything, was unable to stop herself giving in. And by the
time Si left for Cuba, a fortnight before Sarah set off for
Japan, to teach and to travel, despite herself she didn't
want him to go.

Bex is standing on the meridian line, rocking backwards and forwards on her heels, facing west.

'Can you see him?' I ask.

'Not quite.' Bex looks at her watch. 'I'd like to think
he's fast asleep in bed, but I reckon he's more likely to be
crawling home from the pub. Can you see Sarah?'

I look east, up above the park and the trees to the sky,
to the sun. I like the sun, because if it's early morning
here it's late afternoon there, we're nine hours apart but
we're still on the same day, and I like to think that even
though we can't see each other, we can both see the sun
at the same time, it's something we can still share. And
maybe, just maybe, the sun can act as a mirror, its warmth
reflecting our feelings for each other.

My God, I think. Five days in and I'm coming over all New Age.

'Yes,' I say. 'Yes, I kind of think I can.'

Bex stands on tiptoes, puts her hand to her forehead like a sailor looking out to sea. 'It's funny,' she says. 'Here we are, walking up and down nought degrees longitude, like this is the measurement that matters, whereas what really counts,' her smile as she turns to me is a little wistful, 'is how much latitude we've given them.'

Si, I feel, is not exactly living at nought degrees latitude.

'Cheers.' He clinked a beer bottle against mine, the week before his departure. 'Here's to our year of freedom.'

Si is, in almost every respect, bigger than me: bigger bodily, with his rugby boy build (league rather than union); bigger characteristically, more confident and cocky and outgoing and gregarious; bigger boozily, however much I large it, he always larges it larger; bigger collectively, be it CDs or magazines or stories or anecdotes; bigger footed, 'And you know what they say about men with big feet,' he'd wink. Unlike some people whose frame feels too much for them, who bend and crouch and stoop to compensate, Si fleshes his physique out to the full. He has a laugh as welcoming as his eyes, and a baseball cap that never leaves his head, dark blue and emblazoned with two words in white. King Size.

'It's like this,' he told me, not to mention half his local, given how loud his voice was. 'A year without your girlfriend is a long time. Too long a time. And that's not an opinion, Ben. As far as I'm concerned that's scientific, spermatological fact. A man has his needs, you know what I'm saying?'

'Sort of,' I agreed. 'So what are you going to do about it?'

'Well. If you're going to be apart, I reckon you've got yourself three options to choose from. Option one, right, is what's known as "shagging everything in sight".' Si made the inverted commas with fingers as way of an illustration.

'Right,' I said. 'And Bex has agreed to this?'

'If you'll let me explain. You see, it's not as simple as that.'

'It's certainly not,' I said. 'What if everything in sight doesn't want to shag you?'

'Just you cast your mind back to last week. Caesars? The barmaid?'

'Si, the only thing that girl wanted from you was a tip.'

'Well,' Si leaned back nonchalantly, 'it's not my fault if some people find me too big. I'm getting off the point here. The point is, the point is—'

'You're quite pissed, aren't you?' I laughed.

'Piss off. The point is that while it's fine for people like me to go for such an option, for someone like yourself lacking the, how can I put this, the necessary *prowess*, you're only going to end up disappointed.'

'I think you're mistaking prowess for having such low standards you'll sleep with anything that moves.'

'Plus, and here's where even I fall down, the chances are that your girlfriend's not going to agree to this option.'

'No shit, Sherlock.'

'Option two,' Si continued, 'is the opposite extreme. The "holier than thou" option. We're talking a total vow of celibacy here. No nookie of any description, no shufti, no tugging, no blowing, nothing. Nowt. Zero. Zilch.'

'I think I'm getting the idea here.'

'Now I'm not saying this option doesn't have its plus points. For someone like you, having a year without sex is a welcome reversion to type.'

'Ha ha.'

'Seriously though, it gives your girlfriend a great sense of security, reassurance that she can trot off to the other side of the world without her partner packing them in back home. All of this is great, if you're a saint. But as far as I'm concerned, it's just not practical.'

'So?' I asked. 'What's option three?'

'Option three,' Si smiled, 'is to cut yourself a deal. Option one's not going to happen, option two's too much, so you need to strike a balance in between. Say, shagging is out, snogging is in.'

'Are you saying that Bex has agreed for you to get off with people, as long as you don't sleep with them?'

Si smiled as he swigged from a bottle. 'All those Cuban cuties, those mulatto melons, that Caribbean butt . . .'

'I'm guessing you didn't pitch this option in quite these terms.'

'Well, not exactly—'

'How not exactly?'

'We, er, agreed, that this is a last resort, that this was acceptable behaviour in exceptional circumstances.' Si smiled again. 'But this is just detail.'

'Well,' I said. 'I can understand what you're saying, but

I have to say, I'm not sure you've made the right choice. Just supposing, and this is clearly a very hypothetical example, just supposing you meet one of these hot Cuban babes. And let's get really far-fetched and suppose she snogs you. Well, and I know this sounds really ridiculous, but maybe she says, "Si, I want you. I need you inside me now, come on, English lover boy, give me a seeing-to with your big Brummie sausage." And, because of your agreement with Bex, which I'm *presuming* you're going to stick to, you're going to have to say, "Thanks for the offer, but I'm afraid I'm going to have to decline." Now, I don't know about you, but for me I would find such a situation tremendously frustrating. If you're going to have an agreement, how are you going to be satisfied with that? Why don't you just agree that you can fuck other people while you're apart?'

'Because,' Si said, a little quieter, and a little more uncertain, 'because no bastard is going with my girlfriend.'

'Well, you say that,' I continued. 'But what have you agreed to? Bex can't shag anyone, but there's still plenty to do. Think of all those law students feeling her up, copping a feel as they stick their tongue down her throat, slipping their hands down and—'

'Thank you, I think I get the picture,' Si said. 'Of *course* I don't want anyone else going anywhere near Bex, but do you think I'm stupid? Do you think I didn't take her particular circumstances into account?'

'What particular circumstances?' And then I twigged. 'What? The fact that she's living with me?'

'*Absolutement.* Who better than my good mate Ben to keep his beady eye out, to remind any potential suitors just how hard her boyfriend is.'

'Am I allowed to use artistic licence?'

'Funny.'

'You know, I'm not going to be able to chaperone your girlfriend all the time.'

'You can try,' Si offered.

'I guess,' I sighed. 'I think you're mad.'

'I take it that Mr and Mrs Britpop are going for option two then?'

'*Absolutement*,' I parodied. 'And stop calling us that. We've only just got engaged.'

'Well, all I can say is good luck to you,' Si said. 'I think you're asking too much. Someone will crack. Save your relationship and do a deal before it's too late.'

'We've done a deal,' I replied. 'The deal is that Sarah is going for one year and one year only, during which she's going to come back, probably at Christmas, and I'm going to go out there, probably after the election. You're the one who's got the problem, not me. You're tempting fate. All that's going to happen is that one thing's going to lead to another. Rescue your relationship and scrap the agreement now.'

'Bollocks. You're the one who's got it wrong.'

'I think you'll find that's you that is.'

We sat there in silence, both flared up, both looking away. Eventually, and it was a good thirty, forty seconds or so, it was Si who broke the ice.

'Well,' he said philosophically, draining his pint, 'I guess that's somebody fucked.'

Si and Bex called us Mr and Mrs Britpop from the start, the fact that it was the Oasis versus Blur thing that got us together. In those heady early days, it was a joke we didn't mind – as Jarvis Cocker waved his bum at Michael Jackson, as *Morning Glory* turned out every bit as great as *The Great Escape* if not greater, as the nation retuned to Radio One and Chris Evans ruled the airwaves, as *TFI Friday* and *Loaded* continued the feel-good factor, as Paul Gascoigne jinked the ball from foot to foot, over the head of Colin Hendry and into the back of the goal, as Britpop blossomed and bloomed, being young, British and in love seemed the best thing in the world. As Pulp might have put it, being one of the common people was like being in a different class.

But the problem with buying into the joke, with buying into the myth that somehow this was *our* music, *our* time, is, what happens when things start to crack? And at the end of August, a fortnight after Sarah left, the first fissures begin to show. Fifteen minutes before take-off for Chicago and the US tour, Liam decided he wasn't going to the States after all. He was escorted back through customs, his luggage was removed from the plane. 'I'm not doing the tour when I've got nowhere to live,' he told the press. 'I don't care about the tour, I'm sick of living in hotels.'

I don't know about butterflies in China causing tidal waves on the other side of the world, but this rock star refusing to fly is sending a shiver down the spine of my relationship.

Dearest Ben,

Hello, darling, how are you? You must excuse me if my writing is a little bit wobbly in this letter, but I've come up into the countryside to chill out and write to you. Sounds slightly batty, I know, but if you could see what sort of evening it is here, I think you might understand why I'm here.

I wish I had a way with words like you do, because whatever I say, I don't think I'm going to do justice to just how beautiful my current surroundings are. I've cycled out of the village and am now sat on the grassy slope of one of the surrounding hills, looking down to the lake below. It's a circular lake, with a hilly, wooded island in the centre, the whole thing ringed by hills and mountains on all sides. One of the teachers told me the island is actually the tip of a sunken volcano. I assumed he was joking, but actually, it turns out he was telling the truth! (Don't worry by the way; I'm assured the volcano is dormant, unlike some of the others in the area!!!)

It's a beautiful evening. I wish you were here, Ben, and not only because you'd be able to describe it just so. The sky's a lovely pale shade of blue, with streaks of what my granny always called salmon clouds – that mix of silvery grey and pink from the sun. The whole area is bathed in the most brilliant, gentle, evening light, picking out all of the wonderful autumnal colours, so many rich shades of red and orange and yellow. I'm so lucky to be working up here – it's strange, but when I came to Japan, this was exactly the last thing I expected to see! One of the teachers told me that 70 per cent of Japan is mountains and lakes – talk about the small minority spoiling it for the rest of us!!!

Oh, Ben. What I would give for you to be here right now. I think that all the initial excitement of arriving is starting to rub off, and I'm beginning to understand what the year's going to be like, and how long it's going to be. Fuck, it's a long time. I've been wearing out my cassette of Definitely Maybe/ Morning Glory and thinking of you and Knebworth and us standing there, you hugging me from behind as we listen to 'Wonderwall' and all the rest. And I – oh now look what you've done. I'm welling up, just thinking about you. That's no good, that's no good at all. I promised myself I wouldn't do this. Come on, Sarah, get it together.

I'm all right now. Sorry for the smudges – hope you can read it all. I don't know where that came from: this isn't meant to be a feel-sorry-for-myself letter. In fact, it's meant to be the opposite. You see, after weeks of hanging around and waiting and watching, I finally got to teach my first lesson today. And you know what? It was all right. I think I might be able to do this.

Oh, Ben, I was so nervous when I went into the classroom. I was almost shaking handing out the photocopy I'd done. I had to focus on all these odd little details to calm myself: the date on the blackboard, counted in years since the Emperor took to the throne; the school name on the tracksuits, in yellow, gothic letters; the way the class was divided down the middle by sex. Everything felt so different to an English classroom: the mid-blue tracksuits, the whitewashed walls, the orange baseball pitch outside, the dark green island behind – all of it emphasising just how far away from home I was.

Anyway. Here goes nothing, I thought, and launched in, in English as my instructor had taught me. Thirty blank faces. My training instructor had warned me of this, and not to succumb to showing off the half dozen words of Japanese I know: immersion, I remembered his mantra, is everything. But frankly, it wasn't the training instructor who was wetting himself in front of the class. So I started again, and introduced myself in Japanese. This time I got a round of applause.

My lesson was dead simple really. I got everyone to introduce themselves in English, and turn around and shake hands with the person sitting behind them (a very British thing to do: everyone bows here, you see). Not exactly rocket science, I know, but it was all part of my cunning plan – as the handshakes went up and down the rows, I wrote down everybody's name. It was all going so well, until the shaking hands got to the middle row, where the last boy sat in front of the first girl. You wouldn't think it would be a big deal, but the boys and girls sitting on opposite sides of the class was no accident: they were at that age when they didn't talk to each other. And this poor boy was suddenly getting egged on by his mates, because he was about to touch a girl's hand. And when he shook it – I say shook, it was the weakest, limpest handshake I've ever seen – his friend at the next desk, made a kissing noise. At which point, the handshake boy turned round and thumped him!!!

Oh my God, Ben. I was there shouting and trying to keep order as desks and fists flew, but I didn't know the Japanese for 'Stop!' and they didn't understand my English. Thankfully, this teacher from the next classroom heard the commotion and stormed in, and they certainly understood what he was shouting, I can tell you – I mean, I didn't know what he was saying but I was scared myself. Anyway anyway. The lesson finishes, and I'm shaking and thank God I'm a teacher and am allowed to smoke at school. And I've just about calmed down when there's a knock on my office door and the scary teacher's there, with my two prizefighters. The scary teacher says something I don't understand and hands me a slipper, and I'm thinking, Have I lost one? (You have to wear indoor shoes in Japan, did I tell you that?) But no, both my slippers are still on my feet. And then I get it: he wants me to punish the boys.

I shake my head. I can't do that, I'm thinking. And then I have a brainwave. I get them to shake hands with each other, to show there's no hard feelings. My English lesson wasn't wasted after all! I think the scary teacher thought I was nuts, but the boys, I could tell, thought I was all right. A slightly strange way of doing it, but I think I got their respect. I tell you, Ben, it's so different from when I taught at that summer school: it doesn't matter how good a teacher you are, out here there's all the customs you're up against too. And all the time I'm teaching, I'm learning too, exactly what is the 'right thing' to do.

I can't tell you how nice it's been talking to you. If you were here, or I was there, I know you'd take care of me after the day I've had. Maybe your spag Bol special, or a trip to the pub with a whole pound for me to spend on the jukebox. Or maybe hunkering down with a video. Or maybe just hunkering down. (Calm down, Sarah! You'll never get through the year at this rate.) But instead this is as close to you as I get at the moment. I can't tell you how jealous I feel of these words, these pieces of paper that in a few days' time are going to be in your hands. If I could find a way of getting inside the envelope, believe me, I would. I'm going to finish now, it's getting a bit chilly up here, so I'm going to cycle back past the post office and post this. Write to me soon, I can't tell you how much my heart jumps when one of your wonderful letters arrives.

Sarah xxxx

PS Pink. Knickerbox.

4

It's a Tuesday when I meet Annabel Foreman. Or rather, it's a Tuesday when Annabel Foreman meets me.

I don't mean this in an arrogant way, more of in an Annabel way. She's the sort of person who never misses an opportunity to network. Like this morning, for instance. I get the train to Charing Cross as usual, and as I leave the station, straining to see the numbers on the buses as they flash past, I see the one I'm looking for, the 77A. I'm running for it, ducking and weaving among the commuters, then as I skip left to avoid the blur of girl with long blonde hair and a bunch of papers clasped to her red top, something happens. I skip to my left, but somehow the girl swings to her right, straight into my path and I can't but crash straight into her, papers flying into the air.

'Sorry. God, are you OK?' I ask, as her notes flutter down around us.

'Yes, I'm . . .' The girl looks at me inquisitively. 'Hey, don't I know you?'

I look at the girl. Her face, its small, precise features, button nose, and light red lipsticked mouth, seem vaguely familiar. Likewise her long, straw-coloured hair, sweeping down in thick rollered layers, the pair of sunglasses perched on top.

'I don't think so,' I say. 'Here,' I crouch down, scooping up her papers, 'let me help you with those.'

'Thanks,' says the girl, beaming me a smile. There's something about her, about the way she's perfectly, precisely accessorised – the bracelet going with the watch with the ring with the earrings – something about her that hints true blue but beautiful, something about her that says Sloane. But as I pick up her papers and folders, I can't help noticing the red rose logo on the notepaper.

'Do you work for the Labour Party?' I ask, standing up, handing her the notes.

'Oh, *I* know who you are,' the girl says, her face lighting up at the recognition. 'You're working with Gareth, aren't you? Gareth Marks?'

'Yes,' I say. 'I'm Ben. Ben Lawrence.'

'Annabel Foreman.' A hand flicks out.

'Nice to meet you,' I say, shaking it, and as I do so, I have a flash of panic. I hope I haven't crashed into anyone important. 'Look, I'm really sorry about this. I was going for the bus and didn't look where I was going.' I nod towards the 77A, its right indicator flashing, as it pulls away from the bus stop.

'Please. Don't worry about it.' Annabel smiles again. 'Would you mind holding these for a second?' She passes me her crumpled collection of papers. 'Hey, why don't you walk with me?' she asks, straightening her skirt, slim, black and A-line. 'I like to stretch my *legs* in the morning.'

'Sure,' I say, struggling to focus on the papers as Annabel flicks some dust off her red ribbed polo neck. I'm relieved to see that the top few pages at least appear to be blank. 'If I'm not intruding.'

'Goodness no. It'll be nice to get to know each other.' Annabel takes her papers back. 'Everyone's so busy nobody introduces you new boys any more. So tell me. What has Gareth got you working on?'

'I've been doing stuff for the conference,' I explain, as we head for Trafalgar Square. 'We're setting up this thing called the Youth Experience Rally for the twenty-eighth, the Saturday night. The idea is to get together lots of young voters from Blackpool's marginal constituencies, give them a bit of a party, show them how youth friendly we are.'

'Is that *you*? Wow.' Annabel looks impressed. 'You're the guy who's going to get Oasis to play.'

'Well.' Someone had been doing a lot of spinning. We'd asked, and that was about as far as it had got. 'Nothing's confirmed yet.'

'I think they're brilliant. So, so . . . real.'

'Yeah.' I find myself nodding in agreement. Real? 'Yeah, I guess they are.'

'I'd *love* to meet them.' Annabel's voice is softer now, likewise her expression. 'I don't suppose that there'd be any chance that you could, you know . . .'

To be honest, I didn't think that there was any chance that Oasis would, you know, turn up. 'Oh definitely.' I laugh. 'Definitely maybe.'

Annabel looks a little confused at this.

'Definitely maybe,' I explain. 'It's the title of their first album.'

'*Got* you.' She smiles quickly. 'Wow, you're one of *those* people, aren't you? One of those people who really know their music.'

'Bits and bobs,' I shrug.

'I guess that's why you deal with the rock stars,' Annabel sighs, 'while I get stuck with all the moany old journalists.'

'Believe me, it's nothing like as glamorous as it sounds. I spend most of the day haggling over who's going to provide the pizza. Anyway, tell me about you. What is it you do exactly?'

'I'm in rapid rebuttal.' Annabel leans towards me, conspiratorially. 'Though in your case I could make an exception.'

'Right.' I'm not really sure how to react to this. 'So, er, how did you end up working for Labour?'

'New Labour,' Annabel corrects. 'Well, I guess it all started with Neil Kinnock.'

'Me too,' I say. I tell her about the speech, about Gareth's phone call, the flash of recognition in the exam hall.

'How cool is that?' Annabel laughs. 'I know that speech, it was in that party political broadcast, "Kinnock the Movie", the one by the *Chariots of Fire* director. I saw that, rang the party up, and started work almost immediately.'

'Wow. So you've been working here for ten years?'

Annabel laughs. 'Oh good God, no. How old do you think I am?'

I pull a face. 'But you said you saw the broadcast and started work. That video was from the 1987 election.'

'Oh, I didn't see it, then.' Annabel shakes her head. 'God no. I was never into politics as a teenager. No, we studied the broadcast as part of my media studies degree.

I just couldn't get over what a brilliant piece of advertising it was. Did you know it's the only political broadcast ever to be repeated because of public demand? Well, when I heard that Peter was back in charge of things, I just thought, I've got to work with him. And so here I am.'

We're walking down Whitehall, towards Parliament, towards Millbank beyond, when Annabel stops by a familiar pair of thick black metal gates.

'There she is,' Annabel says. 'There's the goal.'

Downing Street. We peer through, past the flak-jacketed policeman to the thin strip of infamous street, home to the prime minister and Chancellor of the Exchequer, John Major and Kenneth Clarke.

'Morning, Annabel,' the policeman says. I sense this isn't the first time Annabel has stared dreamily towards number ten. 'Still no pass to show me?'

'Not yet,' Annabel says brightly. 'But it's getting closer every day. You can't keep me out for ever . . .'

My earliest political memory is Margaret Thatcher getting into power. I remember it quite clearly: it was a sunny May morning during my first year at primary school, and we were sat cross-legged listening to our teacher, Mrs Joseph, waiting for our mid-morning mini-bottle of milk to arrive. Actually, now I come to think of it, the entire class was sat with the exception of me. I was stood at the back of the class in disgrace, because Mrs Joseph had been wanting us to tell the class about other countries that we knew and I had a really interesting story to tell about the campsite I'd visited in Germany where I'd gone into the shop and bought a bar of chocolate *in German* and it was far more interesting than anyone else's boring tale about how they eaten haggis in Scotland, but for some reason Mrs Joseph couldn't see me so I kept on sliding to be near the person who was telling their boring story so she'd pick me next, but instead she told me to stand up and go and wipe my trousers with a paper towel because they were covered in dirt from all my sliding around.

The interesting thing was I actually was quite a good child, which is probably why I remember this incident so vividly. I didn't often get bollocked and so when I did it stuck in my mind. Anyway. I didn't get to tell my tale because Matthew Wilkinson told what in retrospect was a fairly dodgy little story about how French children all smell and his daddy says that's because they don't use any soap. Mrs Joseph decided to move the conversation on and told us that something very important had happened yesterday.

'Can anyone tell me what it was?'

Something had happened the day before which I didn't properly understand. It was a Thursday so it wasn't the weekend and yet the school was shut and I was allowed to go out and play *Battle of the Planets* with Matthew Wilkinson. When I asked my mother why I wasn't going to school, she laughed and said that it was someone else's turn to be taught a lesson.

'Yesterday,' Mrs Joseph said, 'this country had a general election, which means that all your mummies and daddies and every other grown-up got to choose who they want to be for our leader. Yes, Catherine?'

'Miss, I thought that the queen was our leader.'

'She is Catherine, but in a different way. The queen does the important things like launching ships and opening supermarkets, and because she has so many ribbons to cut she has to have a prime minister to do all the other little things, like running the country –' I do wish I had appreciated Mrs Joseph's dryness at the time – 'and yesterday, all your mummies and daddies decided they wanted to have a new leader and they voted for, yes, Matthew?'

'Miss, I know who our new prime minister is.'

'And who's that?'

'She's called Margaret Thatcher.'

'Very good, Matthew. And do you know what's special about Margaret Thatcher?'

'I do, miss,' I said.

'And why's that, Ben?'

I suddenly wished I kept my mouth shut.

'I don't think I should say.'

'It's very rude to say you know the answer and then keep it to yourself,' Mrs Joseph laughed. 'Come on, tell everyone. You're not going to get into trouble.'

Here's where I made my mistake. I believed her. 'My mummy says she's special because she's not a lying shit like the other man.'

The class gasped.

'Benjamin Lawrence!'

'But, miss, you said I wouldn't get into trouble if I told you why she is special. That's not fair!'

'Margaret Thatcher is special because she is the first woman to be in charge of this country, shut *up* about the queen, Catherine Adams, I've already explained the difference, she's not special because she's not a . . . I will *not* have bad language in my classroom.' Margaret Thatcher was not the only woman in charge today. 'Go and stand outside.'

'But, but, miss,' I pleaded. 'What about my milk?'

'Yes, well,' Mrs Joseph snapped. 'I think you'll find it's been taken by the milk-snatcher. You can thank your mother for that when you get home.'

Millbank is laid out like a newspaper editorial office, a huge single open-plan structure, with the main players in the centre, the spiders at the heart of the web. This is where Peter Mandelson sits, at a large boardroom table, along with his focus group gurus and pollsters, and assorted other bigwigs. In the high-ceilinged office, at the opposite end to the river, is the Gordon Brown camp. Gareth and I sit somewhere in between, carving a niche among the banks of telephone canvassers, constantly ringing up voter after voter to check and monitor their ever-changing moods.

The word they're using to describe the mass of people like me, graduates fresh from university who have for whatever reason wangled their way into Millbank, the gleaming campaign epicentre of New Labour, to work voluntarily as the juggernaut shifts through the gears towards the impending general election, the word they're using to describe us bright young minions, which is ironic considering its communist origins, is apparatchik.

'Unless you swan around like this one,' Gareth explains. 'Then you think you're apparat*chic*.'

'Hello again,' says a familiar voice, walking past.

'You've met the Guacamole Girl?' Gareth asks.

'Yeah,' I say. 'I bumped into her this morning.'

'Did you bump into her or did she bump into you?'

'What do you mean by that?' I ask. 'And why's she called the Guacamole Girl?'

'There was this time Annabel went up north on party business,' Gareth explains, 'and she ended up getting lunch with the local MP at the chip shop. As she steps up to order she sees this tub of mushy peas on the counter, and asks for fish and chips once, with a helping of guacamole on the side.'

'I thought that story was about Peter Mandelson?' I asked.

'It's apocryphal,' Gareth grunts. 'You can use it about anyone you like.' He smiles, mischievously. 'Or not, as the case may be.'

I prefer to think of myself as a *domestique* rather than an apparatchik. In the Tour de France, the *domestiques* are the team members there to sacrifice themselves for the stars and leaders, to wind up the pace when necessary, to spoil the chances of the other teams, to stop and help should the team leader be in trouble. I suggested to Gareth that this term was more New Labour than apparatchik, more forward thinking, more European.

'Our leader in a yellow jersey?' Gareth snorts. 'If you've got Liberal Democrat leanings, you'd better fuck off now.'

Gareth, it has to be said, is not in the best of moods today. The reason? Oasis. More precisely, the lack of them.

'What's that line?' Gareth asks. 'About not putting your life in the hand of a rock and roll band?'

Despite the fact that Oasis were professed Labourites, despite the fact that when they accepted their slew of awards at the Brits, Noel Gallagher saying there's only seven people in this country who matter, the members of Oasis, Alan McGee and Tony Blair, despite the fact he went on about voting Labour so much they had to edit it out of the show like they had Jarvis's bottom, we weren't going to get the band, Noel, nothing, for our night at the conference. After a huge argument with Liam during a five-hour band meeting in North Carolina, Noel decided he'd had enough, cancelled the tour, packed his bags and come home. All public appearances were off. Likewise Gareth's chance to impress his bosses, my chance to get in with people like, well, Annabel.

'Maybe we should give Billy Bragg a ring?' I suggest.

Gareth doesn't laugh.

'It's not so bad,' I continue. 'We've still got Alan McGee plus Creation Records on side. There's lots of other great acts we could pitch for. Primal Scream. Super Furry Animals, Teenage Fanclub, Boo Radleys . . .'

'You can try,' Gareth says, 'but Creation are a crafty bunch. Do you know who they're offering us instead?'

'Who?'

'18 Wheeler.'

'Who?'

'Exactly.' He sighs. 'I can't believe this is happening again. One of the first jobs I ever did for Labour was to help out with Red Wedge in the eighties. The Style Council, The Communards, that prat from Spandau Ballet, it was so po-faced and unsuccessful, I thought we'd learnt our lesson once and for all about politics and music not mixing. But oh no, here we go again. Suddenly everything's gone Britpop and we're the political equivalent.'

'What? Bright and positive and British and popular?'

'Empty and derivative and a pale imitation of our major influences.'

I gasp in mock horror. Gareth takes a quick look round to see who's listening.

'Take Oasis,' he says. 'Run by a pair of men whose fates are inextricably interlinked, always arguing, always jealous, each needing the other more than they'd like to admit. For Noel and Liam read Gordon and Tony.'

'What about Bonehead?'

'Who do you think?'

'Oh, will you *stop* knocking John Prescott.' I laugh. 'What about the other ones?'

'Oh, I don't know, they're like the shadow ministers for agriculture and the environment: you know they're there, but you're not really sure who they are.' Gareth's phone rings, but he ignores it. 'It's not just Oasis. Every Britpop band is New Labour.'

'Every band?'

'The lot,' Gareth smiles. 'Come on. Try me.'

'All right,' I say. 'What about Blur?'

'Blur Blair, Blair Blur. A fairly accurate summation of the vagueness of our policies.'

'Elastica?'

'And our ideology.'

'Supergrass?'

'An important component of law and order's armoury to be tough on crime, tough on the causes of crime.'

'Pulp?' I ask. 'Pulp from Sheffield, home of the horrendous rally that cost us the 1992 election? They must be Old Labour.'

Gareth pauses, thinks for a minute. 'No, wait, I've got it. Pulp formed in 1981, but only now, a decade and a half later have they hit the big time. Their long slow rise to the top echoes Labour's years in the wilderness.'

'Bugger. OK. Kula Shaker?'

'All that pseudo-religious shit Tony pours out in his annual speech to the Labour Party Conference.'

'Sleeper?'

'What I'm doing while he's giving it.'

'Suede?'

'What Tony's charms did to Labour members who should have known better.'

I'm struggling now. 'Shed Seven?'

'Well, we've shed more than seven principles but they're going in the right direction.'

'The Bluetones?'

Gareth smiles. 'How much more blue do you want Tone to be?'

'I'm going to stick my neck out here,' I say. 'You're not exactly sold on the New Labour platform, are you?'

'Me?' Gareth shakes his head. 'I'm the red wedge, stuck in the middle of this stupid game of trivial pursuits.'

It's later, when I arrive home, when I'm welcomed by the reassuring sound of our kitchen clocks, that I have the thought about Annabel.

I'm not sure whose idea it is to have the clocks. It could have been Bex's, it could have been mine. It was me, though, who suggested putting them in the kitchen, in a row on the wall above the Formica-topped kitchen table.

They're your classic wall clocks: big and round and white with black numbering and each minute scored with a thin black line. The hour and minute hands are black, the second hand is red like a thermometer at boiling point. The whole is encased behind 'do not break' glass and ringed with a thick circle of aluminium silver.

Each clock comes with a big, brash, brassy tick. A solid, satisfying clunk, clicking away sixty seconds a minute, sixty minutes an hour, twenty-four hours a day, three hundred and sixty-five days a year. Bex and I spent a good afternoon attempting to synchronise them, pushing in batteries on the count of three until the ticks were as close as they were going to get. If you listen carefully, you can just make out where they're fractionally out. The three ticks now form one large, meaty tick, and this thicker tick, this *thick*, weighs the magnitude of every second, marking out the passage of time as stately, important, momentous.

The three clocks are identical with one small exception. The time. The central clock says five thirty, because that's what time in the evening it is. The clock on the left says eleven thirty, because that's what time in the morning it is in Cuba, where Bex's boyfriend Si is. The clock on the right says three thirty because it's the middle of the night in Japan, because that's where Sarah is.

Underneath the clocks, printed on three strips of white card are three words.

Havana. London. Tokyo.

As I place my keys on the table, move across to the sink to fill up the kettle, as the clocks tick Sarah closer to coming home, I replay my meeting with Annabel in my head. Her flash of hair. Her legs. Her red ribbed polo neck and what lay beneath. Gareth's great and everything, and I really like him, but even I can sense that he's not a people person: he's not a bright young thing like Annabel. And the more I become associated with him, the less I'm going to get to associate with people like Annabel.

But what was it that Gareth said? *Did you bump into her, or did she bump into you?* I rewind the footage, pausing it and freezing it. And the more I watch it, the more I think it odd that we collided. I'd clocked her, I'd shimmied left, the only way we could have made contact is if her, no that seems daft, is if her body check was deliberate. I shake my head: for that to be true, she'd have had to see me coming; I laugh, maybe she was waiting for me to arrive. I want to dismiss this, but then I see something else. Her papers. I notice where we collide, the spread of where the papers end up, and then, as I slow the action down frame by frame, I realise something else. By the time we bump into each other, Annabel's papers are out of her hands. Not by much, but by a fraction it's there: the papers are already airbound.

Hail, comrade!

Greetings to you on this most beautiful of mornings, a beauty made more glorious by the smiling faces of small socialist children, flush in the knowledge of capitalism's inevitable collapse. For a humble person like me to be taking part in such a pivotal moment in the advancement of mankind! Why, it makes me weep with gratitude. If only I could find a way to repay this historic fortitude, Comrade Lawrence, I would clasp it firmly to my chest and die a happy man.

So how are you then, my pitiful capitalist scum? Is London, the 'home' of 'democracy', as corrupt and rotten and inevitably on the steep slope to decline as ever? I'm not saying that God is a communist — communists don't believe in God, so God is unlikely to believe in us — but supposing for a second that he's more than just a Judeo-Christian invention propagated by the powers that be in order to subjugate the masses, then how do you explain the fact that Havana is sunny and hot with not a cloud in the sky? Again? Whereas London is suffering yet another day of drizzle/ downpour/ deluge (delete as appropriate)? Do remind me, is Earl Grey the name of the tea you drink, or the government minister in charge of your weather?

Comrade Lawrence, we Cuban people pity you and your petty bourgeois comrades. Being ferried to work in sealed containers underground, crammed in like the rats that you are, squeezed so much so that you cannot even open up the propaganda sheets you pay your pitiful earnings to read, all to go and slave your guts out in the silver skyscrapers of Mammon, to carry out the biddings of your bloody oppressors and overlords. Oh, when I tell my brothers and sisters of the delusions that you suffer, the story of your tragic life, it makes them weep large soapy tears of despair for you. Why, they cry between sobs, why can your pitiful friend not see that the complete overthrow of the entire capitalist system is his one true path, the only way to rid himself of the false consciousness that he toils under, that the time has come to shake off his chains and help return power to where power should be? In the hands of the workers!

So what's hot in Cuba? What isn't? It's fucking roasting out here. If this was Britain, there's be some wacko from the telly claiming you could fry an egg on the pavement. What can you do but siesta and sip long cold drinks in the cool of a Cuban bar? I tell you, mate, I'm already looking about as tanned as you are translucent. Teaching is going OK. Actually, teaching is going very well: my class are cool, well cool actually, especially the sixteen year olds. A couple of them are giving me the eye, I'm sure of it. If only the girls would do the same.

Actually – and this must go absolutely no further than between you and me – there's a new teacher just started and she is hot to trot. She's called Juanita, and let me tell you, she's Juan hot fucking lady. Seriously Amazonian with legs that go on forever and a cleavage you could get lost in for days. Kind of a Cuban Elle MacPherson. When she turned up in the staffroom yesterday, I swear the whole place stopped to have an eyeful. The old guy who teaches science – you know, the one who's so old he went to college with Isaac Newton – he was so blatant, he was fucking salivating at the sight of her.

Anyway, in front of everyone else, she comes straight over to me, and says in perfect English (but with a very sexy, slightly husky Spanish accent): 'You're the new boy, aren't you? Mr England?'

'That's very perceptive of you,' I replied. (This sounds like I was cool and casual, but to be honest, with everyone watching, I was bricking myself.) 'I'm Simon. Call me Si. I'm teaching English here for a few months.'

'I'm Juanita,' she replied, not taking her big brown eyes off me for a second. She glanced round the room, which, unable to follow our conversation, had slipped back into a background Spanish murmur. Juanita turned back to me. 'The old teacher in the corner. Does he always stare at women like that?'

'He doesn't get out much,' I said, and Juanita laughed. A big throaty, sexy head-leaning-back laugh.

From that point on, I knew we were going to get along.

And almost as good as her cleavage, when I invited Juanita round for supper, not only did I discover she likes a bit of a smoke, but she knows where to score some gear. There's only one small problem. Her dealer is her boyfriend. Pablo. Big brick shithouse with a flash set of wheels Pablo. The kind of bloke who by rights should (but doesn't) have a handlebar moustache you could hang off. The only English he knows seems to be the song titles to different Beatles songs, which he peppers the conversation with, I presume for my benefit. Slightly surreal to say the least. You'd be talking about, I don't know, football or something, and suddenly he'll say yellow submarine and laugh in his hissy sort of way. He's got a fucking big knife, a shark one I think, which he showed me proudly, just in case I didn't get the message about Juanita. I showed him my Swiss Army knife, and tried to look threatening with the corkscrew but I don't think he bought it. He just said, 'I juant to hold your hand' and laughed.

I told Pablo I had a girlfriend, which I think is a good move, because he trusts me now. I didn't bother explaining about the 'free snogs' clause. I think he now assumes I'm not a threat. Well, I think he thinks every man within a 500-metre radius of Juanita is a threat, but as threats go, I'm one of the smaller ones. We smoked some of his weed (eye-wateringly strong) and he laughed a lot. Juanita laughed a lot. I laughed a lot. It'd be funny . . . if the stakes weren't quite so high.

Anyway, comrade, the revolution must continue and much as I would like to hang around here and chat, I must get back to my invaluable work. I trust that even with this short missive, I have done something to help destabilise the capitalist system just that little bit further.

Hail Che! Hail Fidel! Hail the workers!

Your comrade,

Si

5

It's a Thursday night that I agree to go to a gig with Bex.

Bex is a guitarist. A folk guitarist. A folkie. She's a big fan of all those seventies singer songwriters – Joni and Carly and Sandy and Dory – and can fingerpick their songs in perfect facsimile. Sarah and I used to lie in bed together, listening to her playing through the paper-thin walls of their student flat. And it's something I'm finding myself doing in Greenwich too – lulling me to sleep with memories of things past. As I shut my eyes, I can almost imagine that Sarah is there with me.

It took a long time for Bex to be convinced that she should go out and play in public. She was embarrassed enough that Sarah and I could hear her through the walls. But slowly, subtly, Sarah waged a very civil war of attrition until finally Bex relented, I think to shut Sarah up as much as anything else. Having agreed, she instantly regretted it and tried to wriggle out of it, but Sarah said it was all arranged even though she hadn't arranged anything and despite Bex's offer that she'd do anything to get out of the gig, Sarah held her to her word. On a chilly November night at the 'open mike' evening in the student bar, Bex and several bottles of Hooch got up and quietly but powerfully played 'Chelsea Morning', 'You're So Vain' and

'Will You Still Love Me Tomorrow'. And buoyed by each round of applause, by the end she was enjoying it.

Bex is determined to play in London. It's a good way to meet new people, she explains as we wait for the train. It's good for the soul – a pressure valve from the stress of her law conversion course: a reminder that there's more to life, to her life, than reading up about court cases and litigation. And so tonight, if the train arrives, we're going on a recce, to suss out the strumming hotspots of the capital.

Charing Cross Road, or more precisely just off Charing Cross Road, appears to be the heart of acoustic London. There's the 12 Bar Club on Denmark Street, down an alley nestling between a row of guitar shops. The Acoustic Café, on the edge of Soho round the back of Foyles. And slightly further down again is the place Bex wants to go, a small club that is signposted outside as an African restaurant.

'Are you sure this is right?' I ask, looking at the dark, narrow flight of stairs descending into the basement. I have a vision of us entering a gambling dive, a porn club, a crack den, nervously ordering a coke and being fleeced for two hundred pounds.

'I think so.' Bex follows her nose, which like mine is picking up a rich, heady scent of culinary aromas. Coriander. Cumin. Chillies. Nutmeg. As we head down, the smells get stronger, as do the sounds of laughter, the clink of cutlery and crockery. We turn a corner and step into a world away from London; a dimly lit cavern punctuated by cellar arcs and people sat around low tables on cushions, eating and drinking and laughing and puffing on those bongs made out of cupolas, waiters whipping past with plates of strange smells and colours that my stomach can't but be pulled by.

'Excuse me,' Bex asks, 'we're looking for an acoustic club.'

I expect the waiter to say, 'A folk club? In an African restaurant? Are you mad?' but instead he nods and points to a back room behind a tiny bar, where a ripple of applause echoes out and, after a satellite link-up time delay, is followed by the sight of people leaving.

'Have we missed it?' Bex asks as we squeeze past in the opposite direction.

'Not at all,' smiles the man on the door, who doesn't look or sound remotely African. He's tall, thirtyish, with hair that matches the thick black frames of his glasses. 'We're just having a break for five minutes so people can go to the bar. It's two pounds to get in. One pound for performers.'

Bex is staring wide-eyed into the room as she hands her money over.

'What?' I ask, wishing my neck would crane far enough to see.

'It's Danny Martin,' Bex whispers.

'Who?' I ask, and Bex bundles me towards the bar.

'Who's Danny Martin?' I ask again, as we queue up at the bar.

I must have said this a little too loudly, because a couple of people look round and Bex kicks me.

'Danny Martin the folk singer,' Bex hisses, embarrassed. 'The son of sixties singer Penny Martin. Have you never heard *Orchard Days*?'

I look equally blank.

'It was an album of her songs that Danny recorded. It was huge a couple of years ago.' Bex shakes her head pityingly. 'You must have been too obsessed with your shoegazing records to notice. Yeah, I was next. Two beers, please.'

'Are you saying this guy is famous? Thanks,' I say as Bex hands me a bottle. 'What's he doing here? Is he down on his luck?'

'Not at all.' Bex shrugs. 'Maybe he's come along listen to other people, to try out some new songs.' She smiles. 'I can't believe he's here. This is so cool.'

The back room is small, square with a wonderfully curved cellar-like ceiling. Everyone is sat around the edge on cushions, Arabic in colour and design, with guitars, cases and mandolins scattered about. On the left sits Danny Martin. Black hair, floppy beyond the fringe, he's sporting a zip-up sports top and is huddled together with his pencil-thin blonde friend, secretively rolling some sort of cigarette. There's a space next to him, but Bex is too modest to take it, so we aim for the cushion in the corner instead.

One by one the other folkies fall in. There's a freckled girl with an explosion of ginger curls, a jazz-wannabe bloke in black polo neck, a well-studded New-Ageish couple in their early thirties, an assortment of nervous-looking men and an older guy with scraped-back white hair and a grin stuck on his face, who plonks himself down next to Danny, looking expectantly at his cigarette.

'Is that everyone?' the doorman asks. 'Right, well

we've had performances from Mark, Jason, Cheryl, River and Poppy, and . . . hi, we're just restarting.'

The latecomer is silhouetted in the doorway for all of a second, freeze-framed like a video, the light accentuating her small, slim body, her mid-length skirt and messy bob, the beer bottle stuck on the middle finger of her left hand. As she moves into the room, into focus, into colour, I see she's Asian, Japanese I think, her cardigan's black and her skirt's purple and that her deep brown eyes are bearing down on me.

'Shift up,' Bex says.

'What?' I say, momentarily flustered. 'Oh, right,' I realise the girl wants to squeeze in next to me. 'Sorry,' I apologise, shuffling up.

The girl nods a small smile of thanks, sits down on the front edge of the cushion. She draws her knees up to her chin.

'Are you OK there?' I whisper. 'Have you got enough room?'

The girl nods without looking round. Like the rest of the room, her attention is taken by Danny Martin, who has picked up a cream-pale guitar and is tuning up.

'As you've, er, probably noticed,' the doorman says, 'we're lucky enough to have Danny Martin with us this evening. Danny's in the studio at the moment, and wanted to come down and try a few new songs out, isn't that right?'

'S'right,' says Danny, not looking up.

'So, has anyone else heard these songs?' asks the girl with the ginger curls.

'Just my girlfriend,' indicates Danny.

Danny's girlfriend waves apologetically at the room.

'Sorry,' Bex says. 'Can I just ask, is that your mother's guitar?'

At this Danny looks up. 'Yeah,' he says softly. 'Yeah, it is. She played here in, um, 1967, I think it was.' He strums a chord, lets it ring out. 'Felt right to bring it along.'

A murmur of approval ripples around the room.

Danny's girlfriend passes him his cigarette. He takes a long drag, then fixes it to the head of his guitar, the smoke and smell curling upwards like a joss stick.

I've never heard Danny Martin before, but in these tiny surroundings, with the rich acoustics echoing off the cavernous walls, I'm instantly impressed. The venue suits his soft, warm, almost whispery voice, the intricate finger-picking of his guitar playing, fingerpicking that from the look of astonishment on Bex's face is skilful in the extreme. When Danny finishes his first song, there's a hushed second of awe, then a rapturous round of applause.

'He's really good,' I whisper to Bex.

'He's fucking great,' Bex whispers back, just as the room has dropped back to silence. Everyone laughs.

'Glad you liked it,' Danny smiles, a little sheepishly. He reaches into his pocket, fishes around. 'Has anyone got a thumb pick I could borrow?'

All the guitarists reach into their pockets in an acoustic version of a gunfight. Bex draws first. When she returns to her seat, she beams at me proudly. '*My* thumb pick,' she mouths.

As Danny continues his set, my mind starts wandering off. I think it's his voice that does it, its soft tones lulling me into thoughts of Sarah, of absence, of longings. I come to, to find my line of sight is lingering right, and I'm looking at the Japanese girl. Her hair is thick, dark, ruffled, carefully layered to look carefree. As I follow the strands down, I can't help noticing the pale glimpses of neck beneath. Likewise the thinness of her black cardigan, the knitting pattern offering tiny circles of skin. The girl shuffles forwards slightly, flexing her shoulders, arching her back as though she knows I am there.

The applause is still continuing as Danny puts his guitar in his case. He apologises for leaving early, but with a sly smile says he's got to be back in the studio. The nervous young men look wistfully on. The room murmurs goodbye as he leaves.

As the girl with the ginger curls starts tuning up, Bex says, 'Hey, he's got my thumb pick,' and scuttles off after Danny. She moves so quickly I'm taken by surprise, and by the time I'm wondering whether I should go after her, the next act is ready to start.

The ginger girl sings a song about love and affection. I think it's a cover, but to be honest I'm not really listening. I'm caught up in the Japanese girl's hair, the subtle distinctions between the colours of the strands, fractional discrepancies like the ticks of my clocks; chestnut, auburn, umber, mahogany. As I watch, her thin slender fingers with their pale purple nails tuck a clump of hair behind her ear; then, as an afterthought, an echo, her middle finger traces the top of her ear, slowly, gently slipping round until finger and thumb are lightly, delicately massaging her ear lobe. So slight, so soft, so nothing you'd hardly notice it at all.

With the faintest of tugs, the girl's hand is gone. I'm

so absorbed I almost don't notice Bex's return, a grin on her face and thumb pick in her hand.

Later, much later, Bex and I are in the kitchen, at opposite ends of the table, two mugs of tea in front of us, two spirals of steam evaporating upwards. The street lamp outside is bathing the room in amber so bright the kitchen light is redundant.

'Si's the bigger shit,' I say.

'No,' Bex replies. 'I think you'll find that Sarah is the bigger bastard. She's further away, the time difference is larger.'

'Yes, but at least Japan has telephones and emails,' I argue. 'Si's chosen a country where he's basically incommunicado.'

'He can write.'

'He *can* write, but how many letters have you had so far?'

'Oh, I don't know. Some.'

'Well, I got one from Sarah that she wrote before she even set off. And I'll tell you another thing. You're going to get jealous of Si because he's basically living in the Caribbean. At least Sarah has had the decency to go somewhere where it is cold.'

'I thought Japan was hot?'

'Not in the north, not where Sarah is. She's going to get months and months of snow.'

'Well, maybe that's worse. Maybe she'll go skiing.'

'I didn't think about that,' I admit.

'There you go then.' Bex raises her mug. 'Here's to bastard boyfriends and girlfriends fucking off overseas.'

'Agreed.' I clink mine. 'Arse to the lot of them.'

Sometimes it's funny to be rude about people. Many years before, I remember watching Five Star being interviewed by Sarah Greene on *Going Live*, and a caller asking the blunt but pertinent question, 'Why are you so fucking crap?' What Bex and I are saying here, it's similarly outrageous, and all the funnier for it. We can tease each other because we both have the same weak spot, both have the same funny bone, both know exactly how the other is feeling. We can be as shocking as we like because we both know the other person doesn't mean it. At least, I'm fairly sure that Bex doesn't mean it. The way she said 'bastard boyfriends' did sound a little pointed.

'You know what,' Bex continues, 'I think this evening's been really good for us. We've got to do this more, go out and get pissed, rather than sitting at home moping. I mean, why should we put our lives on hold for them? We can have fun too.' She smiles, a flicker of inspiration. 'Hey, I know what we should do.'

'What?'

'We should have a house-warming party.'

'A party? Are you sure? What about your aunt?'

Bex shrugs. 'I'm not talking about trashing the place. Come on, it'll be fun.' She grins mischievously. 'It'll nark Sarah and Si off.'

'You think?'

'Oh yes. Neither of them likes missing a good party. And both of them will be paranoid we're organising it to try and get off with someone.'

'Are we?'

Bex pulls a face. 'Course we're not. But that's their gamble, isn't it? Going off and leaving two good-looking people like you and me behind.'

I find myself thinking, with a shiver, of Annabel. Annabel who has an uncanny knack of waiting for the lift, making a cup of coffee, the same time that I do. Annabel who this morning left a Post-It note on my computer that said *Planet Fuck, tonight at 18.00? A x*, which I threw in the bin and fretted about all day until at ten to six Gareth asked me if I was going to the drinks thing in Planet Fuck, and he laughed at my blank face and explained that Planet Fuck was the nickname that Peter Mandelson's people gave to Gordon Brown's office, because they say that's where everything went wrong.

But I think too of Oasis, my very own rock-star sign. How I felt bad about things when Liam didn't get on that plane, how I felt better when three days later he rejoined the band, how it got worse again when Noel quit the US tour, and now how a short sweet press statement about the future of the band has cheered me up no end. 'It ain't over till it's over,' the statement said. 'Keep the faith.' Gareth, who has had it up to here with all things Gallagher, sneered and said, 'Lenny Kravitz and Bon Jovi? Just about sums the bastards up.' But I couldn't help but feel buoyed by the statement, and beg, borrow and steal its meaning for myself. I think of Sarah and think, I've got to keep the faith. As long as I do that, everything should be OK.

Dearest pinko commie scum,

Greetings from the greatest sunshine resort in the Western world. I do hope that the donkeys are walking fast enough to keep your generator going so that you have enough lamplight to read this by. Talking of revolutions, how's your bicycle? I hear it's the 'hip' way to travel in your communist paradise. How lucky you are to be out there. No more nasty HMV megastores with all those horrible records and videos for some corporate whore to force you to buy. No horrible pubs and pints of 'warm beer' for you to be sedated with like the rest of the masses. How could I forget how much you hated being fed pint after pint of Boddingtons. And none of those nasty, horrible football matches to watch on all those disgusting capitalist cable and satellite systems. Or those, ugh, mobile phones to talk into. Or those Gameboys and PlayStations and their horrid, horrid computer games. Or, it makes me sick just thinking about it, that clean water to drink. How I envy your swarms of disease-ridden flies – perhaps you could post some back to me? And maybe some of your rotten carrots, too? What a relief it must be to you to be nowhere near a McDonald's or a Burger King.

It's Tuesday afternoon here in Blackpool and I'm sat in my beautiful en shite B&B bedroom watching Tony Blair's leadership speech. I should be sat with the rest of the delegates in the opulent splendour of the Winter Gardens, but for the second day running I have been unable to get past the ridiculous security ring that surrounds the building. It's stupidly tight: they wouldn't let Barbara Castle in yesterday, so what chance have I got? Apparently Gordon Brown hasn't got a pass either, but I guess he's slightly more difficult to tell to sod off.

'Ask me my three main priorities for government and I will tell you: education, education, education.' Yes, thank you, Tony, we get the point, point, point. It's not a bad speech, actually, but then I guess it shouldn't be. According to Gareth, Tony called in everybody else's speeches, cherry-picked the best bits and sent the rest back. It's a shame you're not here, you'd love the religious shtick, which is high this year. This, apparently, is his 'covenant' to the British people. Next week he's going to be parting the Red Sea. Or maybe he already has?

The one thing that has surprised me about the party conference is how it seems to be just that: a conference of parties. There's so many different types: there are the young things events like the Youth Experience Rally, which Gareth and I helped organise – Alan Partridge, Ministry of Sound DJs, Tony Blair turning up for five minutes, receiving a platinum disc from Alan McGee, waffling on about how Creation Records are so New Labour, then buggering it all up by introducing the band and getting the name wrong.

Then there are the lobbyist parties, put on by big corporate people such as British Airways (lots of free drink, bloody boring); there's the trade union and co-operative parties (all very middle-aged and Old Labour); the media parties (celebrities and influential people only); and finally, best of all, there's the Celtic fringe bashes.

When Neil Kinnock was leader, apparently the big do was the Welsh party. Now, it's the turn of the Scots. This year's happened last night at the Savoy and was a riot of drinking and Scottish dancing. The Gay Gordon, the Eightsome Reel, the White Sergeant, you name it, I massacred it. Actually, I bumped into Tony Blair again there – quite literally: him and Cherie were doing the Gay Gordon in front of us and I went the wrong way. He looked at me oddly, like he vaguely recognised me, and I almost said, 'Saturday night? I was the one with my head in my hands as you got the band name wrong,' before Cherie pulled him away. Yes, probably for the best.

Here comes the big finish. 'Seventeen years of hurt never stopped us dreaming. Labour is coming home.' Very nice, very Euro '96. Let's just hope we don't do a Gareth Southgate and pat the penalty at the goalkeeper, eh? I wonder whose speech that was lifted from.

Anyway. These are testing times. You know I told you about that girl in my last letter, Annabel? Well, she's been at it again. On the Sunday morning, she's knocking on my door, telling me she's got me an invite for 'Geoffrey's party' (she always calls everyone by their first name: Geoffrey is Geoffrey Robinson, owner of the New Statesman). The problem was, I'd sort of agreed to go with Gareth to some fringe meeting about proportional representation.

'Well, if you want to catch up on your sleep . . .' Annabel yawned.

'No, no, I'll try and make it.'

I'd tried to persuade Gareth to come along, but he was having none of it – 'I'm not touching his fucking money,' was his response. So I ended up going without him, and it was probably just as well, because it was all very New Labour: the white wine was free and the 'worker's beer' was £2.20 a pint. And, despite myself, I had a really good time. Annabel's circle – Peter's Friends, they call themselves – were young and funky and good company and, well, to cut a long story short, I got absolutely twatted and Annabel and I ended up crawling back to our B&Bs at two in the morning. At which point she tried to persuade me to come in for a cup of coffee: 'Do you fancy an espresso?' she asked with a smile. Thankfully, though, the walk along the promenade had sobered me up, and I managed to escape.

Because I do miss Sarah. It can be hard when I'm drunk, but so far my holier-than-thou option is, I'm happy to say, still holding up. I have balls like melons to prove it. Well, melonish. One of the offshoots, if you'll pardon the pun, is my rediscovery of Madam Palm and her five lovely sisters. It's like being a teenager all over again: sticky, lonely and a bit sad.

Best go, but before I forget, can you have a word with Bex about walking around the flat naked? I mean, I know how great her arse is, but I think it's beginning to unsettle the neighbours.

Hasta la vista, amigo,

Ben

6

Sarah and Bex were known at college as the cardigan girls. It was a name they got when they both turned up on the first day in almost identical knitwear – threadbare on the elbows, pushed and pulled out of shape, the sleeves stretched over the hands to reveal nothing but a glimpse of fingertips. Sarah arrived with a collection more colourful than Bex's – pink, lemon and tomato red compared with brown, black and olive green – but before long they were switching and swapping as the mood took them. The more worn out the cardigan looked, the more it got worn out. 'Are all your clothes so threadbare?' Si asked. 'Maybe I should check.'

'Maybe it's your jokes that are worn out,' Bex said, shaking her head.

Before Sarah left for Japan we decided to do a clothes swap – one item each to remind us of the other. Knitwear was the choice, for the way it holds on to scents. The cardigan I've got is her pastel pink one. It's hand-knitted, by her gran I think, with thick knitting-needle stitches, small round enamel buttons (one missing, one chipped) and two pockets on the front. Sarah used to keep her Marlboro Lights in the left, her lighter in the right, though I don't suppose she told her gran that. If you hold it to your nose, you can still breathe Sarah in, her intoxicating mix of raspberry-flavoured Body Shop soap, CK perfume, and her skin, with its light, gentle, almost appley aroma.

I haven't told Bex I've got Sarah's cardigan, because I know exactly what she'd say if she found it. 'You soft git,' for one. 'You're just like those blokes who sniff their girlfriend's underwear,' for another. And she'd be right too, in a tangential sort of a way: I'm smelling it to make myself feel better, though I hope in a slightly different manner. The real reason, though, that I haven't told Bex is this – if she found the cardigan, she'd borrow it, and then it would never smell of Sarah again.

The flat is ready. The decorations are up, the furniture is moved, the valuables are hidden, the breakables out of reach. On the kitchen table lies the largest display of plastic glasses I have ever seen. Pints, halves, tumblers, shot glasses. Towers of the things that, if no one turns up, I'm going to stick end to end and get myself into the *Guinness Book of Records*. Those and the tubes of Pringles in all the colours of the rainbow. There's two boxes of wine, one white, one red, a four pack of lager, which is the tip of the Carlsberg. And underneath the three clocks draped in streamers, the three clocks labelled Havana, Party Time, Tokyo, are two small presents. In gold wrapping paper is a parcel from me to Bex. In silver foil is a package from Bex to me.

It's a shame Sarah isn't here. Sarah loves parties. Even though she won't be attending, I still wouldn't put it past her to have sowed the party seed in Bex's mind. As if to make up for her absent friend's enthusiasm, Bex has been buzzing and bursting and brimming with ideas, and despite my attempts to play my normal reticent, slam-the-brakes-on self, I've been out-fought and out-suggested, my every objection overruled. The party is themed. The party is fancy dress. And even though I pointed out that we're not actually on a tube line, Bex has based the whole party on the London Underground.

'What do you think?' Bex asks. She is wearing a shiny silver, low-cut top, her hair tied up with tinsel and glitter in her eyelashes.

'You *shall* go to the ball,' I say as Bex does a twirl.

'I like your shirt,' Bex says, giving the green viscose a brush.

'I should hope you do, seeing as you're insisting I wear it.'

'It's part of your costume,' Bex says, handing me my parcel. 'Go on, open it.'

I tear the package open to find a thin white strip of card.

'It's a dog collar,' Bex explains.

'Right,' I say, trying to think of some religion-related tube stations.

'You're a *parson*, dummy. Parson's Green. Here, I've put a slit in it at the back.' She flicks my shirt collar up, slips the dog collar round. 'There, is that too tight?'

I pretend to choke.

'Very funny. Is it my turn now?' Bex scoops her present up expectantly. She tears it open to reveal a . . .

'Horn?' Bex gives a confused squeeze. Parp.

'What kind of sound would you say that was?' I ask.

Bex squeezes the horn again. 'Parp?'

'To my ears, I hear it more as a toot.'

'Toot?' The penny drops. 'Oh, *I've* got it. I'm Tooting.'

'Almost. What's your Christian name?'

'Ah. Clever. I'm Tooting Bex, aren't I?'

Bex gives me a hug and a kiss on my cheek to say thank you.

'Where's my camera?' She scurries off. 'We've got to take a picture of us.'

Bex fiddles with the timer whilst I fix us a drink.

'Ben, quickly, quickly look this way.' Bex drags me in for the obligatory bad photo.

Flash. I hand Bex a plastic glass of wine.

'To absent friends.' I raise my glass.

'No.' Bex wags a finger. 'That's exactly what this evening isn't about. This is to us.'

'OK,' I say. 'To us. Who cares about . . . what were their names again?'

Bex laughs and clinks my plastic glass.

The guests arrive in a trickle and then a flood. Some of the costumes are more inventive than others. A number of the blokes come in football shirts – Arsenal, West Ham, Tottenham (Hale). A number of girls come as Posh Spice (Victoria) in their little black dresses. There's a fully fledged Paddington, complete with duffle coat, suitcase, and a sign that says 'Please look after this bear'. Someone dressed up in a Womble costume. A few in school uniforms (Grange Hill) and some lawyer friend of Bex's with a can of 'amber nectar', who I'd assumed had forgotten to dress up.

'Not at all,' I hear him leer at some girl, 'I'm Cockfosters.'

'I can see the Fosters, but where's the . . .'

'I thought you'd never ask.'

The evening soon slips into that London party rhythm, where people arrive, relax, then tense up as midnight approaches. Do we get the last train, everyone is thinking, or am I having enough fun to stay on, stay up and splash out for a taxi? It's a dangerous moment for any host, for people pissed are bit like sheep and if a couple of key people decide to call it a night then suddenly you've haemorrhaged half your guest list. If the party gets past midnight in reasonable shape, then you're laughing. For the people who are left are the people who are up for it, doubly so because they've decided to stay. And here – in the early hours of the morning – is where things really kick off.

'Benjamin,' Annabel says.

I'm coming out of the toilet when she calls me. Annabel is sitting legs crossed on the armchair in the spare room where all the coats are. She's wearing her hair up, tight leather trousers that crinkle when she moves, a low-cut red T-shirt. For a New Labourite she wears a lot of red, I think. On the front of the T-shirt is printed a quote from a poem: 'There's some corner of a foreign field that is for ever England'.

'Annabel,' I say, leaning in the doorway. 'How are you?'

'Good.' The cigarette in her left hand is pouring smoke towards the ceiling.

'Who are you?' I ask.

Annabel draws on her cigarette. 'Snaresbrook,' she says.

'Of course. That's from Rupert Brooke, isn't it?' I say. 'So where's the snare?'

Annabel smirks, leans forwards, forwards in such a way as to show off as much cleavage as possible.

'So how are you, Benjamin?' she asks.

'Oh, er, you know.' I recover myself. 'Surviving.'

'It must be terribly lonely, your girlfriend being so far away.'

So this is it, I think. This is my test. I've been waiting for this ever since Sarah left, and now here she is, leaning forwards and emphasising her cleavage in front of me.

The funny thing is, I thought something like this might happen tonight. An inkling. I feel my breath shallow and quicken, as I think, this is real. If you asked me in the cold light of day if I'd do anything, I'd laugh and dismiss the suggestion out of hand. But this isn't the cold light of day, this is the warm glow of night, a night of several cans of lager, which have had their alcoholic effect of loosening some things and straining others. Sarah, I think, Sarah, but my thoughts of her are stripping away in front of my eyes, nothing compared with the lust, the desperation, the sex pulsing. God, I think, shocked at how flimsy my morals are. God. I really, really would like a fuck.

'She's a brave girl, that Sarah,' Annabel continues, 'leaving you in London by yourself. It's very *trusting* of her.' Annabel pronounces the word trusting as though she means 'foolish'.

'I, um,' I waggle my dog collar and laugh, 'I've taken a vow of celibacy.'

'How very noble. But surely even vicars have needs.' Annabel smiles. 'Urges.'

I remember Si's words from all those months before: *A year without your girlfriend is a long time. Too long a time. And that's not an opinion, Ben. As far as I'm concerned that's scientific, spermatological fact. A man has his needs, you know what I'm saying?*

'Come on, Benjamin.' Annabel stands up, pushes the door shut behind me. 'Are you seriously suggesting that you're going to last the year?' She looks me up and down. 'A young gun like you. She can't have been gone more than a few weeks and I'll bet you're desperate already.'

'I am not,' I say. 'I'm not like that.'

'Of *course* you're not.' She leans forwards. 'You must be bursting.'

'I'm *fine*,' I say.

'I'm just a friend offering to help, Benjamin.'

'No you're not,' I say. 'And can you please stop calling me Benjamin.'

'I'm sure Sarah would hate to think of you all frustrated.'

'I think Sarah would hate to think of me getting off with you.'

'You're going to get off with someone,' Annabel says. 'So why don't you get off with me?'

The door opens and a bloke in an Arsenal shirt walks in.

'Sorry,' he says. 'Just got to get my, er . . .' He grabs a couple of coats off the bed and leaves.

On the landing I hear him say, 'It's a tarts and vicars party in there.'

I want to smell Sarah's cardigan. As I stumble out onto the landing, what I'm thinking is, I need help. A smell of the cardigan, a smell of Sarah will see me right. It'll remind me of her, reinvigorate my feelings for her, shut out the thought of anyone else and make me think of her, of us. But as I reach my bedroom, the door is shut, and as I turn the handle, I hear a noise. A squeak of a bedspring. A squeal of something, some*one* else.

I pause on the landing, gather myself, debate whether to go and do my best three bears impression and shout, 'Someone's sleeping in MY bed,' when out of the corner of my eye, I notice a silhouette standing in Bex's room. A girl, alone in the half-light, staring at a picture on top of Bex's dresser.

The girl doesn't look round but I know that it's her, the Japanese girl from the gig. I recognise the shape of her hair. She's wearing a black polo neck jumper and jeans. Her silhouette and tightness of her jumper defines her thinness, her curves. I'm about to go when suddenly I realise the girl's gaze has switched: she is looking at me, watching me in the mirror above the dresser. Staring at me is more accurate: there's a shine in her eyes, a sharpness to her look, like a bird of prey. The moonlight from the window splashes her reflection in an almost ghostly white.

I'm entering the room. I say that, because I'm all but unaware I'm doing it. I'm drawn, almost pulled towards the girl, all the time not taking my eyes off her reflection. The closer I get, the more the moonlight seems to emphasise her paleness, the tiny mole on her chin, the thin strand of hair sweeping down in a concave curve until its end is all but resting on the thick lushness of her bottom lip. Without breaking eye contact she pushes the strand delicately aside. The movement is so smooth, so controlled, so captivating, I can almost feel the soft, silky sensation of the hair skating across her skin.

'Father,' the reflection says. Her voice is soft, gentle, tinged with an accent I cannot place.

'What? Oh, right,' I say. 'I'm a parson, actually. Parson's Green.' I point at my dog collar, my shirt. 'And who are you meant be?'

'Angel,' says the girl.

'Don't you need a halo for that?'

For the first time, the girl's gaze flicks away from me, looks down to the dresser. Sitting there is a small, silver tinsel circle.

'It slipped,' says the girl.

There is something about Angel, about her looks, her dress sense, her demeanour, everything, that exudes calmness and coolness, silences the noise, the thumps, the party beyond. Standing there, looking at her reflection, it's, well, it's almost as if nothing else exists.

'So you were at that gig I went to with Bex, weren't you?' I say. 'The Danny Martin one?'

At the mention of Danny Martin, the girl's face flickers into life. She's nodding and turning round to look at me and her eyes are glistening and she's smiling ever so slightly, a small, subtle, arch smile.

'Oh, he was amazing, wasn't he?' There's that smile again. 'Yes, I'd almost forgotten you were there with Bex.'

'So you know her, then?' I'm a little confused.

'We both ended up at the same gig again last week,' Angel explains, 'and just got talking. She's such a warm person, Bex. Wonderful taste in music.'

Angel glances down again, at the dresser, and it's then that I realise what she's been staring at. On the top of the dresser is a picture in a frame, a picture of the folk singer Nick Drake. It shows the singer leaning against a wall whilst a man hurries by for a bus. The key to the picture is that Nick with his black Byronic locks, is passively, poetically in focus, whilst the businessman running for the bus is perfectly, prosaically blurred. It's a picture of contrasts: art versus commerce, clarity versus confusion, cool versus corporate, passive versus active. Nick Drake is the archetypal anti-establishment figure, stepping back from the rat race and seeing the world as it really is.

'Are you a fan?' I ask.

'Oh, I *adore* Nick.' The girl has picked up the picture, is staring at it intently. The smile, I notice, has gone now. She reaches out and runs a finger down Nick Drake in the photo. As if she's stroking him. 'Do you know *Five Leaves Left*?' she asks eventually.

'Sorry?'

'*Five Leaves Left*. It's the album from which this photo is taken.'

I shake my head. 'Should I?'

'Oh, you must,' Angel says, leaning in, lightly squeezing my lower arm. Her eyes are alive. 'It's just the most beautiful album in the world. So peaceful, so poetic, so vulnerable, so honest. His voice, the guitar playing, the arrangements, it's just amazing. There is nothing more wonderful than waking up and hearing Nick sing. It's perfect morning music.'

There's something about the passion in her voice, the vibrancy despite its softness, that beguiles. There's nothing clever, ironic about what she's saying, there's no pretence about knowingness or one-upmanship. Just a simple, pure, heartfelt opinion.

'I should give it a listen sometime,' I say. 'Chris Evans can get a bit much occasionally.'

'Chris Evans?'

'The DJ?' I pull a face. I'm thinking, She doesn't know who Chris Evans is? 'The breakfast show? Radio One?'

'I never listen to the radio.'

I'm astonished. I thought you couldn't get away from Chris Evans, even if you wanted to. Part of me thinks, She's got to be taking the piss. But looking at her, at the hair that's slipped back down across her face, which almost insanely I want to reach up and push back, I'm in no doubt she's telling the truth. That curiously, captivatingly, she's out of kilter with popular culture.

'So why's the album called *Five Leaves Left*?' I ask.

'I think it's a smoking thing,' Angel explains, brushing the hair back. 'A reference to the note you get in your packet of cigarette papers, telling you you're about to run out.'

'And that's what? His first album?'

Angel nods. 'He did three altogether, plus little bits here and there. Three albums proper before, well . . .'

'Before what?'

Angel flinches. 'Before he died,' she says simply.

Ah. I want to ask more, to ask why, how, when, but before I can, Angel has started speaking again.

'He wasn't successful when he was alive,' she says. 'It was only later that people started buying his records. He died never knowing how popular he'd become.' She puts the picture back on the dresser. 'Fate can be cruel like that.'

'You think?'

'Don't you?' Angel has turned round and is looking at me. I suddenly notice how close together we're standing. 'It's such a capricious thing.'

'How do you mean? Unpredictable?'

'I mean it's volatile,' Angel says. 'Sometimes it can be callous, cutting, almost malevolent. At others it's astonishing, surprising. Whenever you think you know what's going to happen, fate's always one step ahead.'

'And you believe in it?'

'It's what makes life interesting,' Angel says. 'Of course I believe in fate.' She pauses. 'But that doesn't mean I don't challenge it. I think it's important to test it constantly, push it to see how far it can go.'

'And?' I ask. 'How far is that?'

There's that smile again. 'We'll see,' she says. And with an arch of her back, a flex of her shoulders that seems strangely familiar, she turns and is away, brushing past without a look, the faintest of scents lingering behind.

Half an hour later and Cockfosters and whoever he got lucky with have finally left my room. I know it's him because of the empty four pack on my bedside table. I ignore the sheets and make for my chest of drawers, kneel down and pull open the bottom drawer, pulling out jumper after jumper until there, at the bottom, hidden away from Bex, is Sarah's cardigan. I take it out, hold it up to the light, push my nose against it and smell.

Nothing.

I smell it again, but Sarah's scent isn't there. It's gone. Maybe it's me, I think, and grab a deodorant off the dresser to check I haven't got a cold or anything, but no, my nose is fine. Sarah's smell has vanished, faded away until I can no longer pick it out, disappeared until her cardigan is no more than a cardigan. I am, at this point, more than I've ever felt, alone, apart, vulnerable.

I stand up, look at the moon streaming in through the window. Can Sarah see that? I'm not even allowed that: it's morning over there, she's in sunlight and I'm stuck in darkness. I stand there for a moment, holding the cardigan against me and it's then as I look down, down into our yard below, that I see Bex, Bex, to my astonishment, who is kissing, embracing someone else. And then I gasp, and gasp again.

The person Bex is kissing is female.

Dear Sarah,

Oh my God. I feel absolutely awful. It's Sunday morning here. 7 o'clock and I can't sleep. I'm in Ben's room, where I've spent the night, which sounds awful but in fact there's nothing to worry about. Not like that anyway. Basically, when I tried to go to bed last night, there were two lawyers shagging in it and your boyfriend, after a little discussion, agreed to crash on the sofa.

Anyway, that's all boring. I feel awful. This is largely the fault of three lemon Hooches, two Vodka Mules, one G&T that was more G than T, three beakers of cheap £2.99 red wine from the off licence round the corner and a more-than-wee dram of whisky. Plus the best part of a packet of Camels and a generous share of a Camberwell carrot. I threw up last night, which made me feel a little better, but not much. Not much at all.

I feel awful because of all that. But mainly I feel awful because of this.

It all started about midnight. Well, I think it was about midnightish, my timing's a little hazy, I was in the garden having a fag and this girl walks out. She's tall, tartish in tight jeans and crop top, with long brunette hair, all tied up in this magnificent coiffure, that's somewhere between that woman from M People and that bloke from Doctor and the Medics.

'Let me guess,' I said. 'No, you're going to have to give me a clue.'

'High Barnet,' she smiled. 'And you are?'

I parped my horn.

90

'Tooting?' she asked.

'Tooting Bex.'

'Oh, you're Bex.' High Barnet nodded towards my cigarette. 'May I?'

'Sure.' She took a drag and blew out into the night sky. 'You're the hostess, right? I do like your top, where's it from?'

'Jigsaw. It was in a sale.' (You remember, the shiny silver one we bought just before you went away.)

'Suits you.' High Barnet passed what was left of my cigarette back. 'Really shows off your breasts.'

'You think? You don't think it makes them look too big?'

High Barnet shook her head. 'Not at all. They look delectable. Any bloke would be a lucky man to get his hands on those.'

'So who did you come with?'

'Matt. He's the bloke in school uniform pretending to be Grange Hill.'

'Right,' I said. 'He's on my law conversion course.'

'Right,' High Barnet said. 'We did History together at Kent.'

'And what are you doing now?'

'Oh, this and that. I'm working as a runner for a production company. I'm trying to put some basic television experience together, and—'

'Woof!'

'Oh God,' High Barnet groaned as this lecherous bloke who 'came' as Barking stepped out onto the patio, ever so slightly the worse for wear.

'Hi, Barnet.' Barking was a Mancunian, earning what he described as 'a crust' on some graduate training scheme in the city. He was short and suffered from small-person's syndrome.

Though not as much as High Barnet had suffered from it by the sounds of things. Then he turns to me. 'And Tooting Bex too. You know what, you're really horny, you geddit?' He took a swig of lager, some of which made it into his mouth, and wiped his lips on his sleeves. 'Now come on, ladies, don't be shy. Who wants a bit of my tube?'

'I don't think so,' I said.

'It's all right.' Barking winked. 'My travelcard lets me visit all zones, you know what I'm saying.'

'The thing is,' said High Barnet, 'you're wasting your time with us.'

'And why's that then?'

'Well, we're not, how shall I put this?' At this point she looked at me, and winked. 'We're not really into men.'

We're not? I thought. Then I saw High Barnet nodding at me.

'Er, that's right,' I said. 'Nothing personal, but I just don't fancy blokes.'

Barking looked at High Barnet, then he looked at me. 'Oh yeah,' he said. 'Sure you're not. You're just saying that to get rid of me.'

And then it happened. Suddenly High Barnet's hand was round my waist and she was kissing me, a big proper snog, her tongue pushing its way into my mouth, her breasts pressing against mine. I was so surprised that it took me a couple of seconds to realise what was going on. It was all quick and weird and tasted odd and felt strange and not quite right. When I pulled back for breath, I don't know who was more surprised, me or Barking.

'Satisfied?' High Barnet asked Barking. 'Now fuck off and leave us alone.'

Oh my God, Sarah. I snogged someone. I don't know whether High Barnet really was a lesbian or not, but ... oh shit, I'm not, I'm into men, one man in particular, and every time I think about Si I feel physically sick. What have I done? I really, really love Si and I think I might have fucked it up. Has Ben seen? Will he tell Si? I can't ask him in case he doesn't know, but if I don't ask him then I won't know whether he knows or not, and I don't know if that is worse. Shit, shit, shit. I can hear Ben moving around downstairs, so I'm going to have to finish and get this in the post pronto.

Sarah. What am I going to do?

Bexxxxxxxxxxx

7

Should I tell Si?

Such a simple, such a straightforward, such a complicated question. I wish I hadn't seen it. I wish that Sarah's cardigan was still clinging onto her smell and my mind had been lost in that rather than staring out of the window and seeing what was happening in the backyard below. If somehow I could fold the image up, stuff it back into its box, then I would. Because now, whatever I do, I will feel guilty. If I tell Si, I'll be letting Bex down. If I don't, it is Si I'm betraying.

On one level, nothing was wrong. They'd agreed a deal that kissing was allowed, and that was all I'd seen. God knows what Si was up to in Cuba with whatever her name was, so maybe all things were equal. But from where I'm watching, it feels as though these were two wrongs trying to squeeze into a right. What did it say about their relationship? Not much, I think. It seems a little sad, somehow, that here they are, pretending, charading each other. I'm glad that Sarah and I aren't like that.

There is something disconcerting about Bex kissing a girl. As far as I know, and Sarah told me pretty much everything that Bex got up to, she isn't that way inclined. So is this a side she's always had that she didn't let on? Is there something about her that Si doesn't know, that even if he did, he'd be unable to fulfil? Secrets, too many secrets. And now, I have them too.

This is the point of no return, the point where the fairy tale of everything working out all right and Si and Bex and me and Sarah surviving the year starts to slide. Suddenly everything is big and messy and adult and complicated. And, if I'm being honest, it's not just Bex's behaviour that's bothering me. I'm shocked, scared at how close I was to succumbing to Annabel's advances. If that bloke hadn't walked in for his coat ... I'd like to tell myself nothing would have happened, but I know that's not true. I could have and I may well would have. And there's so many things going on, I can't separate out where that came from. Does it say something about me and Sarah? Or does it say something about loving long distance? Either question, I don't think I like the answer. Somehow I've escaped. Next time, well, let's not think about that.

The other thought, the thought I really, *really* don't like, is this. If Bex is getting off with people, if Si is getting off with people, if I'm almost getting off with people, then where does that leave Sarah? If the rest of us are struggling through the year apart, how can I be so sure that she is any different?

The cartoon in the *Guardian* about the design plans for the Greenwich Exhibition starts with a picture of a Millennium Shed. 'Not exciting enough' the caption reads. Next up is a Millennium Ironing Board ('Frankly bor-ring') and a Millennium Boghouse ('Too rude'). The next suggestion is a Millennium Hairy Bottom – 'Still too rude, but perhaps there's the germ of a concept here?' This oscillates into the Millennium Dead Dog, flat on its back, the Millennium Tick with its insect legs sticking up in the air ('At last – maybe we're getting somewhere'), before finally ('Oh yes! Oh yesss! Cut, print and build') there is the Millennium Dome, shallow white bump with its crown of pillars.

Gareth shows it to me with a grunt. 'Typical fucking Tories. Overblown. Over-expensive. Thank God it'll all be over soon.'

'You think?'

'I do think. Which is more than can be said for whoever came up with this.' Gareth looks at me. 'What? You're not telling me you think this is a good idea?'

'I'm not sure,' I reply. 'It's a big thing the millennium, isn't it? Maybe we should be celebrating it somehow.'

'What's so special about the millennium anyway?' Gareth asks. 'It's just a date.'

'It's quite a big date as dates go,' I say. 'Isn't it good to have these sort of things once in a while?'

'Good for who?'

'Good for the country,' I say.

'Good for London.' Gareth shrugs.

'No, this is a national thing. Like the festival in Britain in 1951. If it was good enough for Labour then, why can't it be good enough for us now?'

'Yes, but the point of the Festival of Britain was to celebrate the end of the war, the end of rationing and austerity, and a chance to look to the future. This is just a celebration of a date, a date that, technically, doesn't even mark the start of the new millennium.'

'This is a chance to look to the future. This can be our chance to say to Britain, to the world, what we're about.'

'Why don't we spend the money on health or education or something? Wouldn't that tell the world what we're about?'

'It'll be good for Greenwich, for East London, too,' I say. 'It's a chance to regenerate the area. Think of all the jobs it'll produce.'

'Temporary jobs.' Gareth shakes his head. 'I hear what you say, but I think this is a political stitch-up. If we refuse to co-operate, say we'll ditch it if elected, then the government will accuse us of being party-poopers. If we agree to go ahead with it, we're going to be saddled with a huge unwieldy project that the Tories will take credit for if it succeeds, and will blame us for if it goes wrong. I mean, have you read about the problems?' He glances at the newspaper. 'The whole thing is riddled with holes. The funding is somewhere between unclear and non-existent, the costs are likely to spiral, and no one seems to have a thought about what's going to go in the thing yet. It's a disaster waiting to happen.'

'It could be really *good*,' I disagree. 'Think about Tony's conference speech about this being a young country. What if we harnessed all of the creativity that's about: Britpop, Britart, Britfashion, Britlit. It could be a showcase for our talents.'

'Like who?' Gareth asks. 'Shed Seven?'

'No. Like Blur and Oasis, Damien Hirst and Tracy Emin, John Galliano and Alexander McQueen: you name it, this country is bursting with good stuff.'

Gareth shakes his head. 'It's not going to happen. I mean, not that you'd get them to take part, but this Brit-stuff is all flimflam, superficial shit that'll be gone within a few months. Britpop's an echo of the sixties, nothing more. At least we managed to beat Germany at football back then.'

'Don't you get the vision thing?' I ask. 'The feel-good factor?'

'That's such a New Labour thing to say,' Gareth says. 'And this whole thing has got New Labour written all over it. It's big and symbolic and empty.'

'If New Labour is all such bollocks,' I ask, 'why are you here campaigning?'

'Labour's not bollocks,' Gareth says. 'Deep down, beneath the "new" there's something important. I'm here to help dig it out. Likewise the music.' He reaches down into his bag. 'I bought a proper Britpop album today.'

'You?' I laugh. 'I thought you hated it all?'

Gareth pulls out a copy of *Anthology: Volume 3* by the Beatles.

'Very funny,' I say.

'I'm serious,' Gareth says. 'It may be out-takes and alternative versions and stuff, but it's still by far the best British album that's been out all year. Go on, take it home and listen to it. That is to Oasis what the real Labour Party is to New Labour.'

'Don't you ever worry you're just stuck in the past?' I ask.

'If the past is so crap, why are all your beloved bands paying homage to it?' Gareth asks. 'Maybe I am old-fashioned. But maybe the past has got something, which is why people like me keep going back.'

In the newsagent, I bump into Annabel. Or does Annabel bump into me?

I've nipped in during my lunch hour to buy a copy of *Loaded*, the magazine 'for men who should know better'. Si and I should have known better ever since its launch. But here at last was a magazine for lads like us: funny, irreverent, and a million miles away from the New Man mush of *Arena* and *GQ*, with their pretentiousness and artsiness and their photos of designer clothes I couldn't afford, and wouldn't have been seen dead in even if I could.

Loaded's freshness, its upbeatness, its Englishness, everything about it just seemed to dovetail. It wore its male icons on its cover: Gary Oldman, Jimmy White, Vic and Bob, Kevin Keegan. It had a section called 'Great Moments in Life' discussing catalogue bra sections and having a cold, it honoured 'Greatest Living Englishmen' such as Patrick Moore and the Honey Monster. *Loaded* went to the pub, *Loaded* went clubbing, *Loaded* organised competitions to decide which was the best crisp in the world. There was the occasional woman with no clothes on, sure, but no more so than any other male magazine and besides, this always seemed secondary: Si and I bought the magazine because it made us laugh.

Somehow, somewhere, something changed. Slowly,

surely, as the magazine became more popular, it became stuffed full of all the poncey adverts I bought *Loaded* to escape from. And as the sales crept up, so the female covers started appearing. And today, as I pull the latest edition from the shelf, with its shot, not of a Michael Caine or a Steve McQueen, but of *Baywatch* babe Donna D'Errico leaning forward and bursting out of a small red bikini, for the first time I find myself feeling a twinge of embarrassment. For the first time I think, Maybe I am a man who should know better.

'Hello there.'

I jump and shove the magazine back on the shelf.

'Annabel. Hi,' I say. 'I'm browsing.'

'So I see,' Annabel says, pulls out the magazine from where I've shoved it behind *Gardening Weekly*. 'I guess at least she's wearing red.'

'I wasn't going to *buy* it,' I say.

'What is this?' Annabel asks. 'Relief while your girl-friend's away?'

'This isn't what you think,' I say. 'I buy it sometimes because it makes me laugh, but I thought this was too much and put it back.'

'Why? Ashamed because it's wearing its tart on its sleeve?' Annabel asks.

I smile thinly.

'Bit testy today?' Annabel says.

'Oh, I had a bit of barney with Gareth this morning.'

I explained our conversation.

'You know,' Annabel says, 'I love Gareth to bits but he's, how can I put this, his politics have painted him into a corner. A red corner, if you know what I'm saying.'

I nod.

'Now, I'm not saying that his views aren't heartfelt, I'm sure they are. But sometimes they can be a little, *well*, anachronistic. Don't quote me on this, but sometimes it feels as though he's living his life in the past.'

I nod again.

'Ben, do you mind if I give you some advice?'

'Sure.'

'I wonder whether it would be good for you, for your career, to step out from underneath Gareth's shadow. If you're not careful, people will start associating the two of you too closely together. I mean,' she smiles, 'there's going to be a lot of jobs going round if we win, and you'd want to put yourself forward in the most favourable light.'

'I guess,' I say. I haven't really thought about it.

'Why don't you let me have a word? Quietly, of course. I'm sure we can arrange a secondment to another unit if you'd like.'

'Well, er . . .'

'Of course, I can go back to HQ and tell my female colleagues about what I've spotted you buying.'

'There's nothing wrong with what I was buying,' I say.

'That's why you put it back then?'

'I, er . . .'

'Good,' Annabel smiles. 'That's agreed then. Believe me, it's the right thing to do. Gareth just hasn't got the, what did you call it, the vision thing. You should come and work with people who do.'

Later, I arrive back in the flat before Bex, and pull out Gareth's double CD, the third and final anthology of outtakes and alternative versions of Beatles songs. The front cover is a carefully created montage of different album covers torn together: 'Let It Be', 'Rubber Soul', 'Sergeant Pepper', 'Abbey Road'. I flick it over and start to read the tracklisting: 'Happiness is A Warm Gun', 'Helter Skelter', 'Mean Mr Mustard', 'Polythene Pam'. Fuck it, I think. I've heard all this a million times before. It's my parents' music, not mine. I put the CD back in my bag and reach across for my copy of *Morning Glory*, flick it on and turn it up loud.

Does this mean nothing, Gareth? You're wrong. This is me and Sarah writ large. And as I sit there and sink into the music, I turn it up notch by notch to drown out the rest of the world.

Dear Bex,

Hey there, fellow cardigan girl. Bloody hell! Got your letter this morning and I am writing back at the first possible opportunity, which is my morning free when I'm meant to be preparing and photocopying for this afternoon's lesson, so if my students fail their exams, consider yourself the one to blame.

Now. Listen very carefully: DON'T WORRY. You have done absolutely nothing wrong. Your oaf of a boyfriend cajoled you until you agreed that him snogging half of the Americas would not affect your relationship. The net effect is that you're allowed to snog someone else too. You didn't mean to. It didn't mean anything. So what? It doesn't mean that you fancy Si any less. In fact, the fact that you feel so guilty about the whole thing shows just how much you actually feel for the guy, even though he was keen to have as 'open' a relationship as he could get away with.

But however bad you feel about snogging someone, do not, Not, NOT tell him you have. Although, in theory, he's fine for you to snog someone else, I'm betting that he worked out the clause with himself in mind, and in practice he wouldn't be so relaxed to find that you've partaken in its freedom as well. Blokes are like that. He'll either be pissed off with you despite saying that he isn't, or he'll be spurred into pro-activity so he doesn't feel shown up in the prowess stakes. I've had a letter from Ben who didn't mention it, which doesn't hugely surprise me; his antenna is not the most well tuned when it comes to these sorts of things. But even if – and I mean if – he does know, I'm sure it will still be fine. I'm sure he won't tell Si, at least not without discussing it with me first, and I'll do everything I can to make sure he doesn't. But even if the worst comes to the worst and Si finds out, I'm sure the fact that you kissed someone female will help. I don't think he'd be half as threatened as if you kissed a bloke. Actually, being the kind of man he is, he'll probably get quite turned on by the thought, and ask if he can watch next time.

And anyway, you don't know how lucky you are with this get-out clause. Imagine if I got off with someone – how different would that be? Sometimes I wish Ben and I had agreed something like that, just in case anything happened. A year is a bloody long time, after all. But just as you gave in to Si's instincts for a bit of flexibility, so I succumbed to Ben's need for reassurance and security. The subject, as you know, became 'The unbroachable' before I set off. And now I'm stuck with the thought that any slip, however tiny, is potentially curtains. I may want to spend this year as far away from Britain as possible, but that is certainly one place I don't want to go.

Oh, Bex, if I was there now I'd give you a big hug like you've done for me so many times in the past. And then I'd say, 'Right, you little minx, tell me all about it. So come on. How was it? Did it feel nice? Did it turn you on at all? Did you get her phone number? And how come you've never tried to kiss me? (BTW, I hope you weren't too busy eyeing up the women to notice whether my boyfriend was doing the same. You have sisterly duties to carry out, don't you forget! I want a full report on that slapper Annabel . . .)

I'm going to write to Ben now and find out just what he does know. In the meantime you just act normal. And just carry *on writing to Si as you would anyway. And don't forget, even though I'm thousands of miles away, I'm right there with you.*

Love you, Sarah x

8

And then there's Bex's gig.

I've a lot of work on, but there's no way I can't watch her playing in London for the first time, particularly when I'm her only good friend not half a world away, especially when I know how nervous she's going to be beforehand. And when I meet her at Baker Street station, I'm glad I made the necessary excuses to be here, because she's looking as fraught and anxious as the day Si left for Cuba.

'At last,' she says, passing me her guitar. 'My roadie.'

It takes us a while to find the venue. No wonder the folk music scene's so small, I think, because you can never find where they're playing the gigs. We wander the side roads of Baker Street, a square circle between Marylebone Road and Oxford Street, before we spot a gaunt man in a faded denim jacket with a black guitar case, and at a safe distance, giggling like spies, hiding behind lamp posts, we follow him to a smart-looking Italian bistro, where he slips through a side door and goes downstairs.

'Now what's going on?' I ask Bex as we follow him. 'Why are these places always underground? And why do they always have a restaurant as a front? Is this some sort of subversive movement you're getting us into? Guitarists of the world, you have nothing to lose but your plectrums?'

Like the African restaurant, it's another cellar bar, cavernous with curved ceilings and beautiful brickwork. It's a bigger venue, though, and full to bursting: the bar is off the back by the staircase to civilisation, at the opposite end is the stage, choking with acoustic guitars and mike stands and amplifiers and lots of those thin black boxes with rows of green and red lights. Small round tables fill the room, framed by a horseshoe of three long wooden tables and benches. And firing off in each direction are a collection of nooks and crannies, each cramming in a dozen people or so, each wired up with a set of speakers so that wherever you sit, you can't miss the music.

'Bex!' A girl's head appears from one of the crannies to the right of the stage, calling and beckoning us over. She's got short, fluorescent red hair and a nose ring that catches the light. 'Come and join us.'

The girl is Sal, and she's sat with half a dozen or so folkies, who shuffle up to make room for us.

'Everybody,' Bex says, 'this is my flatmate Ben.'

'Hi,' I say, and try to take in everybody's name as they introduce themselves. What I'm thinking as they do so is just how trendy everyone is looking. This isn't the Val Doonican cardigan brigade with beard and slippers. Not that Val Doonican has a beard, but I think you know what I mean. These are bright young things, hip and urban, funky with a shot of grunge: a strange piercing here, madly dyed hair there. I don't take in people's names because I'm trying to take in this fact. Folk, it seems, is cool.

Another reason why folk is funkier than Britpop: they serve food to your table. In your average back room of the pub indie venue, supper consists of opening up your packet of prawn cocktail crisps on top of the cigarette machine. Here, you're sitting rather than standing for a start, and then a waitress comes and takes your order, delivers the most delicious-looking rustic pizza or earthenware bowl of steaming pasta, and asks if you'd like another drink.

'You don't get this where I go to watch music,' I explain to Mart on my right, all Soho glasses and shiny navy blue shirt, who permanently seems to be smoking a cigarette, rolling one up, or doing both at the same time.

'Why?' he asks. 'What kind of music are you into?'

'I guess I'm a bit of a Britpop fan. You know, Oasis, Blur, that sort of thing.'

'Right,' Mart nods. 'Great.'

'You're not a fan?'

'Not really. Not my thing. I don't mean to diss it or anything. Just doesn't do anything for me.'

'Oh God,' Bex chimes in. 'Ben's musical taste is *awful*.'

'Not as awful as yours.'

'You remember seeing Danny Martin?' Bex asks. 'You thought he was good?'

'Ye-es,' I say. I can recall the evening, but all my mind flits to is that Japanese girl, Angel, pushing a strand of hair behind her ear.

'So you *do* like folk music, then?'

'Well, I liked Danny Martin.' I couldn't really remember Danny Martin. All I could remember from that evening was that girl. 'I don't really know any of this sort of music to know whether I like it or not.'

'Well, you've come to the right place,' Mart says.

'OK,' I say. 'So supposing I wanted to get into this stuff. Where do I start? Who should I buy?'

'Joni Mitchell,' Bex says. 'If you buy one album, you've got to buy Joni Mitchell. *Clouds.* The one with "Chelsea Morning" on.'

'Mart?' I ask.

'Tim Buckley,' he says. 'Late-sixties, early-seventies singer. Extraordinary voice. *Happy Sad* is just my favourite album of all time. His son's great, too: Jeff Buckley? *Grace?* Ben, you've got some treats ahead.'

'Jen.' Bex nudges her neighbour, a pale girl, with her long straight red hair tied back. 'We're helping introduce my friend Ben to some decent music. I've suggested Joni Mitchell, Mart's gone for Tim Buckley.'

'Well, I'm a bit of a Bobcat myself,' Jen says.

'Excuse me?'

'A Bob Dylan fan.'

'Right,' I say. 'Didn't he fall out with the folkies?'

'Only the purists,' Jen says. 'In the mid sixties, he turned up at the Newport Folk Festival and shocked them by playing electric guitar. When he started touring with a band, the purists all turned up and booed. But it's not about whether he's playing acoustic or electric, is it? It's all about the songs.'

'So which album should I listen to?'

'There's so many,' Jen says. '*Blonde on Blonde. Blood on the Tracks. Slow Train Coming. Oh Mercy.* Take your pick.'

'Sal?' Mart asks. 'What about you?'

'Oh, it's got to be Nick Drake,' Sal says.

Everyone nods and murmurs approval.

'Of course,' says Jen. 'You've *got* to listen to Nick Drake.'

'He's the guy you've got the picture of on your dresser?' I ask Bex.

Bex nods. 'He's a strange one. Made three gorgeous albums in the late sixties, early seventies – *Five Leaves Left*, *Bryter Layter* and *Pink Moon*; at the time they did absolutely nothing. It was only after he died that he began to get well known.'

'He can't have been very old.'

'He was twenty-six,' Sal says. 'He took an overdose of antidepressants. Depending on who you listen to, it was either suicide or a terrible, tragic accident.'

'Sorry to interrupt.' A bloke in an orange and purple striped T-shirt, whose stubble reflects his short, shaved haircut appears. 'Is Bex here?'

'That's me,' says Bex.

'Craig,' he offers his hand. 'We spoke on the phone.'

'Hi,' says Bex.

'Great you're here,' Craig says. 'Really looking forward to hearing you play. Now, I can't remember if I explained how it works on the phone, but what we like to do is mix the acts up for the audience. So we get everyone to do two sets of two songs, with the order going one, two, three, four, then we have a break, and then it's the same in reverse; four, three, two, one, if that makes sense.'

Bex nods.

'Now I've got you down as going on second,' Craig

says. 'We're just waiting for Mika to arrive, and then we'll get started.'

Mika arrives while I'm in the toilet. I know this, because the venue had wired even the gents for sound.

'Good evening.' Craig's voice rings out as I'm zipping up. 'Thanks everyone for coming this evening. It's great to see so many faces here, old and new. We've got a great line-up for you this evening so I don't think anyone's going to be disappointed. So please, sit back, have a beer, and enjoy the music.

'So I suppose I'd better introduce our first act to you. What can I tell you about her? Well, she comes all the way from Japan to play for you this evening. Actually, that's not true, she's come from Wimbledon tonight, which may not be as far as Japan, but if any of you use the District Line, you'll know it's no small achievement to get here. I'm waffling, aren't I? Let me shut up and welcome an old friend to the club, please give a hand for Mika!'

The applause is still continuing as I leave the toilets, crane my neck over the crowd and stop, with a jolt, as I realise who Mika is.

The girl from the gig. The girl from the party. Angel.

She's sat on a stool on the stage, her body crunched in, wearing a black woollen cardigan, loosely stitched to show off stripes of flesh between the stitches. A mid-length, mid-purple skirt, with matching nail varnish. I can't help noticing her hair, her large, lazy, funky bob, thick black strands curving in at either side to accentuate her face, her flawless, flawless gothic-white skin. Oblivious to everyone, she's tuning her guitar in a strange, high-pitched way that Bex later explains is called harmonics. For thirty, forty seconds or so, all you can hear is the sound of these notes ringing out, hanging in the air, as delicate as pin-pricks.

'Hi,' Mika whispers as much as speaks into the microphone, pushing a strand of hair behind her ear. For a split second, so short you could miss it, she looks up, skims the room. As her gaze whips past me, I find myself feeling the faintest of flutters.

'Sorry for the delay,' Mika continues, looking down again. 'London Underground. Signal failure after Putney Bridge.' She smiles, ever, ever so slightly, more of a flicker than a grin. 'You've no idea how long I've been waiting for Parson's Green to appear.'

On her guitar, Mika starts plucking a single string on her guitar, the same low note again and again in a hypnotic, rhythmic style, her eyes shut, her body rocking along so slightly you'd hardly notice she was doing it. After a while, she adds a ripple of a run, a tiny triplet of notes at the end of each bar. At this point she starts moving her head from side to side, again ever, ever so delicately. When she starts to sing – no words, just 'mmms' – it's a floating, haunting tune. I can't explain, but it just whistles straight through me. Ethereal, Eastern sounding, almost other-worldly. Like the guitar, it's somehow both gentle and captivating at the same time. And then, just when I'm least expecting it, suddenly the tune has words . . .

> You know that I love you
> You know I don't care
> You know that I see you
> You know I'm not there

And then it stops. There's the strangest silence, for a good five seconds or so, as if the audience can't decide whether that is it or not, whether there is more. And then, with a crash, everyone claps. As the applause continues, I notice Bex waving at me, pointing at me to follow her backstage, the large corner nook, behind the thick blue curtain. As Mika returns to her harmonics, I make my little run of 'excuse me-s' and follow Bex through.

'Wow,' I say. 'What a fantastic song.'

'Nick Drake,' Bex whispers back. 'It's off *Pink Moon*.'

'Right. It was really good. She – Mika's really good, isn't she?' I say, peeking out of the curtain back into the room. From the angle I'm looking, a spotlight lights her up in spectacular silhouette, her body soaking up the brightness to the point that she's glowing.

'Sssh. Yes, you don't need to remind me,' Bex hisses, quietly tuning her guitar. 'I have got to go on after her.'

'Sorry.' I crouch down beside her and squeeze her arm. She's so hyped up, she's shaking. 'You'll be fine. If you sound half as good as you do at home, you'll go down a storm.'

'Do you think?'

'Bex, I *know* so,' I reassure. 'Now. Have you decided which songs you are going to sing?'

Bex looks out to listen to what Mika is playing.

Melancholic, fingerpicked, precise. Neither of us recognises it. One of her own, we decide.

'I think you should do something the crowd recognises,' I suggest. 'Get them going, and sing what you want for the second song.'

Bex thinks. 'I thought I might play a song for Si. "Half a World Away" by REM.'

'That,' I say, 'would be lovely.'

Bex glances down at her electronic tuner, plucks a string. A red light flashes on. She tightens the key and tries again. Green.

From the stage we hear the sound of applause.

'Here we go,' I say, giving her arm a squeeze. 'You'll be brilliant.'

Bex smiles, swallows, grasps her guitar firmly by the neck and heads out. I'm about to follow, return to our table, when there's someone coming in the other direction, and I step back, back into the room and Mika walks in.

'Next up, we have someone playing London for the first time, but I'm sure it's not going to be her last. So please, put your pizza down and give a big welcome to the wonderful Bex Smith!'

I'm standing by the curtain, my head poking out, clapping and beaming my support towards Bex. My mind, though, is straining, urging, begging me to turn round.

'Thanks,' Bex says. 'Wow, what a hard act to follow. This is my first song, which some of you may recognise . . .'

As she starts the song, starts singing, an appreciative murmur ripples round the room, the folkie version of the round of applause on *Stars in Their Eyes*. She's starts fast, too fast, but the murmur settles her down, and in her voice you can hear her relax.

But I'm only half listening. I've heard the scratch of a match against matchbox, the flicker of a flame behind me, and I'm turning round and looking at Mika, leaning against the opposite wall, lighting up. The cigarette's nestled between the middle fingers of her right hand, and she watches me as her left hand waves the flame away, watches me as she draws in, smoke flooding out through her nostrils. I watch, transfixed, watch her inhale, breathe out, inhale, breathe out, and as I do so, it's as though I'm being sucked in myself: drawn in, taken in, dismissed. Everything else seems to stop: only the shrinking of the cigarette hints that time is passing. And it's only when I hear the round of applause from the main room that I come to, and I glance back round, away.

'Thanks,' Bex is saying. 'You're really kind.' She's looking round the room, looking for me. Her eyes skip round in my direction at last, and she smiles. I smile back. 'This next song is one of my own,' she continues. 'It's the first time I've played it in public, so I hope you like it.'

As she begins strumming, I start with a small jump, as I realise that Mika has moved forwards, is standing right by me. So close, in fact, that she's grazing against me, the softness of the wool of her cardigan is tickling against my arm.

'Can you see?' I ask.

Mika looks up at me, and I'm taken aback by her eyes,

their rich, rich chestnut brown, their darkness, their deepness, their intensity.

Mika nods, takes another drag on her cigarette, and then, still looking at me, she lifts the cigarette up towards my lips.

'I'm OK,' I smile. I'm transfixed, I think. Mika nods again, flicks the butt of the cigarette, scattering the ash towards the floor.

'She's good, isn't she?' I glance towards Bex.

Mika looks at me, then leans up on tiptoes, whispers her reply into my ear. I can feel the warmth of her smoky breath tickle the hairs in my ear as she says, 'And you, Ben?'

I'm confused. 'What?' I mouth.

Mika is looking at me again, looking at what I think is something behind my shoulder. But as I glance round and look back, it is my shoulder Mika is staring at, and, with her finger and thumb, I feel the frisson as she outlines the top of my shoulder bone, pulling a hair off, dropping it to the floor.

'Hair,' she whispers. 'Shirt.'

'Right.' I say. 'Thanks,' I add, as the wave of applause washes across the room again, and I come to and realise that Bex's set is over. And I'm caught, trapped between wanting to look for Bex and for Mika, but Mika is suddenly gone, a flash of warmth as she grazes past me, slips into the crowd, and I'm still watching her sweet shape get smaller as Bex's gets bigger and she's beaming and smiling and asking me how was it, how was it, did I think she was OK?

Dear Ben,

Hello mate, soz for not writing sooner, but things have been buzzing here, you know how it is. It's an age ago now, but I'm replying to your last letter from the Labour Party Conference, and your problems with a certain girl named Annabel. Now it may well be that by the time you get this, the whole thing will have blown over. But if it's not, let me give you some friendly, friend's advice.

From what I can tell, you, mate, are quite frankly, and understandably, sex starved. Having had shags on tap for the best part of a year, all of a sudden you have found yourself in a situation where your well of womanly delights has dried up. The technical term, I believe, is 'gagging for it'. Without putting too fine a point on it, you're desperate. You really, really want to go out and get laid.

So when, as was always going to happen, some half-fit bird comes on to you, of course your member is going to go mental. This is your dick talking. 'I need some fucking action!' it's shouting. About bloody time too. This is what you rather quaintly describe as your primeval urge. It's your manhood taking over. Your inbuilt bonking device to go forth and procreate. Sowing the seeds of love.

Does this mean that you don't love Sarah? No, of course it doesn't. This is lust. A very powerful lust, compounded by your current circumstances, but lust nevertheless. And the golden rule is this. Lust doesn't last. Love does. That's what you've got for

Sarah, and that's why you're getting worried. Trust me on this one, mate. When Sarah is back (along with your sex life) you'll have forgotten this Annabel ever happened.

How am I? Thought you'd never ask. You think you've got it bad. Well, let me tell about the other night. I was out in a bar with Juanita and a couple of the other teachers. All nice and gentle and everything. And the evening drags on and everyone comes back to mine and we're drinking and the others go home until it's just me and Juanita there. And we're having another one of those flirty-flirty conversations, you know, all that foreplay by proxy kind of stuff, asking each other about first kisses, first everythings. And Juanita's getting all inquisitive about Bex and grilling me about what our relationship is like, and I explain, and I tell her about our free snogs rule and stuff.

'So if I kissed you,' Juanita asked, 'that wouldn't mean anything?'

'That's allowed,' I said. 'We agreed that in extreme circumstances, we're only human after all, in extreme circumstances a snog would be acceptable behaviour.'

'How strange,' Juanita smiled.

'How come?' I asked.

'Well, if you ask me, it seems odd that kissing is the one thing that's permissible. That strikes me as the most intimate thing of all. You can have sex, and it can be a purely physical activity. Two people going through the motions. But you can't kiss and it mean nothing.'

I disagreed. I said you could have a drunken snog with absolutely no gratification whatsoever.

'But what's the point?' Juanita asked. 'Think about it. Prostitutes don't kiss. Lovers do. What does that say to you? Kissing is private, kissing is personal.'

'So what would you have suggested instead?'

Juanita shrugged. 'Well, I would have thought that the whole point of the agreement was to relieve some sort of sexual frustration. Kissing isn't going to do that. If anything, it's liable to stoke things up further. I would have thought a, what do you say?'

'Handjob.' I translated her sign language.

'I would have thought a handjob or something would be far less personal, and far more constructive.'

'But you've got to understand,' I argued, 'I'd never have got Bex to agree to that. She'd have worried it would lead to something else.'

'Kissing leads to something else. If you have a handjob, and I'm assuming you're like other men, you're going to be pretty much satisfied.' She sighed. 'As it is, a handjob's out of the question.'

I can tell you, by now I was feeling pretty horny.

'Do you have an agreement with your boyfriend?' I asked.

'Only the usual. I sleep with someone. He kills them.'

We sat there, listening to the dark. If there was no Pablo and no Bex, I'm sure we would have been down on the floor and at it. I was trying to slow my heart down when Juanita said, 'What about gratifying other people?'

'What?'

'Well, kissing is allowed. I wouldn't do that because I think it's too personal. You're not allowed to come, so I can't relieve you. But you touching other people?'

This was well weird and well horny. 'It's not something we talked about.'

Juanita looked at me. 'No, I don't expect you did. I don't suppose Bex needed to, because like any other man you wouldn't

119

think twice about accepting a blow job with no reciprocation, but oral sex the other way round? It just wouldn't happen.'

I would have liked to prove her wrong but, as I sat through my sexual history (and I don't suppose you are any different), I couldn't think of any occasion to argue otherwise.

'So what are you saying?' I asked.

'I'm saying that there's a loophole in your agreement. I'm saying that if you wanted to give a woman oral sex, and got nothing back, that would be OK.'

'I thought you said kissing was personal.'

'It is.'

'I would have thought that kind of kissing is very personal.'

'I would think it probably is.' Juanita smiled. 'But then, I didn't write the agreement. I said I wouldn't kiss you, and I won't. But if you wanted to kiss me and are allowed to kiss me, then . . .'

And then, slowly, without losing eye contact, and I swear on my life this is true, mate, she gently lifted her skirt, and with a pair of fingers, pulled her pants to one side.

'Kiss me,' Juanita said.

Fucking hell, mate, I looked at her, and I thought, What the fuck is going on.

'Don't you want a free kiss?'

Juanita looked at me.

'Don't tell me you don't.'

'Of course I do,' I said. I was hardly going to say: Of course I don't if I can get away with it and if that's the only way a blow job's going to happen.

So there I was, going down on her. This is fucking weird, I thought. I'll spare you the details, but I'm sure you won't be surprised when I say, that even out of practice, yours truly is hot stuff. I've never done it for that long before. My jaw still aches.

'Not bad for an Englishman,' Juanita said afterwards. Bastard, I was thinking. Then, then, she said, 'Goodnight'.

'Goodnight? What about me?'

Juanita shrugged. 'I'd feel terrible if I was responsible for breaking your agreement.' She reached over and kissed me on the cheek. 'Think of Bex.'

Can you believe it? Talk about being taken for a ride. I feel kind of, kind of numb (and no, not just my tongue, you unfunny bastard). I don't know, Juanita is right in one respect, according to what I agreed with Bex, I haven't done anything wrong. But at the same time, I can't help feeling bad. Because it was a grey area (not like that. You're disgusting), because we hadn't discussed it, I was taking advantage of what was unspoken in the same way that Juanita, yes, in the same way that Juanita took advantage of me. In a funny kind of way, I feel a bit used. But, and here's the really weird thing, rather than feel angry, it's made me think about the number of women to whom I've done the same sort of thing. Almost into double figures, I reckon. And as much as I feel bad about Bex, I feel bad about that. I can – I've realised – be (quite literally) a bit of a selfish prick in bed. And shit, maybe I'm just missing Bex like you're missing Sarah, but I'm going to start treating women not better as such, but more as equals. Starting with Bex, when she comes over here. And she will, frequently.

This whole thing's really got me thinking. Juanita has a point about the kissing stuff. It is personal. And I think that when Bex comes over here at Christmas I'll suggest we drop it for the rest of our time apart, that we should do what you and Sarah have done. Hard to believe, I know, but I seem to be *getting a bit more respect for women in my old age. I feel really, really strongly for Bex, that's the second point this whole thing has taught me. Odd, I wouldn't have expected to be feeling like this at all. But there you go. Maybe I am a bit of a soppy sod after all.*

Yours thoughtfully,

Si

9

When a band gets as big as Oasis, it's only a matter of time before the imitators start to appear. It's how music scenes work: you get the original groups – the inspiration, the innovation – and then you get the hangers-on, the pallid, paler imitations pulled along in their wake. For every Beatles or Roxy Music or Sex Pistols or Stone Roses, there's always a slew of secondary copycats, the bands who fit the record company's bill of being 'the new Oasis'.

The interesting thing about the Oasis clones is just how carbon the copies are. I mean, even the names – Oasisn't, Quoasis, Noasis, No Way Sis – are derivative. Gareth's theory is that when you've got a retro-sounding scene, the only way for the music to go is to cover what the other bands are playing. If you've got an innovative movement, then the upcoming bands can build on what is original. If you've got a scene that's nodding and winking to the past, then the only things people can build on are the nods and the winks.

'To put it bluntly, Ben,' he said. 'This is the sound of Britpop disappearing up its own arsehole.'

There's been cover bands before, hell, there's even been hit covers of Oasis songs – Mike Flowers Pop's cheesy-listening version of 'Wonderwall' – but this is different to Bjorn Again and Nearvana and Are We Them.

No Way Sis – complete with arguing brothers – have got a five-album record deal. They've got a single out – 'I'd Like To Teach the World To Sing' – the song with the similar tune to Oasis's 'Shakermaker'. No Way Sis doing Oasis doing the New Seekers doing the Beatles. When you think about it like that, maybe Gareth is right.

But here's the thing. No Way Sis aren't playing in the back room of a pub or at some crappy college ball. They're headlining proper venues, venues that real bands have to work their way through years of playing toilets to get close to. There's enough fans out there who are happy to pay to see someone pretending to be Oasis, enough groupies willing to blow someone pretending to be Liam. The real Oasis are holed up recording their new album. Liam's only public appearance in the past few months has been getting arrested for suspected possession of drugs. Liam's response to being stopped was the Liamesque, 'What's it to you, cuntybollocks?' But the nation still wants to see Oasis, and if the real thing isn't around, then the fake version will just have to do instead.

No Way Sis are playing two nights at the Shepherd's Bush Empire, and I've got two tickets. One for me, and one for Sarah. Sarah, who is flying back from Japan for Christmas. I haven't told her I've got them: it'll be a surprise for her at Heathrow, an early Christmas present. And one, I think, that somehow seems appropriate; we saw Oasis just before she left, and now we're seeing the next best thing to celebrate her return.

It's been a few weeks now since I've been moved away from Gareth and have been working for the Audience Participation Unit. Realignment of resources was how it was sold. Diversifying too. Gareth, grumpily, asked if I'd listened to the Beatles CD. I said I had, and thought it was OK. 'You haven't played it, have you?' Gareth laughed, and then he got serious. 'It's up to you, but be careful. I'm not sure you're cut out for their little games.'

The Audience Participation Unit, Annabel explained, is all about awareness. It is about encouraging members of the party to engage with the media outlets that are open to them. So, for travelling programmes, such as *Question Time*, it's all about making local members aware that the show is coming to town and to make sure they get tickets, get into the audience and ask nasty questions to the Tories, nice ones to New Labour. It's about reminding them of telephone votes they can take part in. It's about writing letters to newspapers, supporting the party line.

'The idea,' Annabel continued, 'is to give the impression that the man on the street is in tune with New Labour thinking, or to put it another way, that New Labour is in tune with the man on the street. It's one thing for Tony Blair to talk on the television, but if in every media outlet there are ordinary people endorsing what he says, then it feels as though we've captured the public mood.'

'Captured sounds just about right,' I joked.

'If you think this is funny, then you can always go back and help your friend Karl Marx,' Annabel said, somewhat sharply. 'This is a well-honed, highly successful piece of strategy we're carrying out. This is how it works, Ben. Everyone does it, so why shouldn't we?'

'Right,' I said, a little uneasily.

'Do you want to win the next election?' Annabel asked.

'What kind of a question is that? Of course I do.'

'Well then. And this is one of the many ways we're going to do it.'

The work, I have to say, is more varied than for Gareth. I've been to see *Question Time* three times, the third of which I wore a baseball cap and glasses in case I got recognised. I get to read all the papers, and write as many letters as I can according to their articles. This week has been particularly fruitful, with the printing of an interview in the *Spectator* with the Spice Girls. Posh, Baby, Scary, Sporty and Ginger have done exactly the opposite of Oasis, and come out for the Conservatives. 'As for Major, he's a boring pillock,' Victoria said, 'but compared to the rest he's far better.' Geri, meanwhile, claimed, 'We Spice Girls are true Thatcherites. Thatcher was the first Spice Girl.' I thought that Gareth might be worried about this but he just shrugged. 'Who cares? I mean, it's not like their fans are old enough to vote.'

Anyway. My letters to the newspapers, I feel, have been approaching a work of art.

To the *Telegraph*

Sir,

I read with interest that a popular-beat combo known as the Spice Girls have been quoted as coming out in support of the Conservative Party. While it is always nice to have support, I do wonder if these women are really the sort of people the true blues should be attracting. With their provocative dress sense, surely they are, in the words of one learned judge, 'asking for it'. It can only be a matter of time before some poor gentleman finds his reputation raked through the mud. If that was not enough, one of them, Geri, shares her name with an IRA terrorist leader. As such, I am not sure I will be able to vote Conservative in the forthcoming election and would advise other readers to think the same. Margaret Beckett may not be the most attractive of fillies, but at least she doesn't dress like a whore.

To *The Times*

Sir,
Is it just me, or have other readers noticed that the leader of the Tory-supporting Spice Girls shares her hair colour with that of the failed Labour leader Neil Kinnock? If the Conservatives are now the 'ginger' party of choice, maybe now is the time to vote Labour instead?

To the *Guardian*

For all the talk of Tony Blair moving the Labour Party to the right, it is refreshing to see that 'true Thatcherites' such as the Spice Girls still see the Tories as their natural home. 'Say You'll Be There'? I'll be there for you, Tony.

To the *Daily Mail*

I read with interest that the Spice Girls have come out in support of John Major for the forthcoming election. Interesting because I'm not sure I 'wannabe' living under a Conservative government for much longer. Like most readers, what I really,

really want is a strong dynamic prime minister, who'll deliver better schools and hospitals, and a strong revitalised economy. Perhaps now is the time to give Tony Blair his chance?

To the *Mirror*

With views like that, the Spice Girls can stay at number one for as long as they like. Just as long as they steer clear of Number Ten!

To the *Independent*

Sir,
I note that in a recent article the Spectator *magazine describes the Spice Girls hit 'Wannabe' as 'an anthem to Thatcherite meritocratic aspiration'. Does this mean that their latest single, '2 Becomes 1' is a reference to the ever-dwindling Conservative majority?*

To the *Sun*

Does this mean the Spice Girls will leave the country if Major loses? I know who I'm going to vote for.

To the *Express*

The Spice Girls should think again about voting Conservative, especially as they are such an easy way of remembering New Labour's five pledges for government. Baby refers to the cutting of class sizes for our young children; Scary equates with the fast track punishment for persistent young offenders; Posh is the windfall levy on the fat cat privatised utilities, in order to get 250,000 under 25s into work; Sporty is all about getting the nation fit and healthy by cutting the NHS waiting lists; and Ginger is the gingerly way Labour will treat the economy, offering no rise in income tax and keeping inflation and interest rates as low as possible.

To the *Daily Star*

Everyone should vote Labour because, let's face it, that Posh Spice looks well horny when she's pissed off.

I'm just licking the envelopes when Annabel appears with a new project.

'Did you hear the radio this morning?' she asks, perching herself on the edge of my desk.

My first thought is, What's Chris Evans done now? Annabel, however, hadn't been listening to Radio One.

'It was on the *Today* programme this morning,' she explains. 'The *Today* Personality of the Year. Last year John Major beat Tony Blair.'

'Did he not win the lack of personality of the year?'

'If only. The rumour is that someone rigged it.'

'Who?' I ask. 'Someone like Conservative Central Office?'

'I couldn't possibly comment,' Annabel says. 'But whoever it was, they're not going to get away with it this year. This year Tony's going to win.'

'He is?'

'He is. Now, the way the shortlist gets chosen is that the listeners are invited to ring, write or fax their suggestions in. The ones with the most votes go through to the final round. What I want you to do is drum up some support, get in touch with constituency parties, that sort of thing, get them to contact the BBC, nominating Tony.'

I pause. I'm not very keen on this.

'Are you sure this is a good idea?' I ask. 'It just seems a bit unnecessary. What if we get caught?'

'Relax.' Annabel gives me a smile. 'Why are you so worried about everything?' She squeezes my arm. 'Hey, why don't we go out this evening? I think we could both use a little wind-down time.'

'I, well, I think I might be busy.'

'Sure.' Annabel gives my arm a final squeeze. 'You know where I am.'

I see Gareth as I'm standing by the fax machine. The interesting thing is that I turn my back as he appears.

'What you up to?' he asks.

'Oh nothing. Hey give me that!' I say as Gareth snatches the fax away from me.

'Rigging the *Today* Personality of the Year, eh?' Gareth smiles. 'Ben, you're going up in the world. Do you think you can fix us the election too?'

'It's not like that,' I say. 'This is how it works. And besides you're not any different.'

'What do you mean by that?' Gareth's response is sharp.

'All these stories in the press from a "Labour source" slagging off the Dome, saying we're going to ditch it if we get elected.'

'Are you saying that's me?'

'Come *on*, of course it is.'

'Do you have any proof of that?'

'I just know.'

'You *think* you know,' Gareth says. 'A word of advice, Ben. If you're going to start playing the media, you'd better be extremely careful that you cover your tracks.'

Dear Ben,

All right, now things are really kicking off. I hope the Cuban postal system is working to some sort of level of normality, and you've got this letter after my last one. Otherwise, it's not going to make much sense. Still.

I went to a party last night on the beach, with some of the students and the other teachers. Somebody's birthday, can't remember. Anyway, it was all very chilled. Big campfire, some bloke with a guitar and another with some bongos making the music. Everyone sang and salsa-ed and swam in the sea (not me. I'm not that mad). Very laid-back, very drunken, very chilled.

After a while one of the other teachers is giving me the eye. And no, you unfunny bastard, it's not the lecherous old bloke who teaches science. Far from it. It's this 6 foot 2 Amazonian strumpet called Gloria. A fucking glorious piece of work. Legs eleven out of ten. Anyway Gloria beckons me to do a bit of the old salsa with her, and when I join her she starts really giving it some. Salsa can be a fairly filthy dance if you want it to be, and the way Gloria was looking at me and wrapping her leg around mine, she most certainly wanted it to be. Forget Patrick Swayze and whatever that girl with the nose and the hair was called. This was dirty dancing.

You're up for it, I thought, and truth be told so was I. I know that Bex's arrival isn't far away, and I know everything

I said in the last letter about not wanting to do anything with anyone else, but. But, but, but. I was drunk. She was gorgeous. And I haven't discussed anything with Bex yet, I told myself. The deal still stands. So when Gloria suggested we retire to the woods, I agreed. Yeah, yeah, yeah, so I'm a crap pathetic member of my species, blah, blah, blah. You're not telling me anything I haven't thought of myself, believe me. Would you have done any different, Mr Holier-than-thou?

I follow her into the woods, I'd got a boner so big by this point that it was difficult to walk. She's there leaning against a tree, looking seriously hot to trot, and I move in to kiss her. But before my lips reach hers she stops me.

'Hey,' she says. 'Haven't you got a girlfriend?'

Now the weird thing was, I know I was pissed and everything, but I really don't recall telling her about Bex. Indeed, I would put money on the fact that I probably went out of my way not to tell her.

'It's OK,' I said. I explained about Bex and the kissing thing.

'You're allowed to kiss?' Gloria pulled a face. 'Isn't that the most personal thing of all? I mean think about it. Prostitutes don't kiss. Lovers do. Doesn't that say something to you? I would have thought a handjob or something would be far less personal. Kissing leads to something else, after all. If you have a handjob, and I'm assuming you're like other men, you're going to be pretty much satisfied.'

I was getting a really strong sense of déjà-vu by this point. What was it with Cuban women and kissing? 'All right then,' I said. 'Maybe you're right. Why don't we go in for a little bit of mutual masturbation instead?'

'I'd love to,' Gloria sighed, 'but I thought you promised your girlfriend that you wouldn't?'

'Yes,' I said. 'Well . . .'

'I'd hate to get you into trouble,' Gloria said. 'And your girlfriend is a fellow woman. I've got to stand up for my sisters.'

Well, why did you bring me back here then? I thought.

Then Gloria told me. 'I've just had an idea,' she said, in retrospect a little too excitedly. 'I know you're not allowed to have anything done to you, but it wouldn't be wrong for you to do anything to me, would it?'

'How do you mean?'

'Why don't you kiss me?' she asked.

'I thought you had a problem with that.'

'It depends where you kiss me,' she said, glancing down.

'You want me to . . .?'

'Oh, I'm sorry,' Gloria said. 'I didn't realise you weren't sexually experienced.'

'I am sexually experienced.'

'Yeah?'

'Yeah, I am actually.'

'Prove it.'

So there I was, for the second time in a week, going south. And, for the second time in a week, the woman said thank you very much and sodded off. Women, I decided, could be just as selfish as men. But then, I thought, it's only because of my own selfishness that the situation has arisen in the first place. I have only myself to blame. Least I'm staying faithful, sort of, even if it isn't my own decision.

You may be ahead of me by now, but I'll tell you what happened next anyway. The next day at college, there's a note in my pigeonhole. It reads as follows:

Dear Mr Anderson,

I am a student in my last year here studying history and geography and would be very much interested in meeting you and being given an introduction to English culture. A number of my friends speak very highly of your abilities, and I would be extremely grateful if you could grant me a few moments of your undoubted expertise.

Yours,

Maria Gonzales

When I was queuing up for lunch, this Maria introduces herself. Long straight dark hair, great chest, etc. Did I get her note? I was going to ignore it, but having seen Maria, and the way she smiled at me, how could I refuse? Part of my remit, after all, was this cultural exchange stuff. So, after work, I go round to her room and she's all nice and smiley and friendly, and asking me all these questions about England and London and stuff. And we're sitting on her sofa and she's getting closer and closer, and flirtier and flirtier until I'm convinced she's up for it. But when I make a move, she pulls back.

'I don't think we should kiss,' she said.

'It's all right.' I explained about Bex and everything.

'Yes, but,' she smiled, 'kissing is so, so personal. Think about it. Prostitutes don't kiss . . .'

'Lovers do?' I asked.

'Er, that's right,' Maria said. 'Um.'

'Let me guess,' I'd heard the speech a couple of times now, so could remember it quite well. 'A handjob would've been a better suggestion, and you'd love to give me one but you've got to stick up for your fellow sisters. Cunnilingus, however, isn't covered by the agreement and so that's OK.'

'It is, isn't it?'

'OK, so who've you been speaking to? Gloria? Juanita? What is this? Are people taking me for a mug or something? Come on, tell me what's going on?'

Maria started talking quickly in Spanish. It had gone round like wildfire that there was this English teacher who'd go down, and go down very well, and expect nothing in return because he was in love with his girlfriend. And when she talked to Juanita about me she'd heard just how good the cunnilingus was, and what she had to say to get it. But now she hadn't, she was going to ask for her money back.

'Juanita charged you?'

Maria nodded. Juanita, my friend, was now apparently my pimp.

I feel, as you can imagine, a right schmuck. Taken advantage of, certainly. I don't know what to do about Juanita, but I'm as mad as hell. I'm going to get my revenge somehow. I'm glad the term is almost over. And I'm glad Bex is coming. I've had it with this place at the moment, I can tell you. Women are nothing but trouble.

Si

136

10

The day Sarah returns from Japan for Christmas is the day
Radio 4 announces the shortlist for the *Today* Personality
of the Year. The nominations are all female with one
exception. There's Ann Atkins, a vicar's wife who rose to
prominence by criticising homosexual church services;
Frances Lawrence, widow of the murdered London head-
teacher Philip Lawrence; Ann Pearston, leader of the
Snowdrop campaign against handguns; Lisa Potts, the
Wolverhampton nursery nurse and survivor of a vicious
machete attack; and Aung Sang Su Kyi, the Burmese
democracy campaigner.

Ann, Frances, Ann, Lisa and Aung.

And John Major.

Tony Blair should have been there too. But Tony's
been disqualified, because Annabel's nomination plan
backfired badly. One of the people I faxed my letter to
faxed it straight on to the BBC in disgust. My note, which
said nominations should be faxed from a machine which
did not identify the sender as the Labour Party, was faxed
from a machine which did identify the sender as the
Labour Party, as did the heading on the notepaper I sent.
Rather than gaining kudos for winning the poll, we're in
the mire for being caught trying to influence it.

It's so bad I've even been briefed against. The Labour source in the papers blamed the whole incident on a 'junior' member of staff. The spin is that it was not referred up or authorised by anyone else and nothing of this kind will ever happen again. Annabel's boss made the same thing clear to Annabel, who in turn made the same thing clear to me.

'Oh, Ben,' was Annabel's response. 'I'm so disappointed in you. What were you doing sending it on Labour Party paper? I thought you would have been a bit more subtle in your methods.' Annabel shook her head. 'Oh, why couldn't we have done this properly like the Tories? I'm really sorry, Ben, I know it's Christmas and everything, but I've been asked to move you out of the Audience Participation Unit in the new year.'

The funny thing is that the people who took umbrage and faxed it on to the BBC, the trade union Unison, I don't even remember sending it to them. The even funnier thing is that only person who is enjoying this is Gareth, who smirked when I told him what happened.

'I think you're what's known as a here *Today* and, if I may say so, gone tomorrow politician,' he smirked.

'Benny Boy! Over here!'

Here's where today gets worse. I'm at Heathrow, in the arrivals area, leaning on the barrier with the multitude of taxi drivers and relatives, standing there with a bunch of pink chrysanthemums, watching the steady stream of passengers push their trolleys past, anxiously scanning the crowd for their familiar faces. Sarah's plane has landed, and she's somewhere in the building, waiting for her luggage to glide by on the carousel.

I'm feeling nervous. Anticipatory. A little sick. My stomach has been tightening ever since I got on the tube. It's been what, four months since I've seen her, and I'm worried about how things are going to work out. Will it be the same as before? Will it be better? Or will we be like strangers? Will we even recognise each other? It's one of those occasions when I really feel like my relationship is on the line, that I just hope that everything is OK. I want to see her, to kiss her, to hold her, I want to have sex with her at the first available opportunity. It's been a long, long time since we last made love.

'Benny Boy! Over here!'

And then I hear this ominous shout from across the hall. A shout that sounds suspiciously like Sarah's brother, Jeb. I glance round, blink, and there at the other end of the rail are Sarah's family.

There's her father, Robert, a short, stocky self-made businessman with that flicker of arrogance you get as an alumni of the university of life. The kind of person who doesn't talk, but barks. The kind of person who you can never say the right thing to. He always tries to talk to me about rugby even though, as he would know if he listened to my replies, I have no interest in the sport whatsoever.

Then there's Sarah's mother, Jane, who is perfectly nice, but that's her problem. She's nice to the point of total blandness. She keeps on trying to talk to me about computers and her PC problems (again, I don't know where on earth she gets the notion I'm some sort of computer geek. I must have said something the first time I saw her, and it stuck).

And then there's Sarah's elder brother, Jeb. Like father, like son. He works in some kind of accounting that I have feigned interest in but really couldn't tell you much about. He calls Sarah 'Sis', or more commonly 'Oi, Sis' and me 'Benny Boy', normally supplemented with a hearty, matey slap on the back. Jeb and Robert have an instant hatred of lefties, and never waste any time in winding me up about politics.

They shouldn't, I should state, have been here. The plan, as far as I was aware, was for me to meet Sarah on my own, have a romantic reunion and a night together in London, before heading up to Cambridge to spend Christmas with her lovely folks. The Browns, however, had other ideas.

'Had to come down for a meeting yesterday,' Robert explains. 'Thought we might as well all come down. Hope we're not treading on any toes or anything.'

'We've got a sign,' Jeb shows me, before I can reply. It is an A4 sheet of white card with 'Little Sis' scrawled across it in black marker pen. 'I've always wanted to do this.'

'So how's the election campaign?' Jane asks.

'Benny Boy here's been fixing the *Today* programme.' Jeb slaps me on the back.

'Of course he has,' Robert says. 'It's the only way Labour are going to win.'

'Tell me,' Jeb asks, 'have you met Tony Blair? Is he as smarmy in real life as he is on the telly?'

'Of course he is,' Robert answers for me. 'Now, where's this bloody plane? I told her if she didn't fly BA there'd be problems.'

'She's waiting for her luggage.' I point at the screen.

'Oh God,' Jeb groans. 'We'll be here all day.'

'She never could travel light, could she?' Jane says.

'You're telling me,' Robert says. 'With the amount of rubbish she'll be hoiking around, it's a bloody miracle the plane got off the ground in the first place.'

At the same time, I'm keeping an eye on the passengers coming through with their trolleys, glancing at their luggage labels to see which flight they were coming from. Sarah's plane has been stuck in a holding pattern, and now its luggage seems to be similarly trapped. Me too. I'm nervous about seeing Sarah without having to deal with the family as well. I nip off to the toilet to have a look at myself in the mirror, which is a bad mistake. I look terrible. White and sweaty, and there's a chunk of hair whose earlier flattening with water has all but worn off.

'Better out than in.' Jeb slaps me on return.

I ignore him and look at the luggage labels, which are at last sporting JAL emblems. Come on, Sarah, I think. And then, at last, I see her. I have to double-take, she's had her hair cut short, and she is, like me, looking a little nervous and a little hassled. Weighed down by a bulging trolley of bags, she is scanning the crowd for a familiar face. Then at last, she catches my eye, and I can feel this huge grin start to spread across my face.

And then, and then, I feel this huge shoulder barge past me on my left.

'Oi, Sis!' Jeb lunges past me.

Everyone waiting turns round to see where Noel and Liam are. I'm regaining my balance, when I receive a similar wallop from my right.

'Sarah!' Robert barks in pursuit, with Jane following behind.

Not so much a putsch as pustched out of the way. I look down at the flowers I bought, which are looking ragged in the extreme. Sarah's favourites as well. I dump them in a bin and move to where Sarah is being swallowed up by a Brown family hug.

'Sarah! Hi!' I say.

'Ben!' I hear Sarah reply beneath the melee. I feel redundant, awkward standing there. Then at last, Sarah breaks free and comes over.

It seems like it isn't real, Sarah standing there in front of me. I smile, but also I pause. I want to be consumed by feelings of love but I can't help looking at her tired, sweaty, unmade-up face and feeling slightly deflated, can't help trying really hard to link that to the glamorous, done-up picture I've been carrying round in my head.

It's awkward, and I'm not expecting it. Maybe it's the presence of her father, a founder member of the Lay-Just-One-Finger school, whose daughter is, and always will be, his little girl. I move forward to kiss her on her lips, but Sarah goes for the cheek and a hug, which I do and stroke her back but her body feels unfamiliar and funny.

'Later,' she whispers in my ear.

'Break it up.' Robert claps his hands together. 'There's no excuse for fornication in a public place.'

'Hey, where's my luggage?' Sarah asks.

'Jeb's got it.' Robert points to a fast-disappearing brother. 'He's going to chuck it in the car and then drive round to meet us at the front.'

'I, I thought you were coming back with me,' I say.

'She's exhausted, poor thing,' Robert says. 'She wants to get home to bed.'

I want to get to bed too, I think, though not to sleep.

'Why don't you come up with us now.' Jane say. 'It makes far more sense than getting the silly old train tomorrow.'

'I haven't packed,' I say. 'And Sarah, I've got a surprise for you.'

'You have?' Sarah squeezes my hand.

'Can it wait?' Robert asks.

Sarah looks at me quizzically.

'There's a concert this evening I thought we could go to,' I say. 'No Way Sis. They're an Oasis covers band.'

'The only covers this girl wants are the ones on her bed.' Robert squeezes his daughter's shoulder.

'Dad,' she says. 'I was going to spend the evening here with Ben.'

'Yes, but we're here now, aren't we?'

'Why don't we drive to Ben's flat and pick his stuff up?' Jane suggests.

'Greenwich?' Robert pulls a face. 'That's going to add hours to the journey, and poor old Sarah here needs to get to bed.'

Everyone looks at me.

'It's fine,' I say. 'Really. Look. I've got a few things to tie up at work in the morning. I'll come up tomorrow.'

'Thanks,' Sarah says, squeezing my hand and kissing me on the cheek. 'I'll make this up to you, I promise.'

Later, after I've taken the tube home, done all my packing and last-minute present wrapping, after I've got the train into town and then round on the tube to Shepherd's Bush, after I've stood outside and haggled with a handful of touts until I give in and decide that the most I'm going to get for Sarah's ticket is a fiver, after I've entered the Empire, the down-at-heel, run-down old theatre, dark and dank and rammed with bodies, after I've hit the bar and bought an overpriced watered-down pint of lager in a plastic glass with a split on one side, which means I have to hold it at angle to stop it from spilling, No Way Sis are hitting the opening chords of my favourite Oasis song, Live Forever.

No Way Sis don't look like Oasis. They look exactly what they are: five northern lads who really can't believe their luck. And the audience, too, don't look like the real Oasis audience, the Knebworth crowd. These are the fair-weather fans, the followers-on: Mancunian-style student boys with pudding-bowl haircuts and fake designer gear; skinny middle-class girls who used to like Take That; pissed-up rugby lads with army haircuts who jump and scream and hug each other like their team has just scored; and couples, lots of couples, who aren't even looking at the stage but just standing around and snogging for all they are worth.

It's the couples that are killing me. This could be, this *should* be, me and Sarah. But like everything else today, it just doesn't seem to have worked out right. I thought the band might cheer me up, that coming here might rekindle what seemed lacking this morning. But 'Live Forever', like the whole concert, is just a facsimile of Oasis in the summer. It's bringing out all the wrong associations. And as I stand there and listen to this mangling of my favourite song, I can't help drawing comparisons with my relationship, can't help worrying that my 'Live Forever' is about to become my 'Slide Away'.

Dear Sarah,

*Hola! Merry Christmas from Cuba! I can't believe I'm here –
and not just because the plane was ramshackle to say the least.
I mean Christmas is all about ding donging merrily on high,
sleigh bells ringing, walking in a winter wonderland. And yet
here I am, it's Christmas Eve, and I'm sitting on a bloody
beach!!! It feels all weird and way out of kilter. Anyway. How
are you? I can't believe that we were in Heathrow at the same
time but at different terminals. It seems so unfair. We probably
passed each other on the runway or something. How's Ben?
Was he pleased to see you? He'd been so keyed up about it the
whole week that if your plane was late, I was worried he might
explode! Have you got out of bed yet?*

*Si, I have to tell you, is a changed man. Never have I seen
him so pleased to see me, so attentive, so showering me with
gifts. He should go away more often! He's looking really tanned,
the bastard – I almost fancy him. When I got through the
airport, he was there waiting for me with a bunch of flowers.
Yes! Si bought flowers! I tell you, I was so pleased to see him, I
ran up and jumped on him, almost sending him flying. It's
amazing how quickly everything comes back, isn't it – the way
someone smells, someone tastes, the way someone kisses. For a
fleeting second, I have to be honest, I had a flashback of you-
know-who, but as soon as I touched Si's cheek, and felt his
usual bad shave, it all came flooding back. I realised with a
lump just how much I missed him, and, well, burst into tears.*

That shook him, I can tell you! I don't think he knew how to react to that. He just kind of stared at me for a second, looked really worried. And then I hugged him and it was all right. It's such a stressful situation, isn't it? You're tired from travelling and you so want it to be nice and stuff. And there's all that pressure for things to be OK, when in fact the truth is that you haven't seen each other for months and it takes a little while to readjust.

Anyway, Si, the absolute sweetie, did his best to make the readjustment as easy as possible. We got outside into the car park, and there his friend Carlos was waiting for us in this huge 1950s American car. Si told me the name, but I can't remember. It was open top, green with cream seats – kind of grand and knackered at the same time. Very Cuba. Anyway, Carlos drove us out of Havana and to this massive hotel complex. I thought we were going to stay in Si's apartment – I wanted to see the university and everything – but Si said it was all booked and the university was shut, and, anyway, he said, with a wink and a whisper, his walls were paper thin. Plus, he added, the hotels were guaranteed electricity.

I can't really tell you that much of the journey to be honest. I know it was exciting, being in a foreign country and everything, but all I really wanted to see was Si and so pretty much blotted the palm trees and everything out. I really wanted to snog him but with his friend Carlos in the front, didn't really feel I could. It's a weird place, though. A bit like you imagine it – beautiful buildings, with their imminent collapse only adding to their qualities. Big murals of Che Guevara and Fidel Castro. The hotel complex was different. It was more modern, more European – in a strange kind of way, I kind of felt I could have been in Majorca.

We checked in, went straight upstairs and, not to put too fine a point on it, shagged. I was feeling really tired, but once we got up there, I suddenly felt wide awake again. And Si's generosity hadn't ended either – you wouldn't believe what he did. I was so surprised, I started laughing, which I think he found a bit disconcerting, poor thing, and I had to reassure him he was doing fine, which believe me he was for once. Just a shame the heat seems to have sapped his strength to do it more than a couple of times a day.

Anyway, here I am, a few days later, and I'm here writing to you from the beach, whilst Si has gone swimming in the sea. I'm starting to feel relaxed now. The tiredness from the flight has gone and the stress of seeing Si has settled down. You must have found that as well. It takes a little bit to click back in. In a funny kind of way, I think that Si found that more than me – funny because he's not the one who's just travelled thousands of miles. Or maybe he's used to having Cuba to himself and it seems odd to find someone from home here as well. Whatever, it's almost as if he's been trying too hard to please me. Like on the first night, we walked down to this nearby bar, which to me looked really nice (a shark's head behind the bar!!), just quiet and relaxed and everything, but as soon as we got in, Si decided it wasn't good enough for me, and that we should go somewhere special for our first night together. I tried to tell him that it didn't matter where we went, it was going to be special, but he was having none of it, and even though I said that I wasn't that hungry insisted on taking me to this restaurant that seemed cheap to me but was posh by Cuban standards.

He's beginning to unwind now, though. I think we both are, getting used to each other again. Getting blitzed on rum last night probably didn't do any harm. Inevitably, I think we've both become a bit more independent in our time apart – we've had to be. But when you put two slightly more independent people back into a relationship, it can feel like they're pulling in slightly separate ways. But that doesn't mean we don't care for each other as much, it just means we've changed a bit, and we've got to adapt to accommodate. And I don't think it's a bad thing at all – being apart has made us both more confident, and more outgoing, and that's got to be for the best.

The weirdest thing, I guess, is how these differences mingle with the old routines, which quickly establish themselves again. All those little things that you've forgotten that make up a relationship. Chiding Si for belching. The way he slides his hand around my side to gently direct me where we're going. The fact that he's always ready before me, standing in the doorway impatiently jiggling his keys. And all those little catchphrases that I'd forgotten (absolutement!). I mean, you can get a lot in a letter or an email or a phone call, but you can only get so much, and as we both know, having read Cosmo until we're blue in the face, whatever percent it is of communication is non-verbal. In a letter you can write down what you're feeling, but face to face you can see how the feeling expresses itself. It's a bit like the iceberg thing, you know how you only see a bit of it, and now you can see the whole lot. It makes me happy to see it, it's good to know it's there, but it also makes me sad, because when I'm back in Britain I'm going to lose it for another six or seven months. Maybe if I persuade him to take me to expensive restaurants every night then he'll run out of money more quickly and come back sooner . . .

I should go. I don't know whether I should post this to your house or to Japan – I'll ask Si about the vagaries of the Cuban postal system. Anyway, ciao for now.

Bexxxxxx

11

I want a shag. There, I've said it. Typical, predictable, male me is desperate for a shag. And more than that, I think that I'm owed a shag. Sarah has been away for four months, Sarah is now back after four months, and as her fully paid up boyfriend, I know my rights. I'm due a shag. I know this sounds like the most Neanderthal of responses, that somehow Sarah should be ready and waiting whenever I click my fingers, but the simple fact is this. Sarah wants a shag too. The trouble is we can't.

The reasons? Her mother, her father, her brother and her dog.

Sarah's bedroom is next to her parents, which is bad enough, but what's even worse is that I'm not in there. 'I know we normally allow you to stay in there,' Sarah's mum said when I arrived, 'but Robert's mother is staying and I don't think she'd approve.' I've been relegated to a camp bed in the computer room and when I say room, what I mean is cupboard. It's downstairs, it's cold, and between Sarah and me is Chas, the family dog, a King Charles spaniel who patrols the ground floor like some sort of killer Alsatian, Chas who can detect a kiss at fifty paces.

Sarah won't do anything while anyone else is in the

house, which is a problem because her gran isn't as mobile as she used to be and doesn't get out much. In fact, not at all.

'She might hear,' Sarah says.

'She's deaf,' I reply.

'She'd *know*,' Sarah responds.

It has crossed my mind that Sarah doesn't want to have sex, that for whatever reason she is using her grandmother as a convenient excuse. But the thing is, that after Heathrow, everything is going rather well. Sarah met me at Cambridge station with a warm hug and a kiss and without her parents there, it felt normal and nice, just like when she used to greet me when I came to visit during the university holidays. I feel bad for doubting, that I should have been able to see beyond her tiredness at the airport to the girl I've been going out with for so long. She's back, and somehow she's more real than when she went: the teaching has lifted her, encouraged her, and now she's louder, more confident, more, well, *Sarah*.

'It'll be all right,' Sarah says. 'We'll just have to be patient.'

'I've been patient for four months,' I say.

'Then a couple more days won't kill you,' she says. As she reaches up to kiss me, Chas starts to howl.

'Christ,' says Jeb. 'If I hear one more story about Japan I think I'm going to commit hara-kiri.'

Christmas Day. We're sat in Sarah's parents' sitting room: Sarah, me, Jeb, her parents and her incredible grandmother, who every time I look at her, seems to have shrunk further. Whoever said Christmas is about families got it wrong. Christmas is about your *own* family. Being at someone else's feels like an intrusion, like you're interloping. It's jarring, everything's there, but it's all in the wrong place, done in the wrong order. Sarah's family open their presents in the afternoon rather than the morning. Watching the queen's speech is compulsory. The big film is ignored, for a game of Scrabble. It shouldn't matter that there are only four letter racks, but I can't help feeling it's significant, as I sit there, my pieces propped up against a book, which Chas knocks to the floor every time he sweeps past.

It's strange. Sarah's been away for months, and now she's back it's me who's feeling homesick.

There is a second difference to this year's Brown family Christmas. Sarah. Sarah who is hell-bent on attempting to describe in minute detail every single incident of her four months in Japan. We've had the photographs (several reels), the slide show, the home-video footage of the school concert where Sarah dressed up as a monster ('You didn't need to dress up,' says Jeb). She's taught her mum the tea ceremony, her dad calligraphy, Jeb the basics of kendo using an umbrella as a sword. She's insisted we all try her green tea at least once, which we all did, once, she insisted at Christmas lunch in saying *itaidakimasu* rather than grace. One of my presents, which Sarah thinks is hilarious, is a T-shirt on the front of which is written 'If your mind is being heavy, be a bird fly. Peace! You can break mountains when you think happy'. ('In Japan, everything's covered in this half-literate English.

153

Come on, put it on . . .') And when she talks about these things, she is lit up with passion and enthusiasm, exactly the same as in that record shop all those years before, when she was buying Oasis and I was buying Blur.

'There you go again, Jeb,' Sarah says. 'You're always trying to put me down.'

'I'm not trying to put you down,' Jeb says. 'I'm trying to shut you up about bloody Japan.'

'I'll be glad when I'm back in bloody Japan,' Sarah says.

'Hey,' I say, as Chas knocks my letters to the floor again.

'Come on, Sarah,' her dad says. 'Are you going to have a go or not?'

'Why's everyone picking on me?' Sarah asks. 'Is this pick-on-Sarah day?'

'No one's trying to pick on you,' says her mother. 'Your father just wants to get on with the game, that's all.'

Sarah stares studiously, sulkily at her letters, rearranges them, glances up at the board, and smiles.

'This is the best I can do,' she says apologetically, putting her letters down.

'*Ainu?*' Jeb pulls a face. 'Sarah, what the fuck is that?'

'They're an early Japanese people,' Sarah says. 'Like the Aborigines in Australia. They got pushed north onto Hokkaido by the Japanese, and their numbers have slowly dwindled ever since. Did I tell you about the time that I—'

'I'm sure you have,' Jeb says. 'You told us about ninety fucking five per cent of your holiday.'

'It is not a holiday. I am *working*. And why is so wrong of me to tell you anyway? It's the most exciting thing I've *ever* done.'

'We gathered.'

'Jeb,' her father says.

'Well, I don't think Ainu should be allowed,' Jeb says. 'It's a name, and a Japanese one at that.'

'It's no different from Eskimo,' Sarah argues. 'Or Aborigine.'

'Shush, the pair of you,' Robert says, reaching for the dictionary. 'There's one quick way to settle this . . .'

Sarah and Jeb, I can't help but notice, are glowering at each other. I try to smile at Sarah, but she's not looking at me. Behind, by the fire, her grandmother is starting to snore.

'There's nothing here,' Robert says, turning over a page to double-check.

'It *is* a word,' Sarah says.

'Not in this country.' Jeb takes Sarah's pieces off the board and offers them back to her. Sarah, though, bangs his hand from underneath, and a fountain of letters fly up.

'Sarah,' says her mother.

'No, I have had enough,' Sarah says, getting up. 'No one takes me seriously in this house. Don't you realise how important Japan *is* to me? You just don't get it, do you?'

And with that, she sweeps the letters off the board and storms out of the room. There's a pause, a silence as everyone looks at each other, and then a quiet hacking sound from behind the sofa.

'Robert,' Jane says, 'I think Chas might have swallowed a letter.'

On Boxing Day evening, Sarah and I borrow her father's dark blue Ford Granada and go for a drive. Or rather, a ride.

Sarah is desperate for a cigarette. For four days she has put on the goody-two-shoes act for her parents, carrying on the pretence she has since she was sixteen that she doesn't smoke, and now she is gasping.

'You know when you can have your cigarette?' I say. 'Afterwards.'

And so here we are, driving around the country lanes beyond Cambridge, far enough away from Sarah's family and friends for us both to feel comfortable.

'How does this work?' I ask, prodding at the stereo.

'Oh, I brought some music,' Sarah says. 'It's in my coat pocket.'

I reach across and pull out the tape. The writing is in Japanese.

'It's not what you think,' Sarah says.

It's not. As I slide the tape into the machine, the car is suddenly flooded with the last group I expect to hear.

'You like the *Spice Girls*?' I ask, as 'Who Do You Think You Are?' rips through the speakers.

'I *love* the Spice Girls,' Sarah says. 'Turn it up, this one's great.'

'But this is just poppy rubbish,' I say.

'Oh, the Spice Girls are cool. And they're huge in

Japan. Every time you tell someone you're from Britain, they go, "Ah, Britain, the Spice Girls." And did I tell you that at the school Christmas concert, me and some of the other teachers dressed up as them and performed "Wannabe"? I was Posh . . .'

I sit back, as Sarah drives on. There's something funny about this, something I don't like. I remember that letter I wrote to Sarah before she went, the one about the two different piles of stuff in her bedroom, the things going to Japan and the ones staying behind with me, and I recall writing that although the gap between us was only inches, before long we would be miles apart. And as I sit there, and watch Sarah sing along to the tape, I get the tiniest yet worrying thought that maybe this is true. The Sarah I knew would have loathed the Spice Girls. Sarah, I realise, is changing.

Sarah stops the car. We're in an opening at the side of the road, a country lane by a farmer's field. The night is overcast so there's no moon, no stars. It's pitch black and as I turn the music off, deadly quiet.

'Well,' Sarah says, switching the engine off, cutting the lights. 'Here we are.'

'Yes,' I say.

It is silent, save for the sound of breathing, breathing that is quick, shallow.

'I feel nervous,' Sarah says. 'I feel a bit funny.'

'It's OK,' I say, unclipping my seat belt. I lean across to kiss her. Sarah slowly, hesitantly, responds.

'Come on,' I say, 'let's go and sit in the back.'

We climb through, and for a minute it all seems OK. As I hug Sarah, slip a hand inside her jumper, everything is familiar, as it should be: her smells, her shape, it all comes flooding back. Sarah too, gently at first, then quicker and more insistently starts to respond.

'I've missed you,' she says, guiding my hand.

'I've missed you too,' I say.

'Oh, Ben,' she kisses me. 'Put the condom on.'

'Condom?' I kiss back.

'It's a rubber thing.' Sarah continues to kiss. 'Protects against babies, AIDS, that sort of thing.' She stops. 'You have *got* a condom?'

'I thought you were on the pill.'

'I used to be,' Sarah says, 'but I decided to come off it for a while. Don't you remember? A year without my body being pumped full of hormones? While I'm abroad and not having sex?' She looks at me, a little confused. 'I told you all this. Ages ago.'

I rack my brain. There's the vaguest hum of recognition lurking in there somewhere. We've had this conversation, but I thought it was purely hypothetical. Wasn't it?

'Are you telling me you haven't got any condoms?' Sarah is sitting upright now.

'Why's it my job?'

'Well, it's not my bloody penis.'

I think harder. By now the hum of recognition is getting louder. Shit. We *had* talked about it before she went. It had completely, completely slipped my mind.

'Couldn't we just . . .'

'No, we couldn't.' Sarah is furious. 'Oh, I don't believe you.'

And with that, she opens the door and slams it behind her.

'Sarah,' I say, getting out. 'Sarah.'

'Why is it my responsibility?' Sarah has lit her cigarette and is drawing on it for all it is worth.

'It's not. It's ours. I just. Shit.'

Shit.

'We could go and buy some,' I suggest.

'Like where?' Sarah draws the horizon with her cigarette. 'At nine o'clock at night? On Boxing Day?'

This is not good, but this is about to get worse. As we're standing there uncertainly, awkwardly, a car pulls up.

'Sarah?' shouts the driver. 'Sarah, is that you?'

'Oh my God.' Sarah drops her half-finished cigarette. 'Mark . . . what are you doing round here?'

'I live here.' Mark, fiftyish, with a round face and grey beard, points to a long and hedged-in driveway not ten yards from our car.

'I thought you lived in Norwich.'

'We moved.' Mark notices me. He waves. 'Oh, you must be thingy. Sarah's boyfriend.'

'Nice to meet you,' I say. Sod off and die I think.

'So what's with the car?' he asks. 'Have you broken down?'

'No,' I said.

'Yes,' said Sarah at the same time.

'Sort of,' I lie. 'It was just sounding a bit funny, you know, so we thought we'd stop and let things cool down. It's probably fine by now.'

'Yes,' Sarah agrees, turning the key to start the engine. The car, though, has other ideas.

'What a stroke of luck you broke down near me,' Mark says, pulling his car in next to the Granada.

Luck yes. Good no.

'He's a friend of my father's,' Sarah hisses. 'Shit, shit, shit.'

The door shuts and Mark opens his boot, looking for a torch.

'So what are you doing out here anyway?' Mark asks, as he finds one, switches it on and shines it in our direction.

'Pub,' I say.

'Cinema,' Sarah says simultaneously.

Dear Ben,

All right, mate, how's it going? I hope you've been busy getting your tongue around some rare old bird, helping yourself to your much-deserved quota of breast and thigh (though I bet you baulked at any hand-up-arse action). But enough about Sarah, how was the turkey? (Boom, and if you will, boom.)

It's been a funny old time, I can tell you. Don't know about you, but I was bricking myself about Bex turning up. Unbelievable as it sounds, but the closer it got to her arriving, the more guilty I felt about Juanita et al. (of which more later). I started getting paranoid about how if we stayed at my apartment, we'd end up bumping into someone, so I ended up booking us into some godforsaken tourist hotel for the moment – we start travelling around in a few days. I really laid it on – well, you know what a smoothie I can be with the ladies when I turn the charm on. So I got my mate Carlos to pick us up from the airport in his convertible. I shaved. I even – be prepared to be flabbergasted – bought Bex some flowers. Exactly. Classy guy.

It's a difficult balancing act, I can tell you, between showing someone how much you care about them (Jesus! What do I sound like? I need a lie-down) and concealing the fact that you're trying to make up for something. Like the flower buying – when do I ever buy flowers for Bex except when I've done something wrong? And as I stood waiting for her plane to land, I thought she'd twig instantly. When I saw her, she gave me one of those penetrating looks, like she knows exactly what's going on, and bursts into tears. I tell you, mate, I thought I was dead and buried there and then. I had the words 'I'm so sorry' in my throat waiting to come out when she looked at me again and said, 'Si, these flowers are beautiful.' Saved! Bird Intuition 0 Flower Power 1.

As Carlos drove us to the hotel, things slipped to normal. Suddenly the hotel couldn't come quick enough. I'd been a good boy all week and was absolutely bursting for some action. But I also wanted to prove to Bex – and to myself – how much I felt for her. And so I did for her what I'd done to Juanita et al. (more later – don't be so impatient), and once again I worried about whether I was going too far, but as it happened, just like me, it all went down a treat. And we've been at it like rabbits ever since. Four months is a long time with no nookie, but we've been playing catch-up as best we can. My poor old todger needs its batteries recharging we've done it so often.

Anyway. Here's the worst bit. I thought that getting to the hotel would be all right, but on the second night we went down to this bar. And as soon as we walked in, I looked round and there behind the counter was Maria, the student who I, oh come, you know, get with it. And as Bex was looking around saying what a nice place it was, I saw Maria recognise me and her face drop.

Now, I have a little confession to make. I wasn't best pleased as you might have gathered with Juanita, and it being Christmas and everything, I'd decided to leave her a little present. Some fish to be precise. Now admittedly it wasn't the freshest of fish. And, OK, well, you've got me, I didn't exactly leave it on her doorstep. I kind of, well, Sellotaped it to the inside of her toilet cistern. Juanita, I knew, was going away the *day after I went round for a week or two, and by the time she got back, well . . .*

Now, I don't know if Juanita knew about it yet, or if she did and Maria didn't, or if Juanita did and had told Maria, or if Maria was just going to make some comment or what, but I wasn't going to find out. I think Bex thought it was a bit odd, especially as I'd gone on and on about how nice the bar was before we went but I bought her a slap-up meal to make up for it. This trip is killing my finances. The sooner we get out of here and get on to Santiago the better.

Funny seeing your bird after all this time, isn't it?

Si

12

On New Year's Day we go for a walk in Cambridge. It is a beautiful New Year's Day – crisp and cold, a clear-the-cobwebs kind of a day. Cambridge can be beautiful, but especially so in icy temperatures. A sprinkling of frost, a shiver of ice coating the colleges and cobblestones, gleams in the sunshine like a brighter shade of pale. The sky is the lightest and sharpest of blues, cloudless and clear, save for a smudged set of vapour trails. The streets, similarly, are all but untouched: a single set of tyre tracks slice along the road in front of us.

We're walking past King's College, with its strange, film-set two-dimensional façade, when Sarah skids. I'm holding her hand and all of a sudden I can feel her bodyweight go and through her bright red woollen glove I can feel her fingers clench, squeezing mine for support. Her arm tenses, clinging on, and for a second I think she is going over, and me with her, but instead she spins, slipping on the spot, until her other hand is grabbing my arm and we're clinging and laughing and somehow still standing, somehow still upright.

'You're not exactly Jayne Torvill, are you?' I say.

'Maybe not.' Sarah's face matches her red woolly hat,

which she pulls off to readjust her hair, 'but you're hardly Christopher Dean yourself.'

'How do you mean?'

'I'd squeeze your bicep to show you. If only I could find it.'

'Are you saying that—'

'He's stronger than you? Yes I am.' Sarah replaces her hat. 'Don't even think about making some clever clever cod ballet comment about men in tights and bags of sprouts.'

'It didn't even cross my mind.'

'Yeah, yeah. Look at the way you're shaking your arm like you've just been badly wounded. If I was coming out of a double corkscrew, I know who I'd rather be caught by.'

I was only ten when Torvill and Dean won gold at the Winter Olympics. And maybe it was because I was young, but I got confused by their choice of music, thinking the composer was *Bolero* and the piece was called Ravel. Ravel made more sense to the ten-year-old me: to entangle, to entwine, it summed up what paired figure skating was all about. And even though I know which way round it is now, I still prefer my own version. Sarah pulls a face as I explain this, but it's true. Bolero sounds like a small European car. Or possibly an ice cream.

'You know what I've always wondered about Torvill and Dean?' I say.

'What?'

'Whether they were, you know, doing it?'

Sarah pulls a face. 'What kind of a stupid question is that?'

It's not a stupid question. Torvill and Dean's gold-winning *Bolero* routine involved a storyline about two young lovers, unable to see each other, who agree a suicide pact by jumping inside a flaming volcano. Romance, like the volcano, at its most overblown. And my question about Torvill and Dean is not asked out of masculine curiosity. I'm asking because I want to know during those four minutes and twenty-eight seconds that captured the world, which all nine judges awarded a perfect six, whether that performance of two lovers was just that. A performance.

Can you fool the world into pretending you are in love? Can the world be fooled? Can people see beyond the mood music and the purple costumes and the eighties hairdos and glimpse the truth? Was this love or was this love's opposite, routine? Precise, perfectly practised, superbly choreographed, but nevertheless a routine. There's trust there – Jayne jumps and flips and spins in the anticipation that Christopher will catch her, but is this trust through practice, through doing it time and time and time again, or is this trust through instinct, through feeling that Christopher will never let her down? You've got to be a strong person to be there for someone else. Is Christopher stronger than me?

Sarah and I are skating. We're going round and round in our figures of eight, pirouetting over problems, gliding round our difficulties. It's a flawless display, 6.0s in both technical merit and artistic impression for our avoidance of the issues. Our time together is so short – precious, pressured – I don't think either of us wants to waste it by touching on anything difficult, anything that requires a double corkscrew to flip out of.

There are too many things going on here. We're at the midway point of Sarah's stay, the bit after we've readjusted to each other, but before the worries about Sarah leaving appear, the time where things should be easiest. But the readjustment's been slower, subtler than I expected, and the thoughts about her going back have been more urgent, more insistent, than I imagined. Everything's overlapping. While part of me is still getting used to having my girlfriend around, and all the relaxing and opening up that goes with it, the other half is clamping down in preparation for her imminent departure. And that's not the only pushing and pulling that's going on. Sarah's family and I are tugging the situation to a standstill. We both want her to ourselves, but all our efforts achieve is to cancel each other out. At the same time, I'm pushing and pulling with Sarah too: I can't wait for the year to be over; she wants it to go on for as long as it can.

All these problems are knotted together in a way I can't untangle. Un-Ravel. And the reason, I think, that neither of us is bringing them up is the hope that all of them are of a time, of a piece, are unique to the situation we are in. In the future, they will all seem like a fuss over nothing. Next time I see Sarah, I'm sure we'll both be better prepared. Next time I come to stay at Sarah's parents – well, next time Sarah will be coming to stay at mine.

'I'm fairly sure that Torvill and Dean are both married to different people,' Sarah says, 'though I think that's quite a recent thing. I don't know about back then. I think they once said something elliptical like we're in love for those minutes we're on the ice. Maybe it's good for business to keep people guessing.'

'But that's my point,' I say. 'I'm not asking in some sort of stupid, nudge nudge, wink wink were they doing anything sort of a way. I'm wondering, *can* you keep people guessing? I think people know.'

'All right,' says Sarah. 'Do you think they were in love?'

'Well, I only saw them that one time at the Olympics and I was only ten and—'

'I thought you just knew.'

'But even so, my answer's no. You?'

'Well, of course they were,' Sarah says. 'So our sample survey shows the population split right down the middle on the big question. I'd say that's inconclusive enough to show you can keep people guessing.'

'Or that half the people surveyed are wrong.'

'He could be,' Sarah says. 'He normally is.'

Love is the great unspoken of relationships. And as Sarah and I slip and slide on between the colleges and the cobblestones, its unspokenness is all too vocal. It is silent because of love's myriad of forms, because for each and every one of us it is different, and in those discrepancies, doubts can begin. Love is allowed to speak in the first instant, when the similarities collide: you're enjoying the same feelings at the same time, and that timing is crucial: it's the synchronicity that makes it special. But as soon as the initial burst begins to fade, things start to change. For the unspoken truth is that love lasts different lengths of time for different people. And that switch from being in love with someone to just loving them, the moment when the 'in' becomes the out, is never discussed. This initial, heady intoxicating state, this 'limerence' as it is sometimes called, doesn't last for ever, everyone knows that, but within a relationship itself it is never mentioned. Instead, its passing is passed over, ignored as though it never happened.

But it does happen. It's the way love works after a while. It becomes too precious and expensive and fragile to risk taking out of its box to study it in case someone drops it and it smashes on the floor into a thousand tiny pieces. It's only at the end, when its beauty is about to be passed to someone new that it is touched and handled again, and in the fresh light of day you see the cracks and the chips and the hairlines and fissures you'd never noticed before.

And as love pushes and pulls its partners at different points, it touches them in different ways too. And like Sarah's and my discussion about Torvill and Dean, its many manifestations arise. Our opposite positions are clear: I think Sarah is mistaking love for something that isn't there; Sarah thinks I can't see love when it is staring me in the face. Neither of us can give way without giving fundamental ground, without admitting there's something about love we don't get. But if there's something about love we don't get, what value does that give our protestations for each other? And that's why people in relationships don't talk about love.

We're standing on a bridge, looking back along the Cam as it flows behind the colleges. In the summer the river would be full of punts – students and tourists showing off and getting stuck and falling in. Today it is silent. The boats float stacked by the riverside. The punts have all gone home for Christmas.

We're looking at Newton's wonderful wooden bridge, part of Queen's College kept apart from the general public. The famous, fallacious tale about Newton's bridge is a story of individual genius and human stupidity. Newton made the bridge out of mathematics. With a judicious use of angles, he positioned his planks to perfection, and put them together without a single screw, nail or nothing. Self-supporting, it showed exactly what you could do when you get the numbers right. But later, after his death, lesser men were confused by his brilliance, and took the bridge apart to figure out how it worked. And when they tried to put it back together again, they were about as successful as all the king's horses and all the king's men. And so there the bridge sits today – beautiful designed, brilliantly conceived and stupidly bolted together.

'I think it's to do with the pressure,' Sarah explains. 'One bit of wood supports the next. Everything supports everything else.'

'Interdependence,' I say.

'Exactly,' Sarah says. 'Interdependent. It's like a relationship. I lean on you, you lean on me. I support you, you support me. The thing only works if both people support each other. Otherwise . . .'

Sarah waves her hand goodbye and I'm suddenly transported back to Heathrow, back to late summer when she was leaving me for the first time. I remember watching her disappear behind the sliding doors and thinking of *Stars in Their Eyes*, hoping she might return in a cumulus nimbus of dry ice, made over as Madonna, Kylie or Olivia Newton John. And I remember the other thought I had about *Stars in Their Eyes*, about how its 'magic moment' was nothing more than televisual trick. How the goings in and the comings out must be separated by a marathon makeover in the make-up chair.

It's a deflating thought to have, like discovering how a rabbit is pulled out of a hat or an assistant is sawn in half. The initial thrill of 'so *that's* how it's done' is soon replaced by the realisation that the trick will never be quite so fun again. And as Sarah and I walk on, I find myself thinking, Is love like that? If you sit down and analyse a relationship, does it lose its sparkle? Is it like Newton's bridge, that you can take it apart to work out how it works, but once that's done, all you can do is bolt it back together?

We turn left to walk on, down, to weave our way along the river round the back of the colleges. But just as Newton's bridge is about to disappear briefly from view, I glance back for one last look. And there, walking across the bridge, I see a Japanese girl. I don't see much, little more than a flash of jet black hair, a flicker of a face, but it is enough to make my heart jump. *Mika*, I think.

'Ben?' Sarah asks, ahead of me. 'Are you all right?'

No, I'm not all right, I think. I can feel my heart. It feels big and heavy and thumping and hot. I suck in the cold air, hoping this might cool it down. Mika. It's such a shocking thought to have. Shocking because it's so out of the blue. Shocking because the thought is so sharp. Shocking because I've no idea whether the girl was Mika or not, and because, well, even though the girl is highly unlikely to be Mika, the possibility is enough to make my heart jump to conclusions. Shocking because all of sudden, I really, really, really want to see her.

'Ben?'

'My heart,' I say. 'It twinged.'

'You'd better start doing some exercise.' Sarah shakes her head. 'I don't want you giving up on me now.'

'No,' I reply. I'm really not with it. I look back at the bridge again, but there's nothing there to see.

Ben,

A wobbly hola to you from Santiago. I'm sitting in the most beautiful surroundings, a gorgeous crumbling apartment that has been lent to me by a colleague from university. There's a view out of the window that's overlooking the sea. It's hot, but there's just the thin blast of a cool breeze floating across from a nearby palm tree. It is, quite simply, postcard Cuba. Bex, I'm sure, would have loved it.

But Bex isn't here. We've split up. No – let's be honest about this. She's dumped me and has gone back to England. I feel, in a word, dreadful. One minute everything was going swimmingly, the next, bang.

The evening had started off so well, too. Do you remember I told you that I wanted to change our relationship, to cut out the kissing clause and just stay faithful to each other? Well, we went out for a meal and I explained all this. I told her that I'd been thinking about how important she was to me, and that I didn't want to think of her getting off with anyone else, that I realised our agreement was a mistake. And Bex, well, I thought she was really pleased, she said she was so glad I felt that way, that, as the cliché goes, absence really can make the heart grow fonder.

So we skipped dessert to head back to the hotel and celebrate. Bex is looking happier than I think I've seen her, which makes what happens next all the worse. Bex unlocks the door ahead of me, flicks on the light and suddenly there's just

*this almighty, piercing scream. I rush in, and there, on the bed,
on my pillow, is a shark's head. A shark's head that may or
may not have been from the bar I saw Maria in.*

*The fucking bitch, I think. It's got to be Juanita, hasn't it?
Maria must have told her that we are here and this is her
revenge.*

Then Bex says, 'Who's a fucking bitch?' and I go white.

'Did I say that out loud?' I ask.

Bex nods and starts to cry.

*I try to tell her it's not what she thinks and that I can
explain, when the phone starts to ring. I try to ignore it but it
just keeps on ringing and ringing and ringing until I pick it up.*

Pablo.

'Hola,' he says. 'Hola, English fuckhead.'

*'Pablo,' I say. I try to sound friendly. 'How, er, how on
earth are you?'*

'You fuck my woman,' Pablo says. 'You fuck with me.'

*'Now I don't know what you've heard,' I say, 'but let me
reassure you that—'*

Pablo was not a man interested in discussion.

*'I generous man,' he interrupts, his voice rising. 'I give juan
hour. Juan hour.' And then the phone goes dead.*

Bex by now is upset and petrified.

'Si, just what the fuck is going on?' she asks.

*'We've got to get out of here,' I say. 'We've got to leave
now or Pablo will kill me.'*

'Who's Pablo?'

'The boyfriend of the fucking bitch.'

At this point Bex slaps me hard across the face.

'How could you?' she says. 'One minute you're saying how

much you missed me and the next I've discovered that all along you've been sleeping with some little tart.'

'I haven't slept with anyone,' I say. 'This girl, Juanita, I didn't even kiss her.'

'Then why does her boyfriend want to kill you?'

'Because, because . . . look, let's get out of here and I'll explain.'

'No,' Bex says, folding her arms. 'I'm not moving until I know exactly what you've done.'

By now, I am really bricking myself. Bex has no idea what this Pablo will do if he finds us here. And so, I tell her the lot. Everything that happened with Juanita. And at the end of it, I look at Bex and she doesn't believe a word of it.

'That is the biggest load of horseshit I have ever heard in my entire life,' she says. 'You? Going down on someone and getting nothing in return? Why can't you be honest and admit you've slept with her?'

'It's the God's honest truth. No one's been near my dick,' I plead. 'Now look, if we don't move fast, I'm not going to have a dick left for anyone to touch.'

'Do I look like I care?' Bex says.

'Whatever you think of me,' I say, 'we have got to get out of here right now. Look at that shark. These people don't mess about.'

'Unlike their girlfriends.' Bex is angry, but as she watches me open my suitcase and start flinging in clothes, as she sees the panic in my face, she finally begins to grasp the gravity of the situation.

'Is this Pablo guy for real?' she asks.

'Very real,' I say.

'You fucking idiot,' Bex says, flings her bag open and starts to pack.

'Bex, I'm so sorry, I'll make this up to you,' I say.

'I think you've made up more than enough already,' Bex says. 'No, you've gone too far. You're taking me to the airport and I'm going home.'

And that is exactly what I did. I've spent a couple of days here alone, thinking things through and stuff. I feel terrible about what happened, but I feel angry with Bex too, angry for not believing me, angry for not being able to see that none of it meant anything, none of it matters. I realise how stupid I've been, but most of all I realise just how much I feel for her, that my instincts at the meal were absolutely right. I love her.

But I've also decided that I'm not going to sit around here and mope. I'm meant to be teaching until the end of March, but I'm going to start my South American travelling early. It'll be good to get out of Cuba, good to get somewhere with electricity, somewhere with a Big Mac, somewhere without mad women and drug-dealer boyfriends. I'm not sure where I'm going to go first, but write to me at my hotmail address and I'll try to pick it up.

S'ya. Si.

13

I know I shouldn't use Bex, but I know I'm going to anyway.

It is the Tuesday after Bex got back from Cuba after the Friday Sarah returned to Japan. I'm sorry that Bex missed Sarah. What she needs more than anything is an evening in with her best friend. My support, I know, is little more than surrogate. However warm and friendly and listening I am, I cannot shake the fact that I am Si's best friend. And Bex blaming Si cannot but rub off on me. Did I know? What have I told him? What will I report back? I am the spy in the house of love, and Bex is keeping her state secrets – her state, her secrets – out of my reach.

I'm trapped. Si, I feel, is being similarly cautious towards me. When love breaks down, suspicion starts spiralling, and my proximity can't but drag me into things. For Bex, I am Si's best friend, and my loyalties ultimately lie with him. For Si, I am living with his girlfriend, with all the jealousy that entails. Bex is feeling like the one left behind: the patsy at home, whilst her boyfriend gallivants abroad. Si is feeling homesick: alone and lonely, continuing his travels when I suspect he'd rather be back here. Both are displacing: Bex is ploughing herself into her work; Si is focusing on his travels.

The question is this. Did they split up because Si went abroad? Was their relationship doomed from the moment he stepped on that plane? Was it because of their agreement, the loosening of ties letting in a fatal element of mistrust? Was it just plain and simple messing around? Infidelity, like burglary, is 90 per cent opportunity. And with Si and Bex, by the time Christmas came around, something had definitely, definitely gone missing.

Si hadn't messed around at college, or if he did, he'd certainly never told me. (Bex, on the other hand, had a terrible, drunken, one-night stand three months in, which Sarah had sworn me to secrecy about on pain of death.) And Si, with his own logic, would say he hadn't messed around abroad. Technically, he'd stuck to the terms of the agreement. But Bex had never wanted the agreement in the first place, and technicalities weren't going to win her back. Trust isn't built on technicalities.

I'm thinking about this because I'm thinking about Sarah. I'm thinking about whether we're setting ourselves up for a fall, whether our blind optimism that things are going to work out is dangerously misguided, whether there is something about long-distance relationships that is fatally undermining. Not for the first time, I think, if she loved me more would she have gone? It's an ugly thought, a selfish, self-pitying thing to think and yet it's there in my head and it won't go away.

A long-distance relationship is a risk, a gamble. It's not so much pausing your relationship, I realise now. It's freeze-framing it, putting it to sleep, putting it in a coma. And sometimes people come round from a coma. Sometimes they don't. The trouble is, that whilst your relationship isn't moving, life is going on. And by the time normal relations are resumed, the gap between the two might just be unbridgeable.

Bex is crying. She is shut in her room, with Joni Mitchell blasting out to hide the noise, but I can hear her sniffles between the songs. And this is the strangest thing, but hearing her in there, I find myself feeling jealous. I'm jealous because for her the waiting is over. The agony, the uncertainty, the unknowing, the stress, are gone. And I know she's desperately unhappy, but the lifting of all that weight, well, I feel light-headed just thinking about it. She may be single, but for Bex, life is simple again.

Infidelity, like burglary, is 90 per cent opportunity. As for the other 10 per cent, well . . . I wish Sarah was here. Because life is going on, and if she was here, I'm sure it wouldn't be going this way. It's bad, I know, but I'm blaming her for what I'm about to do. Her not being here makes her culpable. Life is going on, and if she isn't here to stop it, there's not much I can do.

I know I shouldn't use Bex, but I know I'm going to anyway.

Bex doesn't reply when I knock on the door. I knock again. Her record is finished, and I can hear the static thump of needle bumping along the run-off groove.

'Bex?'

I open the door gently and look in. The room is dark: there's a single desk-light on, the curtains are open letting in a particularly murky night sky. Bex is sitting cross-legged on the floor, a yoga position of meditation. Panda rings of mascara circle her eyes. On the floor in front of her are two white piles – a small one of tissues, a larger one of letters ripped into small and tiny pieces.

'Hey,' I say sitting down opposite her. 'Can I sit down?'

Bex shrugs.

'How are you feeling?' I ask.

'Raw,' Bex says. 'Pretty fucking raw.'

I look at the letters. I see stamps, I see snatches of sentences. *Can't wait to. Do you know how much. Wish you were. I want your.*

'Words,' Bex says. 'They're just words.'

I nod. They are just words, but they're more than that too. They're six months of a relationship, of feelings and emotions.

'You don't have to do this now,' I say.

'No, it's good.' Bex smiles, sadly. 'It's cathartic.'

To Bex's left, I suddenly notice more things. A record, snapped in two, all sharp and jagged edges jutting out. Tapes unwound and unwound and unwound. A skirt, red and velvet, scissored to shreds. Photographs in frames, the fractured glass blurring and distorting the smiling faces beneath. A map of Cuba, which had sat above Bex's desk, now lies crumpled in a ball. The clock, the Cuba clock, lies smashed on its side, the hour, minutes, second hands no longer going round. Cards – Christmas, birthday, Valentine's – all ripped apart. A Valentine's card in particular catches my eye. A red heart, torn in two.

'They're just things,' Bex says, picking up part of a record. 'When someone gives them to you, it seems like they're more, like they have meaning.' She gently places the record down again. 'But that's just a trick. At the end of the day it's just a record.'

'No,' I say. 'It's still got that meaning.'

Bex shakes her head. 'You're just sentimental.'

I think about this. 'Maybe. But if these things have no meaning, why are you destroying them?'

Bex cries. They are silent sobs, her eyes are closed, her mouth is open. All there is is the slight shuddering of her body.

'I'm sorry, Bex,' I say and move across to hug her. But Bex waves me away, shaking her head.

'Let me guess. You're all right?'

Bex nods and sobs.

'Sure,' I say and move across to hug her anyway. And as Bex buries her head in my jumper, the howling starts. Big muffled cries.

'It's all right,' I say, stroking her head. I look down at the discarded stuff, at a photo of Si and Bex at a Saints and Sinners party, Si as a devil, Bex as an angel, a split in the glass scoring a diagonal line across the picture. It's shocking, this paraphernalia. Bex and Si had been going out for the best part of a year and a half, and here it all is in front of me, reduced to a small pile of broken goods. In the clear dark of night, relationships seem such a strange way to structure your life, years of effort ending up as this. Here I am, binding my heart to someone on the other side of the world. What the fuck am I doing?

Friends breaking up is one of the worst things that can happen to a relationship. When a couple that seemed so solid suddenly self-combusts, it can't but make you reassess. If they're splitting up, what chance do we have? It's a bug that works the other way too – people getting married sows the seed in other couples for better or for worse – but the breaking-up bug is the one to watch. It can get very contagious.

'Hey,' I say. 'Come on now. This isn't the Bex I know. The Bex I know isn't going to be beaten by this. She's going to dry her eyes and show the world what she's made of.'

Bex stops sniffling. And here's where I take my chance.

'You know what I think? I think you need to do something. Take your mind off things, refocus.'

Bex leans back, looks at me sharply. 'Go on.'

'I don't know.' I try to sound casual. 'Why don't you play some music, get yourself some gigs? It's something that you love doing, it's definitely a way of getting things out of your system – think of all those songs you could be writing.'

'I've written one already,' Bex says.

'Well, there you go then. And the thing about it is, it's something you've started doing since Si has been away. It's nothing to do with him. It's not going to remind you of him.'

'I'm not sure,' Bex says. 'I don't know if I'm up for performing at the moment.'

'Of course you are,' I say. 'Hey, how's about this as an idea.' I speak as though the thought has just come to me. 'We could set up a gig for charity. An evening of, I don't know, Nick Drake songs or something.'

'Well,' Bex says. 'Maybe . . .'

'That's decided then.' I smile encouragingly.

Bex is silent. She's looking down at Si's letters.

'Come on,' I say. 'I know what we can do with those.'

Against the black of night, the tiny shreds of Si's letters look like snowflakes. Bex and I stand there, on the roof, mesmerised as they flurry downwards, flicking and flittering towards the back yard. Bex offers me the carrier bag of words, but I decline, and watch her scoop up another fistful of phrases, fling them into the darkness.

When astronauts are launched into orbit, they are always awestruck by the sight of the earth against the starry sky. Up there, you appreciate that space is literally space – an infinite nothingness spreading its blackness in all directions. And then there's the earth – its blues and greens swaddled in clouds – a single, colourful, beautiful exception. Watching Si's letters disappear below, I think I felt something similar: the shards of paper aren't just words to me, they are the feelings and experiences Si had written about. Like the earth against the starry sky, there is something quietly beautiful about the expressions of love, flickering against the darkness.

Whenever I have one of those 3 a.m. what's-the-point-of-it-all conversations, the conclusion I want to come to is that the answer is love. That in some mystical, magical, unfathomable manner, love touches us, lights us up and lingers on. That love is what marks us out as special and unique, that love gives us passion and purpose. That love somehow outlasts us, that even when we're gone love is still there. It's more of a belief than a theory – a belief I suspect that's born more of hope than experience. For without love, without Si's words dancing in the dark, all there is is nothingness. And however possible, plausible, that might be, it's an idea I don't want to accept.

'This is good,' Bex says, throwing another cluster of comments away. 'This is a really good idea.'

'You're enjoying this, aren't you?' I ask.

Bex looks at me. Her hair is a mess, matted and wound by the wind and the rain, her face is smudged by make-up and tears, but her eyes and mouth are smiling for all they are worth. 'Do you know what?' she says. 'I rather believe I am.'

'I guess this is what's known as falling out of love.'

Bex laughs. 'I prefer to think of it as Si getting dumped.'

'Dropped.'

'Discarded.'

'Chucked.'

'Going down.' Bex pauses. Her mind is racing ahead of her heart. 'Ouch.' She upends the carrier bag, shakes it clear of the remaining words. 'Well, he's going down now.'

Bex is smarting. Bex is also smart. She'll get over this. Maybe not today, maybe not tomorrow, but one day. And for the rest of her life she'll remember this evening: the anger and the upset, the release of ripping up every promise and proclamation Si ever wrote to her. I don't know which way she'll go: she might be cross with herself for letting Si get under her skin like this; she might be cross with herself for not having kept some memento of their time together. But one way or another, she won't forget this night in a hurry.

We peer over the edge, looking down at the backyard, at the relationship sprinkled across the concrete. Torn apart. In shreds.

'He wrote to you a lot, didn't he?' I say.

Bex nodded. 'For what it wasn't worth.'

'There's a phrase for this, you know. All this tearing-up of letters.'

'What's that?'

'Postal traumatic stress disorder.'

Bex laughs, silently. 'There's also a term for people like Si. Second-class male.'

I laugh, but not much. Humour is all about hurting someone. It needs a target, whether its aim is someone else, or whether its jokes are self-deprecating. And though Bex is getting at Si, I find myself feeling pinpricked too. Second-class male. Is this what I am, is this what men are, aspiring to good things but never quite achieving them? I think about Sarah, I think about Mika, I think about me. I think about what might happen.

Dear Si,

I use 'dear', you understand, because that is the convention in letter writing. You are not, however, 'dear' to me. Not in the slightest. You've never been particularly special to me anyway, but after what you've done to poor, dear Bex (now there is someone who is dear), I think I can call you exactly the opposite. Cheap.

I guess I shouldn't be surprised at how you've behaved. It's completely in keeping with your character. Or should I say, your lack of character. It's just all so predictable, you going overseas and being unable to keep your dick inside your garish Hawaiian trunks for more than three minutes. I thought that deal about allowing snogs was bollocks the moment Bex told me. You never had the slightest intention of sticking to it, did you? It was just some sort of cock's charter. If you really wanted to go around Cuba giving the British physique such a bad name, you could have done the decent thing and split up before you set off. But no, you wanted to have your cake and eat it, you wanted your fun and for Bex to play the doting woman back at home, pining and waiting for you.

I believe it is normally the best friend's role at this point to tell you what a stupid mistake you've made and that you'd better start grovelling fast if you're going to have a chance of getting back together. However, far from this being a mistake, I think this the best thing that has happened to Bex for ages (one year and five months to be precise). She was always far, far too good for you, so you screwing up isn't so much a mistake as an inevitability. And as for your chances of getting back together, well, just forget it. I don't think you know how to grovel, so it's probably a bit late to start now. And even if you were world grovelling champion, I still wouldn't rate your chances.

Christ knows what the Cuban women think of you. I remember only too well my conversation with Bex the day after she'd slept with you for the first time. 'Small', she described you as, 'and fast'. My highlight of the week was always her retelling of her latest batch of reassurances to you. 'No, of course it doesn't matter.' 'It's happens all the time.' 'It's more widespread than you think.' If only it had spread a little wider, maybe you'd be in with more of a chance! And I haven't even got on to your technique. One and a half play we used to call it. Which makes your story about the women of Cuba lining up for a spot of your oral abilities all the more ridiculous. It may be a deprived country, but I don't suppose they're that deprived.

You stupid, silly, small, pathetic disappointment of a man. Goodbye. Good riddance. Auf Wiedersehen. Sayonara.

Sarah

14

On Saturday, I go to my local record store and buy Nick Drake's entire back catalogue.

The first single I ever bought was 'Is there Something I Should Know' by Duran Duran. I was nine. I liked Duran Duran because they were a boy's band, rather than Wham! who were largely for the girls. And anyway, as a pre-teenager, George Michael's lyrics of love and unemployment meant nothing to me. Simon Le Bon's lyrics meant nothing to me either, but they sounded profound and so I assumed they were smart. That line about being as easy as a nuclear war. I spent several years trying to fathom the subtleties of that.

There was a definite thrill about buying that first single. It made me feel grown up. I was buying status, cool, credibility. Well, of a sort. I remember ringing up my best friend from down the road, and he came round and we sat there and listened to it again and again and again. There was certainly something about owning the record – Thatcher's child, I'm sorry to say – and something too about the anticipation as you lowered the needle. It was a bit like learning to fly; each early landing was rewarded with a heavy thump of static. But with practice, my needle skills became smoother and smoother, until all there was, was a hiss and a crackle, and the wait for Simon Le Bon's clarion call to come in and kick-start the song.

There's a thrill about buying Nick Drake too, but this frisson is different. It's more reminiscent of when I was fourteen and I bought my first pornographic magazine. Early one Sunday morning, when I thought the world would still be asleep, I 'went jogging' and ran and wheezed and stitched until I found a newsagent out of reach of my parents. Inside, I loitered whilst an old man with a stick fiddled with his change for a packet of cigarettes. I could barely reach the top shelf, and as I stretched on tiptoes for a copy of *Fiesta*, for one horrible moment I thought I would send the whole lot crashing down. I felt hot and sweaty, and so did the five-pound note in my hand. As I approached the counter, my heart was thumping and I half expected the newsagent to tell me to put it back. Instead he gave me a stare, a long hard uncomfortable stare, and took my money.

I'm feeling hot now, queuing up. I want this transaction to be as simple and as anonymous as possible. I don't want to talk to the shop assistant, and fortunately the shop assistant doesn't want to talk to me. He's a punk: no hair, plenty of rings, and is a spectrum away from caring about Nick Drake. He's so bored he doesn't notice how badly my nerves make me write my signature. As I leave the shop, I expect a store detective to stop me, a store alarm to go off, a manager to appear and ask me if I wouldn't mind stepping into his office. Apart from anything else, my demeanour must make me look like a shoplifter. But no one does. I'm free, like the fourteen-year-old boy sitting in the bus shelter as the rain comes down.

Everything about *Five Leaves Left* is English, from the font used for Nick Drake's name to the Robin Hood green of the cover to the folk traditions of the music. The front cover is a colour photograph of Nick looking out of a window in a disused house on Hampstead Heath. With his long black hair, jacket, shirt and jeans, there's something Jaggeresque about the singer. But Nick lacks Jagger's confidence: this is a portrait of a quiet, thoughtful, pensive young man. Inside is the photograph that's on Bex's dresser, the one of Nick Drake leaning back against the wall whilst the blur of a businessman runs past. It's typical of the music too. Quiet, thoughtful, poignant.

There's an unmistakeable melancholy too, in the rich timbre of Nick's voice, also in the haunting arrangements of strings and oboes. There's a shyness in the way his voice wobbles, a naivety and vulnerability on show too. But for all of that, this is a warm album, a morning not a mourning album. A rich, rural, playfully gentle, delicately pastoral, acoustic classic.

Bryter Layter, Nick's second album, is considered by many to be his masterpiece. If *Five Leaves Left* is a morning album, then this is the afternoon. It's a bigger, fuller, lush-sounding record by comparison: the introduction of flutes and saxophones and backing vocals and drums widens the palette. At the same time, the album is suffused with a more urban feel – written when Nick moved to London, the songs are full of city imagery. The sleeve swaps countryside green for purple, with pink and orange borders. The front cover shows Nick sitting with his guitar, his blue-and-yellow-laced shoes in front of him. He's looking at the camera, but the light and slight graininess of the photo make it difficult to work out what he's thinking.

Nick's last album is *Pink Moon*. The evening album. *Bryter Layter* should have made Nick a star, but when it didn't he became withdrawn, retreated within himself. *Pink Moon* is short and stark, the sound of a man struggling with himself. There's no arrangements here, just Nick and a guitar. When he finished it, he dropped the tapes off at the reception desk of his record company without saying a word. It's bleak, but there is beauty there. And in the final song, 'From the Morning', a positive, optimistic ending.

I listen to each album in turn, one after the other. I play again 'Know', the song Mika had played at the folk club. It sends a small sharp rush of cold along my spine. As I listen, I can picture her there, rocking gently as she plays, humming its mysterious tune, her hair, her cardigan, her intensity. I'm surprised at the sharpness of the image: my memory has clocked every single small detail of her performance. I'm surprised too, that as the song is starting to fade and I hear Bex's key scratch in the lock, my response is to eject the CD, and hide all three albums under my bed.

An evening of Nick Drake,
in aid of the African Aid Appeal
Performers £4. Non-performers £5.

Is it a long shot? It's a shot, sure. I'm not a betting man, so I couldn't tell you the odds. That strange person on the TV racing with the sideburns and the funny hat, all his tapping of the nose and pulling of the ear means nothing to me. My poker playing, like me at the end of a poker evening, is poor. My face lights up if I get a good hand, and everyone else immediately folds. So I can't really explain why I'm doing this. To be honest, I'm not really sure why I am. I think it's to satisfy something inside, to sate some nagging doubt before it starts to nag. If I don't do anything, then I'll never know. If I try something and nothing happens, then at least I'll know I've tried. And if I have a go and something does occur . . . Like I say, I'm not a betting man. I couldn't tell you the odds.

For a while, I think Mika isn't going to turn up. I remember the way our family used to bet on the Grand National when I was a child. We'd pick three horses each and put the princely sum of twenty-five pence each into the pot. I never bothered with the form, preferring to pick on the basis of the jockey's colours. I seemed to have a thing for polka dots I recall. I never won. My sister, older and sassier, would always bag the winnings. Maybe right now is like back then; I'm choosing what I fancy on appearance alone. I'm punting on the pretty. And everybody else, who knows how things work, knows I don't stand a chance.

Actually, there was one year when my horse did win the Grand National. The rider of the second favourite just so happened to be wearing a blue shirt with white polka dots. And having held his position anonymously in the pack for the first round, by the time the horses went round again, he was in with a shout. Unlike, for once, my sister.

I've been doing the door for an hour and a half when Mika arrives. I don't see her at first. She's at the end of a short queue, which snakes out through the door, round the corner and up a flight of stairs. I don't recognise her at first. She's got a long black coat on I haven't seen before, and a black woollen hat pulled down almost to eye level. By the time she reaches the table, I've kind of given up hope and am just taking the money. At least some charity's benefiting. At least it has perked Bex up.

Without looking up, I see the end of a guitar case, and say 'Performing? That'll be four pounds please.'

As a five-pound note is held out, I notice something. Her hand. Her small, pale, almost porcelain hand. With a flash I remember that moment at the gig, the pushing back of the hair, the massaging of ear lobe. I look up, and with a leap of my heart I see it is Mika. She's looking down at the fiver and then, with a flick like thunder, her eyes are open and staring at me. I'm mesmerised, lost in the rich dark brown of her irises. Mika holds my gaze, and doesn't let go.

'Hi,' I say, attempting to gather myself. 'I'm glad you've come.' Without losing her look, I take the five-pound note from her hand. Mika gives it the faintest of tugs, the faintest of pulls, then lets go. 'I'd let you in for free, but this evening is for charity.'

'Really?' Mika says. 'I thought it might be for my benefit.'

I can feel my mouth open and shut like a goldfish. I want to say something, but I don't know what to say.

I nod. 'I, er, I want to see you. I'd like to get to know you.'

Mika leans forward, her hand reaching into the Tupperware box that's acting as my till. She flicks up her eyelids to look at me again. Her face is closer now. I can't believe how rich the brown of her irises are.

'Why?' she asks.

I notice her lips. Large, soft, perfectly cushioned. I can feel myself trembling. It would be nothing to push forward and press my mouth against hers. I can't believe I'm thinking about kissing her.

'I can't explain,' I say. 'I don't understand it.'

Mika lets out a little gasp. She looks down again, picks out a pound coin from the box and pockets it. She looks at me, nods, and walks into the room.

Later, layter, after the songs have been sung – 'Northern Sky' and 'Poor Boy', 'Hazey Jane' and 'River Man', 'Time Has Told Me' and 'Day is Done' and 'Way to Blue' and 'Man in a Shed' – after Bex has been applauded and has stood up and thanked everyone for coming and she has made herself more friends in one evening than she has in the previous six months put together, I'm sat there counting up the money when Mika comes up to me.

'Hi,' I say. 'I loved your song.' Mika's choice of song was 'Fruit Tree'. It's a song about fame, the thinness of fame, and how people's true worth is only known when they're gone. An eerily prescient song in retrospect. A melancholy tune, a beautiful flowing fingerpicked guitar part. Mika's voice, as ever, was ethereal.

'You want to get to know me?' she asks.

I nod. 'Yes I do.'

Mika reaches into her coat pocket, pulls out a rolled-up cigarette, places it on the table and pushes it towards me.

'Remember,' she says. 'Five leaves left.'

Then she turns, climbs the stairs and disappears. I watch her go, pick up the cigarette and it's then that I notice. Something is written on the inside of the cigarette paper. As carefully as I can, I split it open, spill the tobacco out onto the table. I unfold the Rizla and read the message, written in small, neat writing. My heart leaps, and then, almost as quickly, as I read on, it falls.

Oxford Street. Tuesday.
I'll absolutely never turn you on.
Understand?

Dearest Sarah,

Thank you so much for your email. Your comments, as ever, are warm, lucid, insightful and considerate. It is a shame that I am still good friends with your boyfriend as this precludes me from asking you to keep your stupid, arrogant, frigid stuck-up nose out of it.

For the record, what I told Bex was the truth. I got tricked into going down on a girl when I was very drunk, and then got tricked into doing it again. It's not something I feel great about, but it falls in (just) with what I agreed with Bex, and I have paid a very, very heavy price for it. I have not slept with anyone while I have been away, which is more, I believe, than can be said for you. Yes, Bex told me everything. The words pot, kettle and black spring to mind. So unless you want me to tell Ben about the night you got shitfaced at the karaoke bar – 'The Time of My Life'? How tacky – can I suggest that in future you keep your stupid fat wonky mouth shut.

Oh yes. And your legs.

Si

15

I'm standing on the pavement outside Debenhams on Oxford Street, watching a man in a kilt and green Peter Storm play the bagpipes. I'm hardly a fan of the instrument myself, but even my unmusical ear can detect a touch too much wheezing and rasping, whining and droning where it should be lifting and lilting. The piper's face tells a story: unshaven, ruddy-cheeked, beads of sweat settling on the forehead. His sporran's seen better days as well. Nevertheless, on a mild, overcast, lukewarm February morning, none of this seems to matter. His tam-o'-shanter in front of him is bursting with change.

I reach into my trouser pocket and pull out Mika's Rizla. *Oxford Street. Tuesday.* Well, this is Oxford Street. It's Tuesday. What do I do now? I read on. *I'll absolutely never turn you on.* A dagger of a sentence. There, in black and white, lies the pointlessness of my position. Nothing will come of this. Every time I read this sentence I find myself feeling chastened, guilty for going behind Sarah's back. I know I don't deserve to feel disappointed, but I do. My only consolation is that it offers me some sort of get-out clause. 'Look,' I can say, if anyone asks questions, 'this is a friendship thing, nothing more. All this is, is a friendship thing.'

And yet here I am. Intrigued. Hopeful. Confused. There's no specific time on the note, no specific place to meet. It's like the vaguest of bomb warnings phoned to the police, the ones the police describe as 'deliberately misleading', the ones designed to cause maximum disruption. The ones that more than often turn out to be a hoax. And yet I'm here, with no search team to help me, no sniffer dogs or disposal experts to hand. It's me versus a million square feet of prime retail space, and I don't even have a magnifying glass. Mika is my needle – literally and figuratively – and I don't know where to begin.

The only people who like Oxford Street are people who don't live in London. It's one of those things, like the tube, that sounds great from a distance, gorgeous in theory, enticing and exciting in a day-out excursion sort of a way. If you live in London, it doesn't take long for the glamour to rub off. Oxford Street is the grubby epicentre of British capitalism. It lacks the style and individuality and the boutiques of Covent Garden or Notting Hill or Knightsbridge: this is flagship central, the biggest stores of all Britain's biggest stores. It feels cosmopolitan, but that's only because of the preponderance of tourists and language students. Like its Aberdeen Steak House, with its stretches of deep-red people-free seats, Oxford Street is, oddly, an empty place.

I can never get over the drabness. Today's blanket of cloud doesn't help but, looking up at the skyline, the monotone rows of three-, four-, five-storey buildings block out the light like back-to-back walls. The only flash of colour is the red river of buses slicing through the centre. Milling round like Lowry figures are the shoppers. They're doing the Oxford Street shuffle, trudging along in sync with everyone else, because if you don't fall into step, you won't so much walk as dodge your way along the pavement. No one ever seems happy on Oxford Street – everyone looks hacked off, wound up, crowded out – but like the coins in the bagpiper's hat, somehow they're there.

There are various theories floating around my head about what is going on. Option one is that I'm meant to be looking for Mika, that in the note is some sort of clue that I've yet to decipher or pick up on. Option two is that I'm looking for Mika, but rather than searching the note for the clue, the clue is somewhere along the stretch of Oxford Street. This option has the luxury of not having to think. All I have to do is to wander along and *I'll know when I see it*. Mika hasn't mentioned the meeting place because it will present itself in its obviousness. Option three is most bizarre: I'm not looking for Mika, Mika is looking for me. Somehow she knows where I am and is watching and waiting for me. Option four is cock-up rather than conspiracy theory: Mika simply forgot to write down the time and place we are meeting. Not a helpful option, that one. Option five is equally useless: I'm not looking for Mika and Mika isn't looking for me. I'm looking for something else entirely.

Part of me feels as though I'm being challenged. Part of me feels as though I'm being tested. And part of me feels as though I'm having the piss taken out of me. Why

Oxford Street? I can't think of a place less in tune with Mika if I tried. Or is that the point, that what I'm looking for is a pinprick of perfection, beauty amongst the drab, colour in the grey, a diamond on a pebbled beach. Maybe the surroundings don't diminish the worth of what I want. Maybe they serve to heighten instead.

I caught the train in from Greenwich to Charing Cross and then took the Northern Line to Tottenham Court Road. Since then I've walked Oxford Street's entire length, past Oxford Circus and Bond Street tubes to Marble Arch, the briefest of glimpses of Hyde Park and now I'm halfway back again. I'm continually looking in front, looking behind for a glimpse of Mika, but it's only when I reach the bagpiper that I see something.

On the opposite pavement, it's nothing more than a flick of hair, but it's enough to make my heart flash and I'm off, skidding across the traffic, almost impaling myself on a passing taxi, flitting in and out of the crowds in pursuit. I think I see her again, and duck into Next in pursuit. Next? I scour the men's, the ladies', but either I've lost her or she's hiding and then there's the back of her head again, out of the shop and turning right. I hare out and then I stop. In reach, in focus, I can see that this isn't Mika. The girl's got similar hair, but she's the wrong shape, the wrong build.

I pause to catch my breath. Is Mika watching me? I scan round. Is she somewhere in this mass of people, enjoying the joke at my expense? I shut my eyes and rub my eyelids. Part of me, the sensible part, can't believe that I'm putting myself through this. I can't believe how vulnerable I am, how vulnerable this is making me. Somehow, Mika is under my skin.

I head into a café on the corner of a crossroads, order a coffee and sip it slowly, staring out onto the street as I try to get my head together, watching the people and the traffic, each trying to jump the other's lights. Across the street is one of those men whose job it is to stand there all day and hold a sign. GOLF SALE it says in thick fluorescent green lettering. You'd think it was the kind of job you couldn't get wrong, but you haven't seen this man. He's listening to his Walkman and absent-mindedly swinging his sign around like a weathervane in the wind. Assuming someone actually wants to go to a fluorescent green golf sale, they've got a 75 per cent chance of heading in the wrong direction. I've been observing him for the best part of five minutes, and I've no idea which way the golf sale is.

I look at Mika's Rizla again. *Oxford Street. Tuesday. I'll absolutely never turn you on. Understand?* I still can't see it. Maybe the clue's in what Mika said. I rewind through our conversation. Maybe I should have just smoked it, got stoned and forgotten all about her. What else did she say? *Five Leaves Left.* No, that was a joke, a pun on the fact it was a Nick Drake evening and that she'd written the note on a Rizla.

Or was it? I recall Mika in the doorway, turning round

and saying, quite deliberately, 'Remember. Five leaves left.' Is that the clue, is that what I'm meant to remember? *Five Leaves Left*. Maybe the answer lies in the Nick Drake album. How many record shops are there on Oxford Street? Four, I reckon: two Virgins bracketing Oxford Street at Marble Arch and Tottenham Court Road, a pair of HMVs in between. It's not going to take me long to check them out, I think. And besides, I think, draining my coffee down to the dregs, it's not like I've come up with anything better.

I've always preferred the main HMV store to the Virgin Megastore. I know the latter is bigger and flashier and more well known, but HMV is always the better stocked. The Virgin megastore on Oxford Street is for the tourists, both literal and musical. The ground floor is all bargain this and bargain that, four for three, three for two of CDs that you really should have in your record collection already. And it may just be my own peculiar taste, but they never seem to have what I'm looking for, just multiple copies of all the obvious albums and empty spaces of all the interesting ones.

Today is no exception. The Virgin Megastore doesn't have a single copy of *Five Leaves Left*. There's two copies of *Pink Moon*, one of *Bryter Layter*, and a thick grey piece of plastic to indicate where *Five Leaves Left* should be. Typical, I think. But when I go to the main HMV store, the lack of song remains the same. No *Five Leaves Left*.

And when I go to the second HMV close to Bond Street, I come out empty-handed again.

I don't hold high hopes for the Virgin megastore at Marble Arch. If none of the other stores have got a copy of Nick Drake, why should they? And when I skim along the shelves from A to B to C to D, I'm not disappointed in being disappointed. This is weird, I think. Not a single shop on Oxford Street has got a copy of *Five Leaves Left*.

It's not normally in my nature, but for once I decide to ask. I've come this far, I've looked for this long, it can't hurt, I think. I wait patiently in line, whilst the bloke in front of me tries to exchange what he alleges to be a faulty CD of *Morning Glory* for a pristine copy of *The Great Escape*. The shop assistant doesn't look like he believes the customer but agrees with a resigned shrug, more to get rid of him than anything else.

'Yes, mate?' he asks me.

'I'm looking for a copy of *Five Leaves Left* by Nick Drake,' I say. 'I can't find one on the shelf.'

'Strange,' says the shop assistant. 'I'm sure that came in just the other day. Hey, Mary,' he shouts across to the girl on the till. 'You haven't seen a copy of *Five Leaves Left* by Nick Drake, have you?'

The girl looks at me oddly. Then says, 'Oh, are you Ben?'

I blink. 'Er. Yeah.'

'Your friend asked me to put it aside for you,' she says, as much to her fellow shop assistant as me. She disappears into a storeroom and reappears with a copy of *Five Leaves Left*.

'Can I, er, have a look at it?' I ask.

'Sure,' Mary says, handing it over.

I step away, and feel myself trembling a little. I look down at the CD, which looks exactly like the one I bought a couple of weeks before. I open the box up, take the CD out and look at it. As normal. I pull the sleeve notes out, revealing the black and white picture of Nick Drake and the blurred businessman. I'm not getting it, but as I pop the CD back, as I'm sliding the sleeve back into place underneath the transparent plastic semi-circles, I notice something. Where the CD clips in, in that hole in the heart of the grey plastic base, I see a corner. I bet that's a Rizla, I think, and as I look closer I can't stop my heart skipping as I see that there's something written on it.

'Everything OK?' Mary asks.

'Yes,' I say, snapping the CD case shut. 'I'll take it.' I reach into my pocket and put a twenty-pound note down on the counter. There's a pause.

'You'll have to give the CD back so I can scan it,' Mary says.

'What? Oh yes. Sorry.' I pass it over, though I can feel my eyes aren't leaving the box. 'Thank you.'

'Enjoy it.' Mary hands me my change.

'I hope I do,' I say. 'I've been searching for it all day.'

I wait until I'm outside before I open the case. I take the CD out and look at the case. The grey base is clipped into place and doesn't want to come out. I slide a fingernail underneath the edge and try to lever it out, but I can feel my nail bending under the pressure and I pull it out and the base snaps back. I put a finger into the small central circular hole but, when I try to pull, all I do is snap off one of the little hooks that the CD clips on to. I run my finger along the raised edge of the base on the left, the spine of the CD, slip a fingernail underneath and then, with a sharp tug on the top corner, with a click, the case comes away.

There it is. My second Rizla. *Four leaves left*, it reads. I pick it up, and turn it over, and there's my second message.

Tuesday. AZ1486D30. You smell.
Stop expecting Christmas, you.

Dear Sarah,

Greetings again from here in Britain, on a crisp, cold winter's day (though nothing like what you are experiencing, I'm sure). Life here, as ever, ticks on. It feels a little like the lull before the storm, everyone waiting for John Major to call the election so we can get going and get it all over with. At the moment, it all seems to be like we're checking and rechecking, making sure we've crossed every 't' and dotted every 'i' on the election plan. It's all a bit surreal: the opinion polls continue to put us miles ahead of the Tories – they're not showing any sign of movement at all, and yet nobody, but nobody, is believing them. I mean, imagine it: Labour with a majority of 100! It's just not going to happen.

Back in Millbank, I'm finding myself oscillating between Gareth and Annabel. Do you remember I got moved from the Audience Participation Unit after Christmas? Well, since then, I've been odd-jobbing like mad. If it's an Annabel day, then I'm feeding information into Excalibur, the computer database that details every single statement ever made by a Conservative ever, which we can call up at a second's notice, rapidly rebutting what they're saying before they have time to finish their sentence. Either that, or I'm helping with the polling and the focus groups, poring over the data to see just how much the man on the street is thinking what we're thinking, and what he'd think if we changed our thinking so we thought what he thought. A Gareth day, by contrast, involves door-knocking and leafleting and talking to people in whichever marginal seat we're visiting that day.

Anyway. That's not why I'm writing to you. The real reason that I'm putting pen to paper is this: Chris Evans has resigned! His breakfast show is no more: never again shall we lie in bed, late for lectures or work, giggling under the covers. I think it's all been brewing for a while now. He's been slagging off the controller of Radio One on air, and had a huge go at the bloke who was in charge of the station's music policy. And ever since he started doing TFI Friday he's been getting more and more knackered: in the autumn it was starting to make him ill, and he had to take time off to recover. Anyway, the BBC, it seems, did everything they could: they shortened the show so it started at seven rather than six thirty and doubled his holiday allowance to fourteen weeks a year.

But when Chris came back after Christmas he'd had a new idea: he wanted to have Fridays off. That way he could recover and relax in time to do TFI. His argument was that in America this was normal practice: DJs often worked Monday to Thursday: by having the weekend DJs do Friday, it upped their profile and everyone benefited. But the BBC, having given him the extra holidays and the shorter show, said no. Chris Evans then upped the stakes and said that unless he got Fridays off he'd quit. The BBC, though, refused to budge, and suddenly, bam, out of nowhere, Chris Evans was announcing his resignation.

This all blew up on the Thursday. On the Friday, Chris Evans did his breakfast show as normal – he still had to do ninety days or something to see out his contract. But he was playing lots of sad songs – 'Please Release Me', things like that. And then yesterday, on the Monday, just before the show,

Johnny Boy Revell rang up to say, 'We're not coming in today,' and that was that. At seven o'clock, a dragged-out-of-bed Kevin Greening played the first post-Chris Evans's breakfast show song. It was – and you'll like this – 'Don't Look Back in Anger' by Oasis.

It's funny really – and maybe it'll all seem a bit odd where you are, but I can't help feeling like somehow it's the end of an era. I mean, I've listened to the Radio One Breakfast Show for as long as I can remember – Mike Read, Mike Smith, Simon Mayo, Steve Wright, even Mark 'Goody Bags' Goodier, but Chris Evans, somehow, is the one that stands out head and shoulders above the rest. That's the one that's my breakfast show, if you know what I mean. The fact that he loved our music, played guitar music rather than dodgy dance, was crucial, surely, for the success of Britpop. For a while it was brilliant – do you remember the Ginger Grand Prix, when he set up an early morning grand prix track, taking in the sites of central London? Or when he was sick of London, and decamped and did the show from Inverness instead? Now radio's going to slip back to just being OK again.

I've put the new Blur album in the post like you asked. Be warned: it's more than a little bit different to their last. In fact, it couldn't be less Britpop if it tried. They've gone all Pavement and American, lo-fi and low-key, and some of it I kind of like, some of it I miss the lyrics and the Englishness and the, well, the tunes I guess. I'll be interested to hear what you think.

Sorry if all this is sounding melancholy. There's no reason why the future shouldn't be great: things can only get better as we keep on telling voters. Maybe it's for the best: all this end of an era stuff tying neatly with the end of the Tories. Except that it's our stuff that's ending, and that can't be right, can it? New

Labour are piggybacking on this young Britain stuff wherever we can – but somehow it's all out of sync, and if John Major doesn't call the election soon, it'll all be over before we even get into power. Hang on: maybe that's his idea? Maybe he's waiting for it all to implode, so he can march on a ticket of tradition and good old Tory values? Christ, maybe he has got his finger on the pulse after all . . .

Anyway. Must go and post this. How are you? How are things? Write soon and tell me all. I miss you. Life would be so much simpler if you were here.

Love, Ben x

PS Green. With Christmas trees on. I know.

16

As I step into St James's Park, having taken the tube to the station of the same name, peeled left over the zebra crossing, slipped past the grimly gargantuan Home Office building, Michael Howard and all, cut through the cut through to Birdcage Walk, waited patiently for the pedestrian crossing to finally go green, as I step into the broad sweeping green of the park, a squirrel runs across my path.

I say run. The squirrel flits in little staccato jumps, bouncing across the path like a stone skimming across water, its tail undulating behind. Three quarters of the way across, it stops abruptly and looks at me, eyeing me suspiciously, checking me out. A bit like when you walk into a dodgy pub and everyone stops to stare at you. My territory, the squirrel is saying. Don't mess. We stand there for a second, staring not moving, and even when I step forwards the squirrel doesn't flinch. Eventually, almost grudgingly, it moves to the side, as if to let me through. It watches me as I walk past, and as I look back, it is still there, until with a flicker it scrabbles away, skipping up a nearby tree.

I walk on, pausing on the bridge that neatly slices the long, thin lake in two. Looking left beyond the trees and the lake resides the familiar image of Buckingham Palace. It's beautifully framed from this angle, the natural world taking the edge off the imposing formal view from the Mall, its thick block, rectangular architecture. But I'm a republican not a royalist, and it's the opposite vista that really impresses. The lake stretches out, widening slightly to surround a small island, the trees and bushes and blue sky and cotton-wool clouds all reflected in the water. Beyond, Whitehall shapes the skyline, an almost continental cornucopia of domes and turrets and twists and turns of design that feel on loan from a Salzburg or a Paris or a Vienna. Strange, standing there, to think that I'm in central London. Strange that the heart of the British establishment should look so European.

I filch Mika's Rizla from my pocket and reread the note. *AZ1486D30. You smell.* I pull out my *A–Z* and turn to the relevant page. The square 6D is the far end of the lake. It features Duck Island, Horse Guard's Road, which forms the perimeter of the park, the Foreign Office and Cabinet War rooms. It is the '30' part I'm not so sure about. If my Duke of Edinburgh bronze award days serve me well, the '3' refers to the '6', and the '0' to the D. I divide the square in my mind from 0 to 10 on each axis, and take 6D to be the top left-hand corner. I drop down three on the horizontal, none on the vertical, and my thumb hits a point where the footpath swings in so it is adjacent to the lake on the north side. Is that right? I'm confused, can't remember whether you're meant to go across before you go down, wonder whether Ordnance Survey maps work the other way round or not. I guess it depends what is down there.

I walk on round the lake. It's mild for the time of year: spring-like for February. Apart from the tourists, there's a plethora of pushchairs and children with bread bags of crumbs to feed the ducks with. One particular chubby child is surrounded by drakes, mallards, geese and swans. A handful of seagulls swoop out of the sky to join in, elbowing and squawking to get food. The most persistent, in an almost deliberate manner, pecks at the child who shrieks and drops the bag of crumbs in fright, whereupon a second wave of gulls swoop in to claim their prize. I expect the child to cry, but in fact he is smiling, proud to be the centre of all the attention.

The path climbs away from the lake before dropping back down to it, flanked by a row of benches looking out over the water. I don't see a Mika sitting there waiting for me. I check the *A–Z* again and reckon that the benches are too far west. The co-ordinates specify the point where the path pulls away from the lake and I walk to where I think that is, by a single tree and solitary large bush, fully in bloom, with its pockets of sharp white flowers standing out against the dark rich green of its leaves. This is it, I reckon. I look at my watch. Bang on two o'clock. No Mika.

As I stand there, wondering what I should do, whether I'm meant to hang around and wait or what, I hear a rustle from above and look up to see the tips of the tree's branches beginning to teeter in a flicker of wind. And as I look up, my nose is suddenly consumed by the sweetest of smells: a richly sweet, sweetly rich aroma of honey. I glance down and realise it is the bush, the fragrance of its flowers that is drifting across on the wind. And as I breathe the honey I think of Mika's note – you smell – and it all begins to make sense.

I walk over to the bush. The wind drops and so does the scent, its delicate smell only apparent as I lean over and deliberately draw it in. And as I do so, I notice something white inside the bush. I look closer and see a rolled-up cigarette Sellotaped to a branch. Mika. Excited, I lean in to take it, but it is only just in reach. I try to unpeel it carefully so as not to tear it and in doing so I feel it slip through my fingers and drop to the ground. I look round to see if anyone is watching before climbing over the fence to retrieve it. But as I spy it among the leaves and the twigs and crouch down to pick it up, as I reach my hand out, there is a sudden noisy rustle in the bush, and I watch in not so much surprise as astonishment as a squirrel springs to the floor and snatches the cigarette before my outstretched fingers.

I let out a solitary laugh as the squirrel zips across in front of me, the cigarette clamped in its jaws like a dog with a stick. I watch it scurry away from the lake, across the path until it sits on a slight slope, flicking its head round on all sides, checking its triumph is not about to be gazumped.

'Hey!' I shout. 'Give me that back, you little . . .' I leap up in pursuit, lumber at the squirrel as if to justify its paranoia. The squirrel's got my number, though, and nimbly springs on, zigzagging left and right as if to throw me off the scent. I pause, the squirrel pauses, and we're both there crouching, eyeing each other from five yards apart.

I feel like I'm the US Army going into Vietnam. I'm bigger, stronger, should really win the battle with ease, but my enemy is smart and quick and knows the territory like the back of its hand. The squirrel is showing no sign of fear and not only that, but the longer I crouch here, the more it's figuring that it's got something good and the more it figures that, the less likely it is it's going to give up its prize.

As I look at the squirrel, it drops the cigarette on the ground. For a second, I think it might scamper away, this may be one squirrel that doesn't smoke, but instead it sits there watching me. And it's then that I realise that this is one clever rodent. The little bugger wants to barter. Come on, it's saying. If you want the cigarette so much, you're going to have to offer for it. What have you got?

What have I got? I feel in my pockets. The only thing edible I have is half a packet of Polos. Without losing the squirrel's eye, I pull them out, hold one up towards the squirrel and put it in my mouth, to show the squirrel it is edible. As I crunch it noisily, I take another one out, chuck it to the right of the squirrel and wait. The squirrel waits. 'OK,' I say. I throw it another Polo. The squirrel still waits. You should take up poker, I think, flinging a third Polo onto the pile.

The squirrel continues to look like it couldn't really give a shit. I resist the temptation to offer it the rest of the packet. The squirrel, for the first time, flicks its gaze across to the Polos. It knows it is a trap but reckons it might be worth a go. Carefully, cautiously, it moves, tiptoeing between the cigarette and the sweets, at every step watching me to see if I'm going to make a move. I'm stationary: I've only got one shot at this, I reckon. I've got to choose my moment carefully.

The squirrel reaches the Polos. It's now as far away from the cigarette as I am. It picks up a Polo and holding it tightly starts to gnaw away. Mmmm, I mouth. Lovely Polo. I wave the packet at it, feeling like a drug dealer, sucking in my prey. The squirrel continues to bite on the Polo. To my delight, it likes it. I watch as it gathers up all three Polos in its paws. I take out one more Polo and throw it just that little bit further to the right.

I wait. The squirrel waits, and then with a dart it goes for it and this is my cue and I spring forwards and dive for the cigarette, but as I reach it, and can even feel it in my grasp, the squirrel has sprung back and, like a striker kicking the ball out of the goalkeeper's hands, it nips me sharply on the finger, snatches the cigarette, scurries across the path and up the tree next to the bush with the sweet honey smell. And then, to add insult to injury, as I sit there, covered in dust and wiping my bleeding finger, it sprints back down, steals a Polo and is back up the tree before I can blink.

If pigeons are rats with wings, then squirrels are rats with big bushy tails. Like koalas, like penguins, there is something about their diminutive nature that suggests sweetness. But their cuteness deceives. They are smart, sharp, vicious little thieves. They know when to attack, when to defend, and when to steal someone's cigarette to survive. And never forget how grey squirrels came over here from North America and took out their better-looking red cousins. They're the animal equivalent of the Vikings. They're the perpetrators of a systematic furry genocide. Yeah. Not so cute now, are they?

My finger throbs. The squirrel bit into the tip of my index finger and every time I wipe the blood off it reappears in a velvety red globule. I stand up, brush myself off, and grind the two remaining Polos into the ground.

This is war.

I walk over to the tree where the squirrel is sitting just out of reach on a branch above. He's nibbling at the Polo whilst holding the cigarette firmly under foot.

'You're meant to do it the other way round,' I say.

The squirrel ignores me.

'Have you heard of Squirrel Nutkin?' I ask. 'No, you're obviously not a well-brought-up middle-class squirrel, are you? Well, let me tell you Beatrix Potter has got your number. She knows what you're really like. Maybe, yeah, maybe I should tell you the story, fill one of the gaps in your deprived childhood or whatever it is baby squirrels are called. Little shits?' I laugh. 'You and your bad upbringing. No wonder you ended up turning to crime.'

I look up at the squirrel. As I thought. He has no response to my put-downs other than to carry on eating his Polo.

'Squirrel Nutkin was always one of my favourite Beatrix Potter stories,' I continue. 'Nutkin lived with various cousins by a lake, in the middle of which there was an island owned by a big old brown owl called, cunningly enough, Old Mr Brown. In the autumn the squirrels would sail across to the island, and in return for being allowed to gather nuts, that's nuts not cigarettes, they would offer the owl various gifts, such as mice or a mole or beetles wrapped in dock leaves and fastened with a pine-needle pin. Everyone that is except Squirrel Nutkin who didn't bring presents but messed around and made fun of Old Mr Brown until one day, *one day* . . .' I look up to see if the squirrel is listening, 'Old Mr Brown decides enough is enough and grabs Squirrel Nutkin. Old Mr Brown is so angry he has every intention of skinning Squirrel Nutkin, that's *skinning* him, yeah, but Squirrel Nutkin attempts to wriggle free and in doing so his tail *rips* in two. You should think about that.'

The squirrel regards me as though I'm mad. Which is fair enough: I'm standing here, talking to a squirrel about Beatrix Potter. With Squirrel Nutkin impertinence, he spits out the Polo, which lands in front of me.

'Litter bug,' I say, but the squirrel ignores me. He's got more interesting things to play with.

'I don't know how you're going to smoke that thing,' I say. 'You haven't even got a light.' But the squirrel has better ideas. Sticking his nose in the end, he pulls out a tuft of tobacco and starts to chew.

'Your teeth'll fall out,' I say, waiting for the squirrel to reject the tobacco in disgust, but to my surprise, he chomps the lot and sticks his nose into the roll-up for more. It's out of reach but then the squirrel has an even better idea. To my horror, he uses a mixture of teeth and paw to rip the cigarette apart.

'You'll regret it,' I say, as the squirrel tucks in. 'You'll be a twenty-a-day squirrel before you know it.'

Shit. It's so farcical I could almost laugh at the situation, at me standing here in desperation hoping that something will happen. I've never been sure what this whole thing with Mika is about but now I guess I'll never know. Who'd have thought it? Kept apart by a squirrel.

But then.

Then the wind picks up. And as the sweet honey smell whispers across, so does the Rizla paper. The squirrel has stuffed so much into its mouth that there's nothing holding it down, not enough to stop it from flying off. And with a flick and a swoop, it's floating towards me on a sweet, honey-smelling current of air. I snatch it and watch as the squirrel thinks about running to retrieve it but his balance and poise have gone and suddenly he's slipping and clinging onto the branch for dear life.

'It's like I said,' I smile. 'Smoking's bad for you.'

Later, much later, when I get home, the first thing I notice is the smell of a cigarette coming from the kitchen.

'Bex?'

She's sat there at the table, an ashtray, a half-empty packet of Marlboro Lights, a smoke alarm with its batteries taken out in front of her.

'I thought you'd given up?' I pull a chair out and round, sit down Christine Keeler-style facing her.

'So did I,' Bex says, sucking deep and slow.

'Si?' I ask.

Bex flinches and nods at the same time.

'I got an email,' she says, as matter as factly as she can, trying to suppress the wobble in her voice. 'You got an email. Sarah got an email. Everyone got an email.'

I haven't heard from Si for weeks. 'Is he all right?' I ask.

'Oh, he's *fine*.' Bex stubs her cigarette out, a little forcefully.

'What, what did the email say?' I ask, but Bex is turned away now, staring out of the window.

'How could he?' she asks me, herself, Si, I'm not sure. 'So soon. So quickly.' Suddenly, she turns back, looks at me intently. 'Did you know about this?'

'Bex.' I hold my palms up, an I'm innocent pose. 'I've no idea what you're talking about.'

'What about the other one? The one in Cuba?'

'Which one?' I ask. I shut my eyes, regret it even before the words leave my mouth.

'There was more than *one*?' Bex shakes her head, laughs. 'Oh, what does it matter? You men, you're all the same.'

'Hey, now come on,' I say. 'That's not fair.'

'Isn't it? He cheated. You covered it up.'

I think about this. 'That's not true. What happened was that I didn't get involved.'

'Well, maybe you should have.' Bex fiddles with her lighter, flicks the flame on and off. Then she says, 'I would.'

'What do you mean?'

'Exactly that. If you were treating Sarah like Si was treating me, I wouldn't be able to stand back like that.'

I flush. What do you know, I think? Is this a warning? I can feel my whole body tense as I try to act as casual as possible. Bex flicks the lighter again and I jump as it whooshes with a big flame, a flame Bex holds up.

'Tell him not to email me again,' she says, flicking the flame off and standing up. I watch her leave the room, watch her slip upstairs, then I find a glass and down a pint of water. I feel nervous, I feel frightened, I feel guilty, I feel torn, and yet, yet despite all this, I can't help my hand reaching inside my jeans pocket, I can't help feeling the rush as my fingers find the crinkle of Rizla paper within.

From: Si
To: Ben (Home)
Cc: Bex; Cardigan Girl
Date: 20 February 1997
Subject: What's hot

Greetings, comrade,

Hello once again, mate, from the midst of the delights of Latin America. I'm sitting in the depths of darkest Peru, sipping my freshly brewed, freshly ground Peruvian coffee, in an Internet café decked out, for the tourist, I presume, in Paddington Bear memorabilia. Maybe it's run by his aunt? Not that you'd be needing your duffel coat here; it is absolutely roasting: if I hadn't already acclimatised thanks to six months of sunning myself in the sun, I might be turning a little pink by now.

It's mad here. Inca this, Inca that. Had guinea pig for breakfast, which was nice if a bit hairy, washed down with a healthy dollop of llama milk. The locals are friendly in a 'we'd like to rip you off' sort of a way, but it's all good-humoured and they like it when you haggle. Am still recovering from a week of exertion, walking to the ancient site of Machu Picchu: five days of trekking at high altitude through the Peruvian jungle. Hard work and dicey at night, as you're not sure what you're going to step on as you nip out of the tent to go for a piss. Still, the site when you get there at the end is absolutely stunning: like walking onto the set of the Mysterious Cities of Gold. You almost expect Mendoza to be there waiting for you!

This is my second visit to the Internet café: my first attempt to write to you having been curtailed by yet another piece of post-Bex action. I tell you, mate, finishing with her was the best thing I've done, especially for my sex life. Rather than another six months of crossing my legs and keeping my fingers crossed, I can hardly catch my breath with a selection of women who are as hot as Lima on a Tuesday afternoon (and believe me that's hot). On my first visit to the Internet café I was writing to you when I couldn't help noticing this absolutely gorgeous piece sat at the computer to my left. Long curly hair, low-cut swimsuit and ethnic sarong. Her name was Claire, a student travelling from Vancouver. Claire had had a fixation with Paddington Bear since she was small and had always wanted to come to Peru.

Let me tell you, it doesn't take long for the Si charm to work its wonders on people like Claire. Especially when I tell them about being dumped by my girlfriend: you should try it sometimes, works a treat. They make the mistake of feeling sorry for you, and bam! In for the kill. Claire was well up for it. I think the giveaway was the sign she was wearing, the one poking out of her more than ample cleavage that read 'Please Look After This Pair'.

Claire was hot. She did stuff you wouldn't believe, stuff I can't write in an email in case I get arrested for sending porn across the web. But believe me, after going with Bex, it was an eye-opener. I thought I knew everything there was to know about nookie – and, as you know, I know a lot – but that night in my guesthouse bedroom was an education. English girls haven't got a clue. God knows what the bloke on the downstairs bunk made of it.

When I woke up, Claire had gone. No note, nothing: that's backpackers for you. And I know I should be heading on, but I'm back here in the Internet caff every day, on the off chance that she returns. Oh yes, mate. Life can be mighty gooood. S'ya.

Si.

17

On the day after John Major finally calls the election, Annabel is running around the office, looking as happy and as excited as I've ever seen her.

'Look at this! Look at this!' She runs up to me, waving a newspaper in her hand.

So this is election fever, I think. The phoney war is over, the battle proper is upon us. We've been so geared up for months, I didn't think the real thing could feel any different. But looking at Annabel, I've obviously got it wrong.

'Come on then,' she says, clasping the newspaper to her chest, hiding the front cover from me. 'You've got to guess what the headline is.'

'Is that the *Sun*?' I ask.

Annabel bites her bottom lip as she nods excitedly. 'Think of the best headline you can possibly think of.'

'Thatcher sectioned?'

Annabel shakes her head.

'Michael Howard ate my hamster?'

Another shake.

'Portillo: my night of lap-dance shame?'

'No, no, no. Better than that. Look.' Annabel turns the paper round to reveal the real headline. And there, in big block letters, are the four words that are getting Annabel so worked up.

THE SUN BACKS BLAIR.

'Isn't it wonderful?' she beams.

'It's, er . . .' It's extraordinary, I think. This is the *Sun* I'm looking at. The 'Nightmare on Kinnock Street' *Sun*. The 'If This Man Gets Elected Will the Last Person Out Of Britain Please Turn Out the Lights' *Sun*. The ' "It's the Sun Wot Won It" for the Tories' *Sun*.

'Everything we've done since last time has paid off,' Annabel continues. 'If the *Sun* are supporting us, then that shows we're hitting the national wavelength.'

'You don't think it shows that we've, you know, moved?' I ask.

'It means we've got a message that's connecting with people. This isn't something we should be embarrassed about, Ben. This is something to be proud of.' Annabel beams. 'Never underestimate the power of the media. It's the *Sun* what won it last time for the Tories and it's the *Sun* that's going to win it this time, but this time it's going to be us.'

Gareth's analysis of the *Sun*'s change of allegiance is slightly more succinct.

'Bandwagonning cunts,' he snarls, and drops the newspaper in the bin.

SW1P 4GT. 1500. 1803. Tirra lirra.
Typical Englishman, privately thinking Mika's excited.

In the afternoon, I make my excuses and slip out, turn right down out of Millbank Tower, away from Parliament towards the Tate Gallery, and my third rendezvous with Mika.

Art galleries and museums always find me feeling tired. I'm never sure why. One theory I have is that the humidity necessary to keep the exhibits in perfect condition is somehow soporific. Another theory is that it is an echo of childhood, a remnant of those bored Sunday afternoons traipsing round stately homes when all I wanted was a can of Coke and a multicoloured eraser from the gift shop. Pavlov's Dog, but with paintings.

Tirra lirra. That's the clue on the Rizla. It means nothing to me. I decide to look around and see what I come across. That might sound a male response, not asking for help, but in this instance it's not like that. I'm feeling like I want to push things. I want to test this, to see how far this is, for want of a better phrase, *meant to be.* These meetings by message, it feels as though my relationship with Mika is a single, fine, beautiful thread, a beautiful thread from which I'm hanging. There's something about its thinness – its finesse – that intrigues: how at any slender second it could break; how this next to nothingness can potentially mean so much. And what I think is that I shouldn't have to search for the thread: if there's some kind of meant-to-be-ness in all of this, then I'll just know when I come across it. If this has any form of meaning, it shouldn't be something I have to work for. It should be an instinctive thing.

Every picture tells a story. I don't remember much from my art lessons at school but I do remember that. Be it portrait or religious or whatever, all good art should have a point. I wander round slowly, soaking up the silent atmosphere, the tall ceilings and white walls, the only sounds the clip of the odd shoe, the scratch of an artist copying a painting onto a sketchpad.

In the first room I enter, I come across a large eighteenth-century portrait of three ladies sat round a small red table playing cards. Their puff-white skirts are so big they border on the ridiculous. The lady on the right is looking out at the painter, at the observer, her cards tilted to let us in on what a good hand she's got. A small, sly smile on her face. The blurb by the picture claims it is a wry nod to competition between women for husbands. The title of the picture is *Hearts are Trumps*.

A second picture catches my eye: *King Cophetua and the Beggar Maid*. A tall, impressive picture dominated by shades of black and brown, it depicts the tale of an African king, Cophetua, who was famously dismissive of both women and love until the day he meets and falls in love with a beautiful, dark-haired beggar girl. In the picture, their positions are reversed: it is the king, resplendent in black armour with his crown in his hands, who sits at the feet of the pauper, gazing straight at her as she sits there barefoot in simple black dress, a small bunch of flowers in her hand. The message is simple, straightforward, reinforcing: love possesses the power to transcend.

I meander on, find myself attracted to a small, appreciative cluster of people crowded round a smaller picture, a picture in a golden frame with the title stencilled in at the bottom: *April Love*. It's a picture of a thin, pale, waif-like Pre-Raphaelite girl with long red hair, her suitor silhouetted in the background, his head bowed on her hand, romantically clutching a rose Romeo-style on the other side of an open window as the girl looks away at the ivy on the wall, the rose petals on the floor. But what catches the eye are the colours: the rich, vibrant blue of the girl's dress, the lush green of the ivy that spirals down the left-hand side of the picture.

'What does it mean?' hisses a girl to my left.

'It's about the fragility of young love,' replies her friend. 'The rose petals on the floor represent both its beauty and brevity. The girl is looking at the ivy because that symbolises longevity, that's what she wishes love was like.'

'Wow,' says the first girl. 'I wonder if love really is short like that?'

'It is where our Jason is concerned,' sniggers her friend.

I hear them giggle away and carry on looking at the picture. There's something about it that is nagging me and something that touches me too: its innocence, its bittersweet hints, its Romanticism with a capital R. Is love nothing but a brief flash of brilliance? Is this Romanticism for effect or Romanticism for real? And then the other thing, the nagging thing, reveals itself. The picture reminds me of Nick Drake, of the album cover for *Five Leaves Left*. The photo on *Five Leaves Left* is bordered by green, as with the ivy. Like the girl in *April Love*, Nick Drake stands by a window, green leaves behind. Like the girl in *April Love*, Nick Drake is wearing a white shirt, a jacket rather than a scarf, blue jeans rather than blue dress. Like the girl in *April Love* he is thin, pale and glancing thoughtfully, melancholically down.

In the centre of another room stands a man with an easel, painting on a large white rectangular canvas. It's moving in an odd way, the artist amongst the art. He's a man in his forties, his hair thinning where his glasses are resting. He pushes them down to look at the painting he is copying, then slides them back up as resumes his work. His cream overall matches his canvas. I think the reason it affects is that it stops the exhibits being pictures stuck on a wall. Because once they were painted on a canvas like this. Once their paint was still fresh, wet. Somehow, the artist's presence makes the pictures come alive.

I wander up behind him to see what he is painting. In a medieval white dress with long straight auburn hair sits a woman in a small boat on a lake. The woman is resting on a rich red tapestry, which hangs over the side of the boat and drapes into the water. At the front of the boat rest three candles, two extinguished, and a crucifix. In the woman's hand is a chain, with which, presumably, the boat was moored. The boat is now set to head out amongst the reeds and lilies into the water beyond. I glance up at the original, which is bigger, bolder, but also finer and more detailed. The redness of the woman's lips, the look of harrow in her eyes, the band of gold-embroid-ered squares on her sleeves, the swallow flying amongst the reeds, centuries on, each stands out in their sharpness. It's a painting that looks familiar, but is one I can't place.

'What's the picture?' I ask.

'*The Lady of Shalott*,' the painter says without looking round, adds yet more detail to the tapestry. 'By Water-house. Based on the Tennyson poem.'

'Tennyson?' I ask.

'Tennyson,' says the artist, standing up, pulling his glasses down to look at the picture. 'Did you do English at school?'

'Sort of,' I say. 'So what's the picture about?'

'It's an Arthurian kind of a thing. She lived in a tower on the island of Shalott, just down the river from Camelot, and was only allowed to look at the world via a mirror.' The artist smiles. 'No, don't ask me why. One day the knight Lancelot rides past and the Lady is so struck by him she can't stop herself from looking at him directly. As she does so, the mirror cracks and she is cursed. Her punishment is to sail towards Camelot, to die before she gets there.'

'Right,' I say. Then I have a thought. 'Tirra lirra.'

'Tirra lirra indeed,' the artist smiles. 'So you *do* know the poem.'

So this is it. I stare at the painting, soak up its Pre-Raphaelite Romanticism. Very Mika, I think. That mix of love and death, doomed by life, like Nick Drake holding a mirror to the world, like Nick Drake that odd, out of kilter relationship with reality. There's something desperately sad about the picture, the way that love damns the Lady. And once again, like the *Five Leaves Left* cover, like the honey-smelling bush by the lake in St James's, greenery and nature is everywhere.

Death, love, fragility, sweetness, melancholy, nature.

'Excuse me,' the artist says, 'is that your, er, cigarette?'

I follow his gaze to the floor to my left. A joint. I reach down and pick it up.

'Is it yours, or was it that girl's?' the artist asks.

'What girl?'

'There was a Japanese girl here a second ago.'

My heart flips.

'Where?' I ask. 'Which way did she go?'

The artist nods towards the door to his left.

Mika is here. My heart thumps. She is here, she was behind me, watching me. I step out into the main hallway, look up and down, look for Mika. Now I *do* feel like a spy. The main entrance is a stretch down to my right, she hasn't gone straight for it, I would see her. That means she is somewhere in the building. I'll cover the entrance, I think. I walk slowly, carefully, checking the doors off left and right but then I hear a noise behind and see a flick of black hair disappear in a room behind me. That's got to be Mika, I think, slipping across the hallway. I make to follow then stop. No, better to slip right myself, corner her off.

The room is early-twentieth-century art. In the centre of the room is Salvador Dali's famous telephone, the one with the lobster for a receiver. I crouch down behind it, pretending to tie my shoelace, watching the door, waiting for Mika to appear. But as I wait and wait, I realise I've made a mistake and as I stand up and make for the door where I'm expecting her to arrive something makes me look round, and there she is again, the back of her head, disappearing behind me, down the main hallway for the exit, and by the time I double back all there is to see are the revolving doors, spinning to a stop. I race out, hare down the steps, only to see a hundred yards in front of me the back of her head again, as she disappears inside a red double-decker bus.

'Mika!' I shout, but by the time I reach the stop, the bus has long gone, heading for Parliament and the centre of town, swallowed up in the traffic.

Dear Ben,

Konnichi wa once more, my love! I'm so sorry you haven't had a letter for a while, but I've been wanting to send you the photographs I've enclosed, and I've only just had them developed. I hope they're worth the wait! As you can see, the snow and ice is still here, and is likely to remain so for the rest of the month. On a good day, it gets just above freezing. On a bad night it gets down to about minus fifteen. That's when I wish you were here, so I could snuggle up to you during the night, sharing a bit of body heat . . .

It may be cold, but it is beautiful, isn't it? And I've been more than making the most of my very own winter wonderland: I've taken skiing lessons with the children from the local school, which they all think hilarious, because everyone here can ski before they can walk, and so all the other people in my beginner's class are about five years old! I've been skating lots, too: the school froze over their baseball pitch to make an ice rink, and I've been getting better. No pirouettes yet, but it can't be far off.

I guess I should explain about the photos. They're from the Sapporo Snow Festival, which is this huge do in the island capital, full of these jaw-dropping sculptures and buildings — whole buildings! — made out of ice. They're made by the army who, because of Japanese law, aren't actually allowed to do any fighting and so, I guess, don't have much to do. They're amazing, aren't they? The replica of the White House is extraordinary.

The not so impressive sculptures are from the local snow festival, where I took part in a team competition to make a monkey from a 6 foot block of snow. Isn't ours terrible? I was never much good at art at school, as our attempts with the ice and snow confirm! I wasn't helped by the fact that drinking on our team seemed to be compulsory, and I swear that by the time the final whistle sounded, some of our crew thought we had made two monkeys not one.

The good-looking girl in the kimono is me! I can't remember whether I told you or not but, since Christmas, I've been taking lessons as well as teaching them. Originally, I tried my hand at shyodo, Japanese calligraphy, but I ended up falling out with my teacher because, even though I'm left-handed, he insisted I draw the characters with my right – some aesthetic I offended or something. So I swapped his lessons for Sado, the tea ceremony, which, let me tell you, is a little bit more complicated than tea bag, brew, milk! In the photos I'm being taught how to 'otomae' or serve. No jokes, now!

Anyway. How are you? How's Bex? I had a long letter from her the other day, after we all got that email from Si. I know he's your friend and everything, Ben, but he can be a bit of a prat at times. Tell him to put a sock in it next time you write to him, will you? He's certainly not doing himself any favours. From the sounds of things, the email has snapped Bex into action, and far from moping around she's going to get back out there and enjoy herself. Good on her! I told her to go for it, just as long as she doesn't keep my darling boyfriend awake in the process!

Do you know when the election is yet? Does John Major not realise that the longer he leaves it, the longer I have to wait to see my boyfriend again? There's this week here called Golden Week, which is all these bank holidays bunched together at the beginning of May, which would be perfect. Do you think your politicking will be done by then? It's going to mean so much having you out here, I can hardly wait. I've got it all planned. It's going to be like that holiday we had in Barcelona, except this time round you're going to be relying on MY language skills. And yes, I do know the Japanese for 'extra chilli'!!!

Write soon, Ben. I want all the goss on Bex, on what her new blokes are REALLY like. Keep safe, won't you, and keep thinking of me. I miss you.

All love, Sarah x

PS White. CK.

PPS You didn't tell me last time, spoilsport. Or weren't you wearing any?

18

192 Kita, Thursday 7.30
I want a no trouble time, OK? Friendship's everything.
Entertaining love, you'd only ultimately regret this.
Only unhappiness could happen.

I'm leaving Tottenham Court Road tube station and head-
ing north. There's a symmetry here – how my first leaf,
my five leaves left, found me pacing up and down Oxford
Street, how my journey ended up at Marble Arch, and now
I'm here, exiting the tube station at the opposite end.
There's a second symmetry too, I think, as I climb the
stairs, say, 'No thanks,' to the *Big Issue* seller, and step out
into the street, the criss-crossing shoppers in front of me.
As I cross Oxford Street, glancing briefly up towards Oxford
Circus, Marble Arch, I pause and look back down Charing
Cross Road heading south for Leicester Square, where in
that African restaurant, all those months before, I first saw
Mika, her silhouette in the doorway, watched in awe at
her delicate lightness of touch. It's funny, I think, how I'm
mapping out London in terms of Mika, how you can draw
a line from the African restaurant and Marble Arch and
they meet here, at Tottenham Court Road tube station,
here where I head north for my next meeting.

The more 'leaves' I get from Mika, the greater the guilt when a letter from Sarah arrives. The sound of post on doormat used to be one of the most tantalising noises I knew. Now, though, the thud feels heavy, cumbersome. It's terrible, but whereas I once looked forward to a letter from Sarah, now I feel a tangible sense of relief when one isn't there. And whereas once I'd read her letters again and again, now I skim them quickly, awkwardly. If only Sarah would say something, touch my heart somehow, remind me of how things were. But she never does. Is she like that because my mind is elsewhere, or is my mind elsewhere because she's like that? It's chicken/egg time, and I think I know which I'm being.

192 Kita, my fourth note had said. *Thursday 7.30*. I'd gone to a bookshop and found myself a Japanese dictionary. Kita means 'north', which didn't make any sense to me at all, but then I had a thought. 192 was directory enquiries, wasn't it? And so I rang them up, said 'Kita, that's k-i-t-a, London,' and then there was a pause, the sound of the gentle clack of keyboard, and then the woman with the Scottish accent said, 'The only thing I'm getting is a Japanese restaurant on Tottenham Court Road. Does that sound right?'

'Yes,' I replied, scribbling the address down. 'Yes, I think it does.'

It's appropriate, somehow, that Kita is on Tottenham Court Road, nestled in that semi-seedy area north of the tube station full of all the electrical goods retailers, the bit before it poshes out into Heals and Habitat. I don't know much about Japan, but hi-tech and the Far East feel as though they go hand in hand. And there, amongst the CD

Walkmans and the MiniDisc players, the camcorders and flat screen TVs, I see a small red lantern above a doorway, swaying ever so slightly in the evening breeze. Kita, I think, and walk down the steps inside.

At the bottom of the stairs, I push aside the red curtain that hangs across the doorway to enter. The restaurant is long and thin, its darkness exaggerated by its black wooden decor. As I look along the two rows of diners, I can't help noticing that everyone is Japanese. To my right, through a cream curtain with Japanese characters painted down the left-hand side, a curtain beyond which I presume is the kitchen, a waitress appears. She's young, Japanese, dressed simply in white shirt and loose black trousers, her hair tied back in a ponytail.

'*Konban wa*,' she says, nodding rather than smiling at me in acknowledgement.

I look blank. 'Hi,' I reply. 'I'm here to meet someone.'

'Ben San, *desu ka*?' she asks.

'Benson? No, my name's Lawrence. Ben Lawrence.'

'*Hai*,' the waitress nods. 'Ben San. Mister Ben.'

That's with one n, I almost say. Though as I follow the waitress through the restaurant away from the kitchen, I can't help feeling a little like the children's television character. Like Mr Benn, it's as though I've opened the curtain onto another world, left London behind for somewhere new, exciting, intriguing. As if by magic, I think. As if by magic.

Beyond the rows of tables is another room, a raised

area marked off by thin white paper screens. All I can see inside is a silhouette, a silhouette of a girl, a girl whose slender shape I can't help but recognise, who can't help but make my breath shallow ever so slightly, a girl sat perfectly still, kneeling in front of a small, low table.

'*Kutsu*,' says the waitress, blocking my path.

'Sorry? I don't understand,' I say.

'*Kutsu*,' the waitress says again, looking down. I follow her gaze, but I still don't get it. Then I see the pair of shoes sat on the step outside the screened room, small, black, female, ballet-like. I remember that letter from Sarah, the one about the slippers. Sarah, I think, with a small, silvery shudder.

'You want me to take my shoes off?' I ask, pointing at my feet.

'*Hai*,' the waitress says. '*O-negai shimasu.*'

I bend down, undo my laces, slip my feet out, glad my socks are normal, glad there are no holes with toes poking out. I tuck the laces in and place them next to the other pair of shoes: by comparison they seem big, ugly, cumbersome. I look up at the waitress and smile nervously.

'*O-negai shimasu*,' she says again, bows slightly, slides back the screen door, and as she does so, the silhouette becomes a person, becomes Mika, the black and white becoming colour as I take in her dress, traditional and eastern, dark blue and gold trim, long sleeved with a stiff high neckline, a succession of gold buttons travelling down the centre of her décolletage, her bust, her stomach and onwards, a tight row of tiny buttons that by the time they disappear below her hands, resting gently on her knees, must be numbering into the hundreds. Her hair is different

too, the messiness of her bob removed: now it is straight-
ened, coutured, pulled back off her face, slickly slid behind
her ears. Her eyes, though, the rich, dark, intensity of her
eyes, remain the same.

'O-negai shimasu,' the waitress says again, and I step
up and into the room, kneel down opposite Mika, not
losing her gaze as I hear the screen door slide shut behind
me.

We sit there like that, quietly looking, quietly watching,
quietly waiting, our eyes, our posture mirroring, matching
each other. I'm trying, really trying to soak it all up, take
in as much as possible. Mika's fabulous, flawless skin. The
small, rich, lusciousness of her lips. The succulent straight-
ness of her neck, her back. The soft crackle of the
atmosphere. The way her breasts gently rise and fall with
the lightness of her breathing. She is, I think, perhaps the
most perfect, the most picturesque woman I have ever
seen. I'm gathering myself to tell her so, when Mika
moves.

She leans forwards, to the table, the table, which in
my focusing on Mika, I've barely noticed. Sitting there is
a small, square black tray, a tray that turns up at the
corners like a piece of paper, a page from a book that had
been burnt to a crisp and curled up at the edges. In two
rows sit eight pieces of sushi, six are slices of white and
red fish, the seventh of what looks like egg held on by a
thin belt of seaweed, and an eighth of two pink and white
prawns, their small fan tails hanging over the end of the

piece. Behind them, in two rows of three, sit six further, smaller pieces of sushi, upright and wrapped in seaweed, the mottled green contrasting with the fluffy white rice inside, the strips of pink and yellow and green of fish and egg and cucumber poking up in the middle. There's a small pyramid of a pale green paste and a larger pile made up of thin slices of almost translucent pink, wrapped together so you have to peel one layer off at a time.

To the left of the tray is what looks to my uncultured eye like a small, cream earthenware vase, a vase whose clay is rugged and creased, and with a thick piece of brown thread tied round its neck. But it isn't a vase, it's a jug, a carafe of some sort, and Mika leans forwards and picks it up, pours its clear liquid into what I assume is the Japanese equivalent of a shot glass, small and round and earthenware. She picks one up between finger and thumb, waits, watches me until I do the same, and then, without losing eye contact, puts the tiny cup to her lips, tilts and drinks until it is empty.

I follow suit. I don't recognise its sweet taste, am surprised by the fact that the drink is warm, hot without being scalding as it slips down my throat. What I do recognise is the kickback of the alcohol. This stuff is *strong*, I think, as I feel my eyes glisten with water.

'Wow,' I say putting the cup back on the table. 'What is—?' I start my sentence, but stop as Mika raises a finger to her lips, holds it there until I am silent.

Mika leans forwards again, picks up a second jug, this time with a lid and a narrow protruding spout. From this she pours a thin brown liquid, what I presume to be soy sauce, into a small shallow white dish in front of her. By its side, I notice, is a pair of dark brown chopsticks, their tips resting on a small china stand. I also realise that on my side of the table there's nothing there. I'm about to say something, when I see Mika's finger, pressed against her lips once more.

'Itaidakimasu,' she says, bowing a little and picking up the chopsticks. Nimbly, expertly, she uses the chopsticks to pick up a piece of sushi, one with a topping of white fish. I watch as she douses it in the soy sauce, first one way, then the other, then with one swift action, lifts the sushi up and into her mouth without dropping a single grain of rice, sliding the empty chopsticks out.

'Oishi,' she whispers, looking at me. 'Oishi.'

Without pausing, the chopsticks move forwards again towards the tray, picking up an identical piece to the one she's just eaten. The sushi is dipped in soy sauce again, but this time the piece is held out for me.

'Kudasai,' Mika says.

I smile, lean forwards as Mika lifts the chopsticks, and I eat the sushi. As I feel the chopsticks in my mouth, I pause, can't help but look at Mika as she slowly, slowly draws them out.

'Oishi?' she asks, as I start to chew.

The sushi is the strangest sensation. The fish, fresh and raw, tastes nothing like fish. The white rice it sits on is sweet and sticky. And in between, the 'glue' that holds the two together is sharp and hot like horseradish. The combination of tastes – the fresh, the hot, the sweet – is unlike anything I've ever tasted.

'That was nice,' I say. 'Really, really nice.'

Mika nods, continues her delicate performance, taking, dipping and eating another piece of sushi.

'You look stunning,' I say. 'That dress, your hair, everything. You look absolutely spellbinding.'

Mika doesn't reply, not a flicker of response crosses her face. Instead, she selects me another piece of sushi, and we both lean forwards across the table as I take it, her chopsticks withdrawing then moving forwards again, picking off a single grain of rice still stuck on my lip. I stay forwards to eat it, but Mika leans back, eats the grain herself.

I try to start a conversation again, but my words just echo round the room. Mika, for whatever reason, doesn't want to talk. Every time I speak, the chopsticks dart forwards, tapping my cup, ordering me to drink. And so we continue this strange, silent, intoxicating tableau, the taste of the food continually surprising me, the alcohol making my head feel lighter and lighter and lighter. By the time the sushi is finished, a mixture of drink and nerves and the way I am sitting makes me desperate for the loo.

'I must go to the toilet,' I say.

Mika looks at me, a little sadly, then puts the chopsticks down, back on the table, the tips back on their rest. Her back straightens, her hands return to her lap as they were when I first entered the room.

'*So desu ne*,' she says.

'Excuse me,' I say, feeling the pins and needles in my legs as I get up. I slide the door open, shuffle into my shoes. I look at Mika, feel the heat of her eyes burning into me, feel my face burning in response. With a gulp, I slide the screen door across, watch as Mika slips back from colour to black and white, her silhouette sitting silent and still. I stand there for a minute, taking in the slimness, the elegance, the sweet curves of her shape, watch for as long as my body will allow before slowly, reluctantly, I relent, and turn to find the toilet.

I half wonder if the toilet will be Japanese, but I'm relieved to see it is English. As I wash my hands I glance at myself in the mirror above the basin. What do I look like? Flushed, from the alcohol. Nervous, from the situation. Unsteady, from both. I can't help feeling both captivated and bewildered by what is happening. There's method here, I'm sure: some underscoring reason as to what is going on but it's one that's out of my reach, one that at the moment I am unable to grasp. This is unlike anything I've come across before, it's simply beyond my experience. As such, I don't know how to play it.

As I slip back out, past the clank of the kitchens, part the cream curtains into the restaurant proper, pass the other eaters, back towards the tatami room, I can't help noticing something. There's no silhouette behind the bamboo screens. My pace quickens, and it's all I can do to stop myself running across the restaurant. I slide open the bamboo door and, with a pause and a sigh, my worst fear is confirmed. Mika has vanished.

Fuck, I think. Fuck. I glance round the room, which is as I left it, except for one small addition. On the table, on my side, sits a small, flat, solitary Rizla paper. I'm about to go into the room when I remember my shoes and so I find myself leaning on bended knees and stretching across to reach it, but even so, it's tantalisingly out of reach. I pull my shoes off in frustration, slam them down on the floor and step in, snatching up the Rizla. My last one. My five leaves, like Mika, have gone.

Greetings, comrade,

Hullo once more from the wonderful delights of Latin America. Where have I been since I last wrote? Well, there's not many places me and my trusty motorbike haven't been, Che Guevaring around, and I haven't even got time to tell you the number of women I've had clinging onto the back of the bike for dear life as we bomb down the motorways. Since I last wrote, I've travelled in a not particularly logical way from Peru through Venezuela, Paraguay, Colombia and spent three weeks in Chile picking grapes at some vineyard. And having had the pit stop, I've ridden on, down down deeper and down, until finally I'm here, in Brazil, on Copacabana Beach.

Mate, this place is like heaven on earth (and no sign of Barry Manilow either, though the guy behind the bar does not have the world's smallest nose). It's exactly as you could wish for: acres of perfect sandy beach, brilliant blue sea and sky, gorgeous birds (more in a minute) and fantastic football. The Brazilian skills are a sight to behold: I was sat there yesterday, watching this five-a-side barefoot game on the beach, mesmerised at the flicks, the kicks, the curves, the swerves, the Cruyff turns and banana bends, when one of the players, despite the protests of the others, pointed at his watch and made to leave. I thought that was going to be it, but then they noticed me sitting there watching.

'Hey!' they called, waving me over.

'No, no, no,' I protested. 'I'm English.'

'England!' The Brazilian with the ball, an Amazonian of a guy wearing nothing but a pair of denim shorts, nodded enthusiastically. 'Bobby Charlton! Kevin Keegan! Paul Gascoigne!' He kicked the ball over in my direction.

If only I was Bobby Charlton, Kevin Keegan, Paul Gascoigne. Carlton Palmer, Geoff Thomas, Gareth Southgate more like. Still, when you've got an opportunity like that, you don't say no, do you? I mean, the Brazilians may be great, but who invented the beautiful game? And you don't get to be your college third team substitute without a modicum of skill, do you? So there I was, an English player, transferred to Brazil.

The player I was replacing was the centre of defence, so there I went, the bastard offspring of Tony Adams and Bobby Moore. It wasn't long before I was tested: the opposite striker, small, mazy, dribbling away like he was son of Zico, bore down on me, feinting one way, then the other. And then, just as he had me mesmerised, just as I was about to tackle him, he collapsed on the ground like he'd just been shot, groaning on the floor in a heap of agony.

'Penalty!' His teammates rushed up and grabbed the ball.

'Hey!' I said. 'I never touched him.'

But no one believed me. I watched as the little dribbler, slowly, painfully, got to his feet, miraculously shook his injury off in time to take the penalty and then, just to test his leg was OK, did a triple double backwards somersault to celebrate.

I was furious: at such blatant hoodwinking, at how the other players all but applauded mini-Zico's ability to put one over on Johnny Foreigner. Well, screw you, I thought: you may think we're shit, but we can play football too. I remembered England beating Brazil 2–0 in the Maracana Stadium in 1984, the icing on the cake being John Barnes's brilliant solo goal, doing what the Brazilians did but better, dribbling round half the team before slotting the ball into the back of the net. If John Barnes can do it, I thought, then so can I.

By now, I couldn't help noticing the small crowd that had gathered to watch the match. Here was my chance. I collected the ball from my goalkeeper and made for the opposite goal. I shimmied past the first player, dummied the second, nutmegged the third – I remember thinking I wish someone was videoing it. I could hear the murmur ripple round the crowd as I bore down on goal, as I prepared to slot the ball coolly past the keeper into the corner of the net, when from nowhere, from behind, I felt a lunge, a late tackle, and my legs were whipped away from beneath me and I collapsed onto the floor, receiving a face full of sand.

'Hey!' I looked up to see mini-Zico dribbling away with the ball. 'Penalty!'

But the other players just looked at me and made diving motions with their hands.

'I did not dive!' I tried to stand up, but felt a sharp pain in my leg. 'Ow! I got taken out!'

But no one was listening. They were watching mini-Zico do his dribbling thing, his slotting the ball past the goalkeeper thing, his triple double backwards somersault thing. I hobbled off the pitch to recuperate.

And here's where things really kicked off.

'Are you OK?' a voice asks, and I look round to see the most bikini of bikini babes standing there: bronzed tan, long *dark curly hair, and this itsy bitsy teeny weeny yellow polka dot bikini, a bikini that was having real problems in staying on.*

'I, I think I may have broken it.' I hammed it up.

'He is bastard.' The girl gesticulated towards mini-Zico. 'Come.' She points to a beach hut just off the back of the beach. 'I very good massage. Do you think you can walk there?'

'I can try,' I said.

And so me and this girl — Paola her name was — make it back to this hut, where she tells me to lie down and starts massaging my leg. And as she does, I'm looking at her and wondering if she's up for it, and then slowly she's massaging further up my leg until, well, I think you can guess. Paola was amazing. Let me tell you, that Brazilian flair doesn't stop at football. Who needs Bex when you can get properly laid by someone who knows what they're doing? Finishing with her is the best thing that's ever happened to me.

But enough about me. How are you? How's tricks? Write soon, Si.

19

319 feet. Wednesday, 3 p.m.
Give over. Romantic gestures – exaggerated
or understated – soon backfire on you

By the time I climb to the top of Parliament Hill on
Hampstead Heath, the torrential rain that has accom-
panied me since I stepped out of the tube station has
soaked me to the bone. It's the kind of downpour that
drowns you in an instant, its calming sssh as it hits the
ground fading out the distant sound of police sirens and
car horns. I'm so wet that I've reached the point of not
noticing it, save to push my matted hair from my face, to
wipe my eyes to stop the water stinging down.

On a different sort of day, I would not have Parliament
Hill to myself. Normally there would be an abundance of
people 319 feet high, looking out over London, through
the bank of branches to the skyline beyond, to the Nat
West Building and St Paul's Cathedral and the Telecom
Tower and the hazy image of the Crystal Palace TV
transmitter, looking at the silver grey map or sitting at
one of the many benches at angles on the hillside. And
on the other side of the hill, on the slope to the north,
there'd be people flying kites, staring at the sky and tugging the string to twist the kite in a downward corkscrew,

swooping it back up before it hits the ground, getting tangled up in someone else's kite.

Today, with the rain and the never-ending carpet of thick grey cloud that hangs heavy, almost burdensome in the sky like a mist refusing to clear, the London skyline is an outline at best, a preliminary pencil sketch waiting to be defined and painted in. The only kite on display is lodged among the branches: the diamond blue body in one tree, the tail in another. I slide my hand into the dry of my jeans pocket, feel the Rizla that rests there, and wait.

I have a slight sense of trepidation about today. What happens now? What happens next? I know that today, in some way, is the end of something. But is there a beginning here as well? I feel a shade sick thinking about it. So far along this strange and wonderful and intoxicating journey, everything has been contained. It has all been hint and sleight and suggestion – nothing has actually happened; no difficult decisions have been made. Today, though, feels different. Today feels like there might be no going back.

I hear the noise of a train. I look down, and beyond the trees and grassy slope, the orange-red running track and children's playground, the familiar livery of a Silverlink train slides from right to left, west to east, Richmond to Woolwich, Hampstead Heath to Gospel Oak. And as I follow it along, something, some*one* catches my eye. On the path at the bottom of the hill, in a long cream belted mackintosh and thigh-length black boots, looking up at me, is Mika.

She may be three or four hundred metres away, as small and as far away as Oasis were at Knebworth, but there's no doubt it is her. She stands there watching me, and I watch back, waiting to see what she does next. Instead she's still, implacably still. I should go down to her, I think. I should go down.

There's a set of steps carved into the hillside, curving their way through a gap in the trees. All the rain has turned the ground into mud, chewing it up into puddles and footprints, and I have to watch where I'm putting my feet to stop myself from slipping. I hold my arms out like I'm an aeroplane, to help keep my balance. As I descend among the trees, Mika disappears briefly from my eye line, but when she should come back into view, I notice to my horror that she has vanished. I wipe the rain from my face to double check, but suddenly she's not there. I look left, then right, and then there she is, running for the far corner of the Heath, where the path disappears into a row of houses.

I run after her, skidding and slipping in the mud, splashing through puddles, but it's no use. She's got too much of a head start. By the time I reach the corner of the Heath she is long gone, gone into a maze of streets and houses. Fuck. I bend forwards, hands on knees, and gulp in huge breaths of air. I spit on the floor in despair. I'm wet and I'm cold and I'm wheezy and I really don't know what is going on. I look up at the Heath and shake my head in defeat, and then, there she is again. At the top of the path that runs up the left-hand side of the Heath, the path that runs parallel to the row of terraced houses that climbs the slope to the left of Parliament Hill.

Somehow she's cut up through the streets and doubled back.

I stand up straight and stare at her. Mika stares back. This time, it is her turn to move first. With a flick she's off, up and over the crown of the hill, off and out of sight. Fuck, I can feel my body groan, here we go again. I race up and by the time she's back in view, she's the same distance away again. She's looking round at me and walking. I make to run and she speeds up too. I have a thought: I stop, and so does she. I walk and she walks. I run and she runs. I understand, I nod, slowing to a walk as Mika follows suit. You want me to follow, I'll follow.

We walk for what seems like miles, away from the noise and the city into the heart of the Heath. There is not a single other soul in sight. Uphill, downhill, switching and skipping the criss-cross of paths that score the ground like veins. As we continue north, the grass gives way to muddy ground, open land to more wooded territory. Mika continues to pick her way upwards, not even bothering to look round now and stops to wait for me on a wide bridge overlooking a large pond. By the time I get there, look down at popping circles of water splashing down on water, she has peeled left, continuing over another smaller bridge into the woodland beyond.

By the time I reach the woodland – a clearing dotted by large trees, their branches knitting together – I have lost her again. And then I hear a voice.

'Ben.'

I turn round and Mika is there, ten yards to my left, one foot up, leaning against a tree. The jet black of her hair, the darkness of her eyes, the leather of her boots, the paleness of her skin, of her coat, standing there in the rain, it is almost as if she is in black and white. As she looks at me, she is panting slightly, her body rising and falling gently in rhythm. I can't work out if she is short of breath or if she is nervous.

'Mika,' I say.

'Ben,' she says, waving a hand up to stop me coming closer. As I stand there, she smiles. 'It's different in Japan to England,' she says. 'When you think I'm pushing you away, I'm wanting you to come closer.'

She waves me away again. This time I move forwards and she nods.

'Five leaves,' she says. 'This is your fifth.'

'I know,' I say. 'So what happens now?'

There's a pause. Mika is looking at me intently. 'That's up to you,' she says.

'How do you mean?'

Mika smiles, but this time her smile feels different, like it's frayed at the edges. 'Ben, I've got to go away for a little while.'

'Where?' I ask. 'How long?' I feel panicky as I try to take this in. 'Are, are you coming back?'

'Oh yes,' Mika says. 'I should think so.'

'Will, will I see you when you return?' I ask.

Mika smiles again. 'No more questions, Ben.' She beckons me to come forwards. 'Close your eyes. Close your eyes and promise me you won't open them until I say so.'

I take one long last draught of her. 'I promise,' I say, shutting my eyes.

There's a pause, and then I can feel Mika's hand on

mine, one by one uncurling my fingers, placing a note there, wrapping my fingers against it. And then, against my lips, I feel the soft warm touch of a fingertip, gently, faintly outlining the shape of my mouth.

'Five leaves,' Mika says as her finger continues to trace my lips. I hear a soft crunch of further leaves underneath, the crinkle of her coat, feel the warmth of her breath as she leans forwards and up on tiptoes, hear her voice gentler and softer as her mouth rises towards mine. 'Five, four, three, two . . .'

There is nothing as simple, as sensual, as intimate, as a kiss. Artists, poets, playwrights, directors, each knows the symbolic power a kiss can have: a Judas kiss of betrayal or a Juliet kiss of love; a godfather's kiss of death or a saviour's kiss of life. In a single intimate instant, the greatest of emotions can be encapsulated. No other action, no other act, can symbolise a feeling in the way that a kiss can.

A kiss can be delicate. Think the song of the same name by Prince. Light, delightful, playful, fun. So light, in fact, that you can send it by air – hold it in your hand and blow it in the breeze like a Marilyn Monroe or a Holly Golightly. A kiss can be dirty. Think of Prince again, the mucky funk of 'When Doves Cry'. Imagine the picture he wills you to 'dig', the kiss in which he wants to be 'engaged': two sweat-drenched bodies in a courtyard full of violets, so electrically entwined that various animals looking on can't but feel the heat.

The posh word for kissing is osculation: to osculate.

It's a word whose second meaning sums up the first: to have close contact with. Even the mathematical derivation makes sense: 'contact of a higher order . . .' Indeed.

It's not a pretty term, though. Osculate me, Kate just doesn't cut the mustard. And I know Hardy was a sailor and everything, but if Nelson had asked for a dying spot of osculation, his friend may well have turned the other cheek. Instead, from the Old English *cyssan*, the Old German *kussen* and the Old Nordic *kyssa* came the Middle English *coss*, which by Renaissance times had had a reformation into the four-letter word we know today. There the etymology of this slightest of touches, this closest of contacts, remains nestled in the dictionary between kismet and Kiswahili – an Arabic word for destiny, an African language found in Kenya and Tanzania.

It's a word in its rightful place. For nothing is as fateful, as riven with destiny, as a kiss. And kissing may not be Kiswahili, but if it's done right it's got a language all of its own. There's a French influence for sure, but I'd say Hispanic too – Latin as in lover rather than O Level – Italian, Swedish, Oriental and, if you're lucky, a hint of Basque. It's a doublespeak if ever there was one: gobbledegook if wrong; linger franca if right. A language with its own phrasing, its own expressions. Out of all the languages the modern world has to offer, kissing is truly the universal tongue.

It starts before any lips have locked. The second before, when the heads are drawing in, locked in with the magnetism of the moment, there's that pause, that final delicious lingering pause, crackling with the frisson of what is to follow. There's nothing between the mouths but a fraction of space, a few square millimetres of air, nitrogen and oxygen and whichever inert gases make up the atmosphere. It's the same silent beauty that's shared between two telephone lovers: the emptiness is everything. Nothing can be as romantic as nothing.

Lips are a little like football management. It's all about pressure. Forget Hardy: kiss me hard or kiss me hardly. I like the briefest of grazes, the driest and lightest of soft, cushioned touches: the flick of the lips, top bumping top, bottom nudging bottom, playfully pushing and pushing away; the thrill as you *feel* with your lips that your partner is starting to smile. But equally I love it when the lips are locked, not so much engaged as wedded in a kiss, when passion is pressing down for all it is worth, sucking the air until someone is breathless. And the longer you leave that fraction of space intact, those few square millimetres sealed with a kiss, the more exciting it is.

Later, I can be found in a small quiet pub just off the Heath called the White Bear, drying off in a squeaky leather green armchair by a fire. On the small round table in front of me is a pint glass, a pint glass that is half empty rather than half full. To its side is what Mika pressed in my hand as she kissed me and disappeared: a green Rizla packet.

It's empty. Of course it's empty, I think. My five leaves, like Mika, have gone. But there's a message, a message inside, a message that makes me sag as I read it, a message that makes me reach for the alcohol and swallow. As I read and reread Mika's delicate, distinctive handwriting, my heart slowly, sadly, punctures, deflates.

> *Mouthing, entwining, embracing, touching . . . magic-ally exciting, obviously not nice. I can't keep denying reality: all kisses end sometime. Ben, I realise this hurts – despite apologising. Yet, Ben, your heart is Sarah's. Good relationships are very exceptional. Maybe I don't dare aggravate yours. x*

If this was a fly-on-the-wall documentary, this would be the point I raise my hand towards the camera lens and tell the director to stop filming.

From: Ben
To: Si (Hotmail)
Date: 29 April 1997
Subject: So near . . .

Dear Si,

Greetings again to wherever you are from a place on the edge, on the cusp, on the brink. It's polling day the day after tomorrow, and I almost can't believe I'm writing this and maybe I'm tempting fate by doing this, but bugger it: I think we're going to win. It's a dangerous thought to have, and if I'd said so at Millbank, I'd have been given a lecture from whoever was in earshot about this being no time for complacency. And I know the polls last time said we were going to win and we lost, but surely, surely this time is different. Apart from one rogue poll that whittled the Labour lead down to 5 per cent, we've sat there high and dry and dozens of points clear. And even given all those people who lie in opinion polls and say they're going to vote Labour because they're too embarrassed to say they're Tory, even taking those people into account, surely we've got enough of a cushion to squeak through.

According to Gareth, it's not so much that we're going to win, it's more that the Conservatives are going to lose. John Major went for a long campaign in order to show us up, but I think it's done his lot the bigger damage. To be fair (and there's no reason why we should be, but still), the economy is in far better shape than when he won last time, but no one's interested: all the press want to talk about is Europe and is he for the single currency or against and will he rule it out in this

Parliament or for all time and so on, blah, blah, blah. Major's stuck in the middle: there's countless Tory candidates openly publishing pamphlets against the official line, not to mention the Referendum Party threatening to cream off a potentially vital couple of Tory percentage points, and on the other side there's Heseltine and Clarke, who'll walk if Major comes over all Eurosceptic.

And then there's the sleaze. First there was the Tory MP for Beckenham, Piers Merchant, up to no good with a 'teenage nightclub hostess', whatever one of those is, I'm sure you know better than me. And secondly, and more importantly, there's Neil Hamilton and his lovely lady wife Christine. Hamilton, accused of taking cash from Mohammed Al Fayed in return for asking questions, despite intense pressure from Tory high command to stand down, stuck to his guns. All the other candidates dropped out, to be replaced by Martin 'white suit' Bell, who is standing as the independent anti-sleaze candidate. All of which is terrible for the Tories: the two things that drag them down – sleaze and divisions over Europe – are the two things they can't get away from.

Annabel, by contrast, doesn't think it's so much that the Tories are going to lose as that the country is caught up in the ideas of New Labour. 'People love Tony,' she keeps on saying. And certainly, compared with John Major, he looks young and dynamic and a breath of fresh air. But I can't help siding with Gareth about the manifesto. 'It's fucking empty,' he says. 'You can't vote for New Labour because there's nothing there to vote for. It's all either too vague, or so small as not to make any difference.' It's not so bad, I always argue back. 'No,' Gareth says, 'but it's not so good either. You know those posters we've been running? Enough is enough? What worries me is not so much what we're going to do as what we're not going go to do. I'm worried that we're not going to do enough.'

I'm going to Japan on Friday. Did I tell you that? I'm going to see Sarah for ten days; we're meeting in Tokyo and then heading down on the bullet train to Kyoto and Hiroshima and on to Nagasaki, I'm not really sure exactly, Sarah's booked it all. And I know I should be excited and everything, but I'm really worried about it: firstly that, after the election I'm just going to be absolutely knackered and in no fit state to do anything; secondly, that seeing her at Christmas was funny and I'm not really sure why and I worried it's going to be funny again; and thirdly, well, I don't want to talk about the thirdly. It's complicated, it's messy, and it's over. I wish you'd been here, mate: I really could have done with a blokey chat and a pint. I tell you, you don't know how lucky you are, living the life of Riley out there in Latin America. Every time I read about your latest conquest I kind of feel jealous, miss Sarah, and thirdly, well, I don't want to talk about the thirdly. Maybe you could it tone down about the shags a bit? I'm chuffed for you, but reading about them is kind of getting me down.

It's been a long few weeks: I think I'm getting overtired, because today Neil Kinnock came up to Millbank, to thank everyone for all the hard work they've done over the campaign, and it took everything I had to fight the tears back. Everything was stripped away: all Gareth's cynicism about New Labour, all Annabel's spinnery. For a moment I remembered what it was we were doing, how long we'd been out of power, how far we'd come. I couldn't help remembering his speech, you know, the one about not playing politics with people's lives, and as I watched him work the room, I could feel the tears welling, the lump in my throat. And I felt for him, that he'd come so close to winning, but he was big enough to be here and be pleased that someone else was going to do it. And when he came round to us, he smiled when he recognised Gareth, and gave him a big bear hug, and Gareth gave him a big bear hug back and I may be wrong, but there were tears in his eyes too.

'Hey,' he said, shaking my hand, clasping my elbow with the other. 'Chin up, lad.'

Yes, it's been a long few weeks. I think this one might be a bit long too. Thursday's going to be nerve-wracking, but hopefully, hopefully, Thursday night's going to be a good one. And then there's Friday, the day when things, hopefully, hopefully get better. Fingers crossed.

By the way, if you haven't got your postal vote sorted and we lose, I'm never going to speak to you again.

Ben

20

This is it. This is the moment that I've been saving up and waiting for – my post-election holiday to Japan, my meeting up with Sarah, my once in a lifetime journey from Tokyo to Kyoto and Nara, to Hiroshima and Miyajima and Nagasaki. Relaxation, recuperation, reinvigoration.

It's a dream that's turning into a nightmare because everywhere I look, everywhere I glance, all I see is Mika.

In front of me, behind me, to the side, I can't help myself. I'm continually flicking round, each and every time my heart rate rising, my eyes locking with a total stranger until I turn away. It's an instinctive reaction and despite knowing, knowing that the person I'm standing behind in the queue isn't Mika, there's nothing I can do to stop my body responding.

'Are you OK?' Sarah asks. 'It's like you've never seen a Japanese person before.'

What's worse is that it never *is* Mika. I see flash of hair, or the sunlight on someone's skin, a profile, a look, but then, as I glance on, I see the nose isn't right, the neck isn't as elegant, the girl is fatter or thinner or older or younger and each discrepancy, each difference, only goes to highlight how slim, svelte, sharp, sultry, sexy Mika is. All it does is heighten her hold over me.

I can't eat. I can't sleep. I feel headachy. Nauseous. Sarah thinks I'm jet-lagged but I'm not. I'm lovesick. I'm lovesick and overtired and in severe culture shock and I don't know, I really don't know, how I'm going to get through the week. And the worse thing is that Sarah is worried, Sarah wants to help, and the more she is trying the further I can feel myself withdrawing because, in the strangest way, every time she touches me it sort of makes my skin crawl.

'Maybe you've got culture shock,' she suggests. 'Maybe it's the food.'

This should be happy. This should be a celebration. Labour have won the election and I'm here in Japan, in Kyoto, in one of the cultural capitals of the world. We're standing by the side of a small lake, and across the water, on the opposite side, is Kinkakuji, the golden temple, and it actually is – a small, square double pagoda temple with its walls covered in gold leaf, gleaming in the sunshine, reflecting with a shimmer in the lake below, and Sarah is positioning me, trying to take my photo, telling me to relax, and the temple is one of the most beautiful things I've ever seen in my life and Sarah is telling me to smile and all I want to do is curl up into a small, little ball and disappear.

I've never been a Billy Bragg fan, but a review of one of his albums has always stuck in my mind. The album, *Don't Try This At Home*, was released in 1992, a few months after the last election, and the reviewer suggested that after many years of politicking and posturing, Bragg had finally grown up, he'd learnt that, and I paraphrase, politics may get you down, but only love can break your heart. It's something that has always struck me as having the smack of truth to it, but one which, if I'm being honest, I've never properly understood. Now, though, I think I'm getting it.

Labour, New Labour, Tony Blair has won the election. We've won the election. After eighteen years of hurt, of waiting, we've walked in and walked all over the Conservatives. A 179-seat majority. 179! As we sat there in Millbank, watching and waiting and cheering as 'Lab gain' after 'Lab gain' after 'Lab gain' flashed up on the screen, the atmosphere got more and ridiculous. When rumours starting flying that Michael Portillo might lose his seat, no one would believe them. But then there he was, his famous quiff wilting, his smug grin frozen on his face, false and glassy as he stood there, stiff rubber-lipped, and announced what a truly terrible night it was for the Conservatives.

It should have been a truly wonderful night. And for everyone else it was. At one point I watched with a lump in my throat as Gareth and Annabel embraced. He gave her a comradely hug. She gave him a New Labour kiss on both cheeks, but for a moment there they were, united and together, smiling and joking and, for one night only, singing from the same joyous hymn sheet.

But as for me, well, somehow I felt strangely divorced. My mind, it has to be said, was at a different place. It's like when you've been working hard and go on holiday and your body relaxes and suddenly in the sunshine you find yourself with a streaming cold. Well, here, having worked and harried and phoned and balloted and door-stepped and campaigned and leafleted, now it was all over, like a floodgate opening, all I could think about was Mika.

There was a huge celebration party organised at the Royal Festival Hall, but as we walked along the Thames from Millbank to the South Bank, I suddenly didn't feel like going. I watched the others head in, and then doubled backed, back along the south side of the Thames, under-neath Hungerford and Westminster bridges, until I found a bench opposite the Houses of Parliament, sat in the silence and the dark, watched the silhouette of Big Ben and Westminster gain shape and colour as the sky changed from black to navy to blue in preparation for the morning, I sat there and tried to take it all in.

Mika dominated my mind. I could see her hair clearly, feel the gaze of her eyes and, if I closed mine, the taste of her kiss. Every glance, graze, brush, flick, every little thing she did was captivating. Every little thing. Being with her was like a door opening into a different world. Simple, strange and beautiful. What was it Si had said? Lust doesn't last. Well, my thoughts of Mika felt as fresh as if they were yesterday. The simple, strange and beautiful thing about her was this. I didn't want to admit it, but I knew it was true. In a way I had never experienced with anyone before, I was, am, headily in love with her. A simple, strange and beautiful love.

And it was a love more powerful for its impossibility. I was engaged to Sarah. Mika knew that, Mika understood, Mika had withdrawn. That's why she had kept our rela-tionship so slight, so brief. Could you call it a relationship?

An affair? Frisson seemed more appropriate. A brush maybe, a brush of something better. I felt for her, knowing the situation, having the courage, the grace to give way. *Good relationships are very exceptional*, she'd written. *Maybe I don't dare aggravate yours*. That warmth, that sensitivity, that understanding, it made it all the harder to take in the fact that whatever we had was no longer there, that she was elusively out of sight, out of reach, out of touch.

Can you be in love with two people at the same time? My feelings for Sarah and for Mika seemed almost diametrically opposed. Sarah and I had grown up together, shared so many occasions and experiences together that the thought of being without her didn't seem possible. Our relationship felt safe, solid, secure: we were a good team, partnership, that's the word, we balanced out each other's good points and bad points. We had the same interests, liked doing the same things, had the same friends. But here's the thing: I knew Sarah inside out, I'd hardly met Mika at all, and yet somehow, in some strange way, I knew her too. I could tell you Sarah's favourite album, her favourite food, what kind of film she'd like to go and see, what she wanted for breakfast, what made her laugh, what made her cry, what her thoughts would be on any myriad of topics. Mika? I couldn't tell you any of that. But I could describe for you in intimate detail the way she gently, slightly, delicately draws a hair off her face and slides it behind her ear. Sarah? I guess Sarah doesn't have that sort of hair.

As the sky lightened and dawn crept up on Westminster, the faintest sounds of 'Things Can Only Get Better' drifted across from the Festival Hall. As I sat there, all I could think was that I fucking hope it does. Mika had flitted, flickered across my world, and now she was gone. In love, in politics, the campaigning was over. Decisions have been made. The candidates have been chosen. It's time to respect the people's wishes and get on with getting on.

Sarah is insistent on sightseeing. For about a thousand years from the eighth century onwards, Kyoto was the Japanese capital before Tokyo, and there is plenty, plenty to see, especially when you have a guidebook and a pencil. We have been to Kyomitsu Temple, with its wonderful red multi-level pagoda nestling out among the trees, drank from its holy spring and gaped at its wonderful views across the city. We've been to the Heian Shrine, the holiest of Shinto places, with its enormous pillar-box-red Tori gate straddling the road in front like a giant pi sign. We've seen the Imperial Castle and Nijo Castle, complete with its 'nightingale floors', designed to squeak to detect intruders. We spent a day in nearby Nara, capital before Kyoto, dropped our jaws at Todaji Temple with its 16-metre-tall, 500-tonne statue of Buddha. All of it is a breathtaking blur of gardens and pagodas and temples and statues. It's too fast, I can't take it all in, but at the same time I'm happy to let Sarah continue, let her take control, because it means she isn't stopping to think or question me about why I'm down and withdrawn and preoccupied.

On our second night in Kyoto, Sarah wants to take me to a sushi bar. I try to put her off, but she is insistent.

'You're not coming all this way to go to McDonald's,' she says. 'Come on. Be adventurous. Take a chance.'

It's not a question of not wanting to be adventurous. It's a question of remembering. But the sushi bar is different: it's more modern than the place I went to with Mika, and I try to relax. We sit on stools round a large conveyer belt as pieces of sushi roll by on different-coloured plates – the colours reflect the different prices.

'Can I choose for you?' Sarah asks. 'There's so many different things I want you to try.'

I want to try too. I want to try to make everything all right. But every time Sarah passes me something and tells me its Japanese name and how it's really delicious, I can't stop myself from thinking back to the Japanese meal I had with Mika: its sensual simplicity. And every time I eat a piece of sushi, the taste resonating around my mouth, tastes that seem stronger because of the freshness of the fish, as the wasabi lights up the roof of my mouth and I douse the flames in Asahi beer, the memories keep coming back.

'Did you know that in Japanese cooking,' Sarah says, 'there are five factors to consider. The smell of the food, the look or the appearance of the food, the sound of the food – the fresh crunch of the vegetables, the slurping of the noodles – the texture of the food, what it feels like to the touch, and, of course, the taste of the food. It's all to do with the five senses,' she concludes, her eyes darting across from one piece of sushi to the next, debating which one to eat.

I watch the way Sarah is eating, her adeptness with the chopsticks, the dissolving of the wasabi into the soy sauce, the single mouthful without spilling a single drop of rice. But however daintily she does it, there's something that doesn't quite hold true. And down the other end of the conveyer belt, I see a short, petite Japanese girl eating hers, and there's something in her movement, in the sweep, the strokes, the grace, which makes me think of Mika. And it's then, as the thought of her flickers across my mind, that it all begins to make sense.

The five elements of Japanese cooking: sight, sound, smell, taste, touch. That's what this whole thing with Mika's been about, isn't it? The Rizlas represent the senses. Nick Drake's *Five Leaves Left*, that's the sound. *The Lady of Shalott* in the Tate: that's the sight. The bush in St James's Park? The smell. The sushi meal on Tottenham Court Road? The taste. The kiss on Hampstead Heath? The touch. I remember what Mika had said before she'd given me the first roll-up. *You want to get to know me?* With a flutter, I realise that's exactly what she's done. These five things encapsulate Mika: the music, the romanticism, the sense of nature, of Japan, of intimacy. It's a shocking, stunning revelation, the force of which is so strong that suddenly it seems like the whole room starts to shake.

'Look,' Sarah says, pointing at a picture on the wall, a long thin strip of Japanese calligraphy, descending characters in beautiful black brush strokes. The picture is swaying ever so slightly.

'What's happening?'

'Earthquake,' says Sarah, eating on as the tremor causes the plates on the conveyer belt to rattle. 'Well. More of a quiver than a quake.'

'Does this happen a lot?' This is hard: talking to Sarah, thinking about Mika.

'Oh, all the time.' Sarah shrugs. 'You get used to it.'

A murmur goes round the room as the rumble stops. I look at the picture still swaying from side to side.

'But I thought you were petrified of earthquakes?' This isn't the Sarah that I know. 'Isn't it one of your recurring dreams that the earth will swallow you up?'

'It used to be,' Sarah says. 'But I think I figured it out. When I was a little girl, we used to live near this railway line. I think the trains rumbling by worked their way into my dreams.' She helps herself to another piece of sushi, a tube of tuna coated in rice and wrapped in seaweed. 'It's just the way it is.'

'What? You mean that there's always a rational explanation for things?'

Sarah shakes her head as she finishes her mouthful. 'I was thinking more about the earth and earthquakes. That it's the natural order for things to rub up the wrong way, readjust and settle down again. When you think about earthquakes like that, they don't seem so scary somehow.'

I hope that's what this is, I think. A readjustment rather than a fault.

'It's an interesting question though, isn't it?' Sarah continues. 'That there's always a rational explanation for things. I reckon there probably is.'

'Do you think?' I ask. 'You don't think there are some things that we can't understand, that we can't explain?'

'Like what?'

'I don't know. Like. I don't know.'

I don't want to say it, but Sarah presses.

'Like what?' she asks.

'Like. Like love or something.'

'I think you can reduce anything down,' Sarah says. 'Love's all about chemical reactions in the brain, the release of pheromones, that sort of thing. It's just a process like anything else.'

'You don't think there are points where science stops?' I ask.

Sarah shakes her head. 'I think there are things that science hasn't explained yet, but that doesn't mean they aren't explainable.'

'It doesn't sound as good though, does it?' I say. 'I chemical reaction you.'

'That's because you've got a sentimental streak a mile wide,' Sarah says, taking my hand. 'Ben. It doesn't mean I feel any differently about you. All I'm doing is describing how it actually divides down. This is how it works.'

Reduced. Divided. I smile at Sarah, squeeze her hand, but I can't help hearing her words echoing around my head. Is she right? Is that all love is? Is everything as explainable and reducible as she suggests? Maybe she's right – maybe all this is, is that we're coming to the same conclusion from different angles. Either that, I think, or one of us is badly missing the point. And as I sit there, there's something else that's bothering me too. *This is how it works*. Where have I heard that before? I think and think and then I remember. Annabel. The day she inducted me into the ways of her department.

I glance across at the picture on the wall. It's stationary. Askew, but still. In my mind, though, in my mind's eye, the picture is continuing to sway.

From: Si
To: Ben (Hotmail)
Date: Wednesday 6 May 1997
Subject: Latin America

Dear Ben,

This is probably going to sound a bit barking to you, mate, but I have a small confession to make. Well, quite a big one actually, and for some reason, I find it easier to tell you while you're out of the country. I don't know why. Maybe if you're that far away, then you're not going to shout at me.

OK, deep breath. Here we go. The truth, Ben, is that for the last few months I've been having you on. I've never been to Latin America. All the emails I have been sending you have actually been from my dad's computer back here in not-quite-so sunny Birmingham. I know it sounds crazy, but it's true. Since January I have been back here living with my folks, paying off my debts and stacking up the shelves in my local Kwik Save.

The reason I came back is because after Bex dumped me I felt really gutted and suddenly travelling around South America didn't seem as appealing as it did. I didn't tell you, I didn't tell anyone, because, well, I felt a bit crap about giving up. I thought everyone might think I was soft. And also, because I was hurt, I didn't want Bex to have the satisfaction of knowing that she'd ruined my year. And because you lived with Bex, I knew that I could write to you and she'd find out that I'd got over her and was having a good time.

But the truth is, there was no good time. I haven't been shagging my way round anywhere. I don't want to screw around: what the whole Cuban thing has taught me is just how much I feel for Bex. Ben, this is going to sound really soft, but, what I've realised is that I really love Bex. I would do anything to have her back.

I'm sorry I've led you on. I know it was crap of me big time, but it felt easier to bury my head in the sand than be honest about what was happening. And I'm sorry for using you to get at Bex: I had my reasons but it's still bad form. I just hope you're not too mad at me because I really need your help, mate. You've got to help me get Bex back. I know, I know. Si, the shagmeister, asking for relationship advice. But the fact is that you and Sarah have succeeded where Bex and I haven't; you're still together and going stronger than ever, and I need you to tell me how you do it. I really envy you, mate. I would give anything to be in your shoes right now.

Christ, I can hardly believe this is happening. Me getting hung up over a girl, and a girl who dumped me at that. I always thought that you were just a bit mushy about Sarah, but I was wrong. I guess it gets us all in the end.

Whatever you do, don't tell Sarah. Don't tell Bex. Let's meet up when you get back and have some – lots – of beers. I think it's probably my round.

Si

273

21

This is what happens when an atomic bomb explodes. It begins by producing a fireball of several million degrees centigrade, an atmospheric pressure of several hundred thousand bars. The temperature drops as the fireball expands; at 0.1 seconds it falls to 7,000 degrees, at three seconds 1,500. After one second, the fireball has expanded to its largest point, reaching its maximum radius of 230 metres. At the hypocentre, the point on the ground directly below the explosion, the energy of the thermal rays is such that the ground temperature rises to between three and four thousand degrees.

The atmospheric pressure, meanwhile, creates a shock wave that travels at 740 metres a second, more than double the speed of sound. After 30 seconds, the blast has travelled 11 kilometres. Behind the blast comes a wind of supersonic velocity. The bomb that exploded above Hiroshima on 6 August 1945 was the equivalent of dropping 15 kilotons of TNT – an amount that would have taken 3,000 B-29 bombers to carry. The combination of the blast, the thermal rays and fire obliterated an area within two kilometres of the bomb's hypocentre.

This is what happens after an atomic bomb explodes. About 10 per cent of the energy of explosion is accounted for by residual radiation. People within one kilometre of the hypocentre during the first four days after the explosion are exposed to a substantial amount of gamma rays. People in areas where rain falls after the explosion are exposed to a large amount of fallout radioactivity. People who ingest food or water contaminated by radioactivity, or who inhale dust while handling the dead or clearing up the wreckage, receive a significant dose of internal radiation.

As well as the more obvious external wounds and burn, 'atomic bomb disease' displays the following symptoms: general malaise, susceptibility to fatigue, headaches, nausea, vomiting, anorexia, diarrhoea and fever. As well as these, those particularly associated with radiation include epilation or loss of hair, haemorrhagic diathesis, or bloody discharges, oral and pharyngeal lesions and leukopenia, or abnormally low white blood cell count.

The symptoms of people who escape death appear to clear up after four months. But later, protuberant scars or keloids begin to appear over wounds and burns, particularly among teenagers. Two years on, cataracts caused by radiation begin to appear. Between five and ten years afterwards, leukaemia due to radiation reaches its peak. Twenty-five years on, cancer among survivors becomes prominent, in particular thyroid, breast and lung. Those who survive, apart from psychological and mental suffering, must wonder if every time they fall ill it is about to turn to atomic bomb disease.

It is difficult to put an exact figure as to the number of people who died as a consequence of the Hiroshima bomb. Out of a population of 350,000, approximately

100,000 died on the day of the bombing. Within two weeks, this figure had risen to 125,000. After four months, it had reached 140,000. The number of people who have died as a result of the after-effects of the bomb is unknown.

When Sarah and I arrive in Hiroshima, having travelled from Kyoto by bullet train, we leave our rucksacks at the left luggage office, take a tram to the Hiroshima Peace Park, and the first thing that we see is the dome.

The Industrial Promotions Hall next to the river was 200 metres from the hypocentre of the Hiroshima bomb. It has been left exactly as it was on that August day, a surviving selection of walls standing oddly, adjacently and awkwardly at right angles to each other, pale, fragile and windowless. In the middle is the building's centrepiece, a round tower rising up towards the sky, empty yet strangely intact, the dome's metallic framework somehow still there. It is bold silhouetted against the blue sky: stark, symbolic and as I look at it, even though it is a hot, humid, energy-sapping day, I feel a shiver wriggle down my spine. What it reminds me of, more than anything else, is a skeleton.

I feel a nudge at my side and look across at Sarah, Sarah who has taken her sunglasses off and is looking up at me, her eyes brimming with tears. And it is as if it is a chain reaction, because suddenly I can feel my eyes fill too. There's nothing to say, no words that I can think of that are big enough, and so we just stand there, holding and watching, watching and holding, trying to take it all in, trying to make sense of it all, trying, if only a little, to guess what it must have been like.

This is history, I suddenly remember Liam's shout at Knebworth. As I stand there, stare at the sky through the shape of the dome, I smile to myself at the memory. Noel's response was right. Knebworth isn't history, Knebworth isn't even close. I think too of Labour, of Gareth's phone call to persuade me to help. *This is it, Ben, this is your chance at a little piece of history.* I'm not sure that Gareth's got it right either. We'd like to think our hard work and effort is important, but really, how important has it been?

This, I think, this is history.

Sarah and I walk on into the park. We haven't, I realise, spoken a single word since we got off the tram. The park is large and flat, with trees and gardens and water and pavements. At the opposite end to the dome is the museum, a large single first-floor building, and as we walk towards it down the middle of the park, there's a rectangular lake to our left, at the dome end an Olympic-style flame, a flame of peace that will flicker as long as another atomic bomb isn't dropped. At the museum end of the lake is a shrine, a shrine said to contain the souls of all those who died from the bomb, a shrine covered by a thick grey arch, an upturned 'u' to protect the people from the rain, and if you stand in front of the shrine, you can look through it, to see first the flame, and then the dome beyond.

I'm looking at this when I hear a child's cry, and we both turn round to see, in front of the museum, a children's play area, sandy rather than grassy, full of young Japanese schoolchildren wearing their distinctive bright yellow sunhats, children running and playing and laughing and chasing the pigeons, of which there are many, who strut and peck and follow the children around for food. There's something about the children and the brightness of their yellow hats that seems incongruous, yet there's something moving about their presence too. Their youth, their playfulness, their innocence. I glance back across at the dome, and the contrast between the children and its skeletal frame could not be sharper. I hope your generation has more sense, I think.

I can't take the museum. The photos and descriptions and stories of people from that fateful day are too much for me, and I leave Sarah in there and go back to the Peace Park to gather my thoughts.

As I step out, a young schoolboy runs past, his yellow hat hanging on for dear life by its plastic thread. He's running and carrying what looks like the tail of a multicoloured kite, a strip of red and yellow and orange and pink and blue and green fluttering in the breeze behind him. I follow his run to a statue, like the arch above the shrine, simple and stone and with subtle sweeping curves, but this time shaped like a giant pebble standing upright, with its bottom half scooped out to give a trio of legs, on top a statue of a figure with its arms in the air. At the foot of the statue, the boy adds his tail to a mound of colours, like flowers heaped in memory.

But the colours aren't flowers. As I reach the statue, crouch down and look, I realise what all they are. Birds. Lines and lines of paper origami birds, hand-made with messages of peace from the schools around the world that have either sent or brought them here.

The boy has disappeared, but standing to my left is a Japanese man, fifty or sixty, smartly dressed in a dark blue suit. I hear the rustle before I see the piece of paper in his hands, the paper he is folding and twisting and shaping. He senses me watching him, looks across, and I see his well-worn face, which wrinkles further as he smiles at me.

'Excuse me,' I say. 'Sorry, do you speak English?'

The old man continues his folding and nods.

'What's the meaning of all the birds?' I ask.

The old man looks up at the statue, at the figure on top. Above her, in her hands she is holding a bird, a silhouette frame of a bird, a frame that echoes the frame of the dome.

'She,' the Japanese man says, 'she Sadako. Sadako Sasaki. When atom bomb come, Sadako is little girl, two years old. Bomb explode, many people die, but Sadako OK. Then, when Sadako twelve, Sadako very sick. Sadako has atom bomb sickness. Sadako go to hospital.' The Japanese man looks across at me, a little sternly. 'Old Japanese legend. Person make one thousand cranes, Gods give good luck. So Sadako makes cranes. Sadako make six hundred cranes, but Sadako very sick. Sadako dies. Now, we make cranes for Sadako.'

He returns to his piece of paper. Skilfully, adeptly, he folds, flips it until there in the palm of his hand sits a small white origami crane. He bows slightly at the statue and adds it to the pile. Then, looking at me and smiling, he pulls out of his jacket pocket two pieces of paper.

'Please,' he says, and hands one to me.

And so here I am, in Hiroshima Peace Park, making an origami crane. The man folds his piece of paper in half, and I follow suit. As I follow his nimble fingers, the piece of paper twists from being folded in two, first into a pyramid, then into a square, then into a long, thin diamond. Neatly, swiftly, the man bends down the tip of one of the flaps. Suddenly, and with a flicker of excitement, my paper diamond has a head, a crane's neck and head, and as it does so, I see where its pair of wings are going to come from. I open them out and pull up the bottom of the diamond to make its tail. And then, with a twinkle in his eye, the man cups his crane in his hands, and as he blows gently into it, the bird blossoms, fills out and expands. I try to copy but I blow too hard and the bird flies out of my hands, pushes upwards briefly, then is spinning downwards as I reach and catch it. I blow again, holding it firmer this time. It's not perfect, but it's recognisable.

I show it to the man. 'Is good,' he says, and smiles. I smile back.

Later, Sarah and I visit nearby Miyajima, a tiny island off the coast considered one of the three most beautiful places in Japan. But even as the boat approaches it and we pass the jaw-dropping sight of the floating tori gate and floating temple, as we approach its seductive mix of chalky white cliffs with their lush green woodland topping, my thoughts remain with the white origami crane that is nestling in my pocket.

As soon as we step off the boat, we see the notices about the monkeys, the wild monkeys on the island that we should be beware of, that we shouldn't feed. But as we walk along the path that cuts through the forest, spiralling up to the island's centre, it isn't the monkeys that I'm thinking of.

I can't take Hiroshima in. Its weight, its magnitude, is simply too much. There's lots of conflicting thoughts flickering through my head: anger, sympathy, frustration, empathy, pity, fury, but none of my feelings is focused – I haven't had long enough to think it all through, to digest everything, to make it all make sense. And somewhere in the midst of it all sits Mika, Mika who I don't know what the fuck is doing there, Mika who I can't help feeling achingly sad about. Like I say, at the moment, none of it is making sense.

'Ben!' I snap to, to hear Sarah shout and feel a pull in my left hand, and there, tugging and gnawing and chewing, a small but insistent deer is eating my map. It's young and male, with a pair of stubs where a set of antlers will later appear, a complete lack of shyness and a hell of a grip.

'Give that back,' I say, but the deer isn't letting go, and as I tug the map rips in two. I watch as the deer chews on, spitting the map out into small balls of papier-mâché onto the path below.

'Ben!' Sarah says.

'Sorry,' I say. 'I thought it was the monkeys we had to be wary of.'

'Only the ones holding the map.' Sarah snatches what remains of the map from my hand and opens it up. It is as if a giant woodworm has chewed a huge great hole through the middle. Sarah looks at me through the hole and sighs.

'Well,' she says. 'I wonder where we go from here.'

Labour Headquarters
Millbank Tower
Millbank
London

9 May 1996

Dear Ben,

Welcome back from your much-deserved holiday jaunt to Japan. I hope your girlfriend was well and that you had a good time. While you've been away, some of us have had a country to run (how nice it is to say that!). It's more or less in one piece, thanks for asking, but it would be nice if we could have your help. So give me a ring when you get this: I think we might have a job offer for you.

Yours,

Gareth

283

22

I meet Si in the Chandos, a Sam Smith's pub at the end of
St Martin's Lane heading down from Leicester Square to
Trafalgar Square. I would have thought that he'd have
gone for the upstairs 'opera' bar with its deep green
leather sofas, but when I can't see him there, and double-
check downstairs, in the dark and dingy spit and sawdust
bar, I hear a cough. Leaning against the corner of the bar,
wearing a familiar blue baseball cap, the remnants of a tan
still faintly visible, is Si.

'Comrade Lawrence, I presume.' He grins and holds
his hand out.

'Simon Anderson. It's been a long time.' I can't help
myself grinning back. I shake his hand firmly, and then,
and I think this is the first time I've ever done this, give
him a hug.

'Manly pats on back,' Si says slapping me firmly.
'Good, strong heterosexual pats.'

'So how are you?' I ask, pulling back.

'Oh, you know.' Si shrugs. 'Shall we sit down?'

Downstairs, the Chandos has lots of nooks, pews
facing each other in small, thin, private booths. It's a pale
echo of that famous pub in Belfast, the Crown, which

goes as far as having a door into each booth, to guarantee total anonymity.

'This is a terrible pub,' I say. 'Why do we keep coming here?'

'Because it's the only pub in London I know how to get to,' Si says. 'Because it's cheap and the beer is nice.'

'No, the beer is nice if you like bitter.' Si raises his half-finished pint glass. 'Unfortunately,' I continue, 'Sam Smith's isn't as great at making lager or stout. This Ayingerbrau isn't exactly Kronenbourg. And have you ever tried the stout? Oh no, of course you haven't. You're still alive.'

'So how are you?' Si asks. 'How was Japan?'

'How was Latin America?' I ask.

'Oh, don't start. Look, I'm sorry.' Si looks sheepish. 'I screwed up.'

Si is looking away as he speaks to me, looking down. It's not a Si I've seen before. The Si I know is a showman, never short of full of it. This Si is a repentant, humbler version.

'I screwed up,' he repeats. 'I didn't want to admit I failed.'

'I thought screwing was the one thing you didn't do.'

'Ha,' Si says. 'Ha. Look. If we're going to have a laugh at my expense, can we get it out the way?'

'You could have bloody told me, mate.'

'I know. But I wanted to piss Bex off and using you was the only way I could do it.'

'Well, you succeeded there,' I say.

'Did she read the emails?'

'You know she read the emails because you kept on "accidentally" cc-ing her.'

'I didn't know whether she read them or not.'

'Of course she read them. Wouldn't you? Wasn't that the plan?'

'Yeah,' Si says, a little guiltily.

'It was counterproductive anyway. All it did was spur her to go out and find someone else.'

Si looks at me for the first time since we've sat down. 'Has she . . . ?'

'After what you wrote? Of course she has.'

I'd met Michael when I got back from Japan. He was sat forwards on the sofa, naked except for a pair of checked boxer shorts, reading the paper and smoking a cigarette. Tall, with a matt of thick black curly hair on his head and his chest, his grey-blue eyes flickered in startled surprise when he saw me. This may have been due to the fact that when he'd heard the door go, he'd shouted in his thick South African accent, 'Gorgeous, get your ass in here.'

'Who are you?' I asked, not unreasonably.

'Michael. Bex's boyfriend.' Michael stood up, in more ways than one. He held out his hand, but somehow I didn't fancy shaking it. 'What are you doing here?'

'I live here.'

'Yeah, but you're not meant to be here. You're meant to be in China.'

'Japan,' I corrected. 'I've come back.'

'Right.' Michael nodded thoughtfully, picked his cigarette up off his ashtray, took a drag. 'We weren't expecting you.'

'So I see. Where's Bex?'

'Supermarket. Gone to get some breakfast.'

Michael sat down again, turned over the page of his tabloid.

'I didn't know Bex had a boyfriend,' I said.

'Neither did she. Not until I picked her up.' Michael turned over another page, and his face cracked into a smile. 'Look at the tits on that.'

'So what do you do, Michael?'

'I'm in TV.'

'In what way?'

Michael doesn't come across as someone who works in TV. And he doesn't.

'I'm a decoder. Go round people's houses, retuning their videos so they can get Channel Five.' He reached for his cigarette. 'It's good work. Get to meet a lot of people, lots of housewives.'

'Right.' I remembered that what I'd been looking forward to ever since the plane took off from Narita Airport was a good, decent, cup of ordinary old English tea. I was about to put the kettle on when I noticed that on the floor by Michael's foot was an empty carton of milk.

'Oh, sorry, mate.' Michael followed my line of sight. 'I was a bit thirsty, you know?'

Unfortunately I did.

'Christ,' says Si. 'He sounds a right jerk.'

'He's a total jerk. As far as I can work out, that's the only thing he's got going for him.'

Si shakes his head. 'Have they. . . ?'

I nod. 'The real pisser is that I still haven't got over the jet lag, so I'm there at three in the morning, wide awake while they're, well, you don't need the details.'

'I certainly do not.' Si takes a sip of beer. 'So what do we do? How do I get her back?'

'I don't know,' I say.

'Course you do. You're the one who knows what you're doing. You're the one who's still got a relationship.' Si takes another sip of beer. 'Do you remember that conversation we had, before we went to Cuba? I've thought about that a lot. I think I was wrong and you were right. I should have listened to you, Ben, I should have stayed one hundred per cent faithful.'

I think of Mika. 'You know,' I say, 'the funny thing is that I think you were right and I was wrong. I wish I'd got your leeway.'

Si pulls a face. 'How can you wish you'd done what I did? I got dumped.'

'Yeah, but you were unlucky. It doesn't mean that you didn't do the right thing.'

'You're missing the point. Agreeing to anything at all is asking for trouble. It opens the door. The only thing it succeeds in doing is undermining what you've already got.'

'But maybe a good relationship should be strong enough to take it? I mean, if any couple are going to last the distance, then the chances are that sooner or later something is going to happen: a good relationship should have the flexibility to deal with it and move on.'

Si shakes his head. 'That sounds like some sort of

cheat's charter.' Then he pauses. 'Is this about that Japanese girl? I thought that nothing happened?'

'Nothing has happened. Well, nothing like that. I've hardly seen her at all, and yet at the same time we've had this really weird thing going. I mean, you could call it an affair, but I don't think it is an affair. I don't know. Can you have an affair without having sex?'

'Of course you can,' Si says. 'It's just that rather than down here,' he points to his groin, 'it's all about up here.' He taps his head.

'Not this one,' I say, and touch my heart.

Si looks at me, straight in the eye. Then, quietly, he says, 'Ah.'

'Here's the thing,' I say. 'I have never, ever met anyone like Mika. The way she looks, the way she moves, every single small thing she does is marked with a grace and a beauty that just locks itself in my mind, and in my head I can replay them again and again, and I do, and I sit there and watch in absolute awe. Just thinking about her moving a hair off her face blows me away. Sarah's good-looking, but she's a different kind of good-looking. She's pretty, and I don't mean that in a derogatory way. Pretty is good, pretty can be great. But Mika isn't pretty. Mika is beautiful.'

I take a sip of drink. 'You know what you said about lust?' I continue. 'That lust doesn't last? Well, this isn't lust. This isn't fading. If anything, it's crystallising and getting stronger. I don't want to admit it, but the more I think about it, the more I have absolutely no doubt that even though I hardly know Mika, I am falling madly, passionately, completely, almost pathetically in love with her. And obviously, this somewhat throws a spanner into my life.'

'A graceful spanner.'

'A *very* graceful spanner.' I smile sheepishly. 'Actually, I can't help wondering if the spanner in all of this is me.'

Si pauses. Then he asks, 'Does Mika love you?'

I shrug. 'All the notes she left for me, all of them are telling me nothing's going to happen. The first one said that she would never turn me on. In the last one, she said she didn't dare get involved and mess my relationship up. But what does that mean?'

'What they say? That she doesn't dare get involved?'

'It could mean lots of things. Is that telling me to back off, or is she suggesting that if Sarah wasn't around that she'd give it a go? Maybe she hasn't told me she loves me because she doesn't want to complicate the situation.'

'Or maybe she hasn't told you she loves you because she doesn't love you.'

'That's the thing I don't get,' I say. 'I know what the notes say, but I also know what I feel when I see her. There's a connection there, an irresistible instinctive connection that I can't believe doesn't mean anything. I can't believe that it's only one way.'

'And what about Sarah?' Si asks.

'It doesn't compare,' I say. 'It's a completely different relationship. Sarah and I are simple, straightforward, comfortable. I don't have to pretend to be anything that I'm not. We get on well, we have a laugh. This year, well, this year's complicated. How can you have a relationship when you're half a world away? When we're together, we're good. We complement each other.'

'What? Like telling her how pretty she is?'

'No, I mean that we balance out each other's good and bad points. We're a good team.'

'What about that, though?' Si asks. 'What about the other sort of complimenting?'

I trawl for an example, but can't recall any. 'But that's because we've been going out for a while. You don't after a bit, do you?'

Si thinks for a minute. He blows out deeply. Then he asks, 'Do you want to know what I think?'

I nod.

'I think you've got to tell Mika how you feel,' Si says. 'If she doesn't fancy you, then fine. If she does, well, then you're going to have to make a decision.'

'What about Sarah? What about going behind her back?'

'Oh, I wouldn't worry too much about Sarah for now.' Si smiles, almost mischievously. 'For all you know, she may have been up to some dirty dancing herself.'

I shake my head. 'Not Sarah.' I sigh. 'I don't know where Mika is. She's gone away, I don't know where or for how long. I don't have her telephone number, her address, nothing. I don't even know her surname. All I have are these stupid little notes telling me to go away and stick with Sarah. The only person who might have an idea of where I could find her is Bex, but there's no way I can ask her without it looking suspicious.'

'But I could.' Si smiles. 'Listen. You help me get back together with Bex, and I promise I'll get you Mika's address.'

Dearest Bex,

Hello there, it's me. Don't hang up, or whatever the letter equivalent is, screwing this up into a ball and throwing it away. At least read this letter before you do so. Hear me out: give me two minutes of your time first. If you still want to screw this up into a ball after that, then fine. That's your choice.

Where to start? With an apology. I'm sorry: deeply, unreservedly, sincerely sorry for the way I've behaved. I could come up with a string of excuses or fancy semantics to attempt to justify my behaviour, but that's not the point: the only thing that matters is that I hurt you. I screwed up big time and I deserve everything I've got. If I could turn the clock back to before I went away, before we went time zones apart, if I could do that, I'd never have come up with the idea of an agreement. I thought it would help keep us together by giving us some leeway while we were apart, but I was wrong, big time.

I'm sorry for all the emails I've sent since we split up. They were mean and spiteful and uncalled for. Again I could attempt to offer some justification but, again, I'm not writing to defend myself. I've behaved like a twat. What I will say is that none of them are true: when you left me in Cuba it knocked the stuffing out of me. I never went to Latin America, I didn't feel like going. I came home. For the last four months I've been paying off my debts by working humiliating, back-breaking long hours at the local Kwik Save. I felt lonely and upset and my way of dealing with it was to lash out at you, to make you think I was having a good time without you.

But the truth, Bex, could not be further away. I've missed you so much. I missed you in Cuba, but back home and single, I've missed you even more. And the more this has gone on, the more I've realised precisely how much you mean to me, how much you are a part of me, just how grey life seems without you. I can't begin to describe the colour and the joy and the comfort and fun you inject into my world. I love you, Bex, I love you in more ways than I could possibly begin to describe. But there's no harm in having a go, though, is there?

Number one. I like your smile, the way your face crinkles when you laugh. Number two. I like your hair: its shiny, smart sheen, its sharp, sexy cut. Number three. I love your skin: smooth, soft, tanned, gorgeous. Number four. I adore your sense of humour, both the way you laugh and the way you make me laugh, your delicate teasing and perfect put-downs. Number five. I love the way you dance, the way your hips swing and shimmy along to the music. Number six. I admire your determination, your hard work and discipline and drive in everything you do. Number seven. I love your body, especially when it's next to mine. I'm not going to get smutty because that's not what this is about, but allow me one example. The small of your back is exquisite. Number eight. I love your passion, be it for your music or your goals or Tottenham Hotspur or whatever. Number nine. I love your sensitivity, your vulnerability as you sing to strangers, daring to allow them a glimpse of the inner you. And number ten. I love you. All of you, from the hair on your head to the tips of your toes. It's something that when we were together I didn't tell you enough. And now we've been apart, I realise just how strong these feelings are and I want to be able to tell you again and again and again.

Bex, I would do anything to have you back. You name it, I'd do it. I'd run naked through the streets for you. I'd stand up in the middle of a crowded tube train and tell everyone how much I loved you. I'd shave off my eyebrows, eat a dozen Marmite sandwiches, however horrible, however humiliating, it would be worth it, just to have you back in my life. We were so good together, Bex. We belong together. That, more than anything, is what this year has taught me, just how precious and perfect and important you are to me. And if you have any of the above feelings for me, then I beg you, let's give it a go again.

I love you, Bex. Let's make up. Life's not the same when you're not around.

Si *x*

23

I'm making a cup of tea when I find Si's letter. More specifically, I've made the cup of tea, squeezed the tea bag against the side of the mug with a spoon, and am about to dump it in the kitchen bin under the sink when I see the letter, ripped in two, unopened. I sag, I can't help it, as I pull it out, wipe the remains of last night's pizza off the back, place it on the table.

'Bex,' I call.

'What?' Bex shouts back from upstairs. 'What?' she asks again, as she crashes down the stairs, stands in the doorway.

'This,' I say, indicating the letter on the table.

'Ah. That,' says Bex, a little guiltily, a little defiantly.

'Yes,' I reply. 'That.'

'So what about it?'

'Don't you think you should open it?'

'Not really.' Bex shrugs. 'Now, have you seen my bag? I'm going to be late.'

'Oh, come on,' I say. 'Don't you think you should read it at least?'

'What could he possibly say that would interest me?'

'I don't know,' I say. 'I haven't read it.'

'Well, that makes two of us.'

'Look, it's none of my business—'

'That's right, Ben. It's none of your business. Now if you don't mind . . .'

'Bex,' I say, which comes out a little sharper than it should, as though I'm telling her off or something. 'Bex,' I repeat, a little gentler, picking up the letter, holding it out to her. 'It *is* none of my business, but if it was, I'd really recommend you at least looked at this.'

'I'm not going back there,' Bex says. 'I've moved on.'

'To what?' I ask. 'To Michael?'

'And what's wrong with Michael?' Bex asks.

'Well,' I say. 'He's not Si, is he?'

'You see, I'd have that down as a plus myself.' Bex snatches the letter out of my hand, tears the two halves into quarters, rips the four quarters into eighths. 'I don't care what Si's got to say,' she says, returning the letter to the bin. 'Whatever it is, it's too little, too late.'

'I think you're making a mistake.'

'No,' Bex corrects. 'I think you'll find it was Si who made the mistake.'

'Oh, come on,' I say. 'It's not as if you're Snow White, is it?'

'And what do you mean by that?'

'I mean that you got off with someone too. That girl at our party.'

Bex's jaw drops. Her face reddens. She spits out short staccato sentences. 'How do you know that? Did Sarah tell you? She kissed me. This bloke was bothering her. It was nothing.'

'I saw you,' I say.

296

Bex's vocabulary has gone. 'No, that's not, I didn't, you can't have . . .'

'You and Si are as bad as each other,' I say. 'You're both skulking around moping and missing the other person, when it's clear that you both still really care for each other. And if Si's had the guts to break that stalemate and apologise, I think you owe it to him to hear what he's got to say.'

'No, Ben,' Bex says. There are tears in her eyes. 'I've moved on.' But her voice isn't carrying the same conviction as before.

'Well, maybe you haven't moved on as far as you think.'

Bex shakes her head. 'He's hurt me,' she says. 'He's hurt me too much.' And with that, she's turning round, grabbing her coat off the banister and is out of the front door with a slam.

'Shit,' I say out loud. I pick up my mug of tea and take a sip. It's gone cold.

Later, I meet Gareth for lunch in Smith Square, a quiet corner hidden away between Westminster and Millbank, dominated by St John's concert hall.

With its four corner towers, St John's is a beautiful piece of baroque design, and equally famous for its classical music. It's sometimes known as 'Queen Anne's Footstool', because the then queen kicked her footstool over to show the architect how she wanted it. The restaurant in the crypt underneath is one of Gareth's favourite haunts, not,

I feel, because he is a fan of either Beethoven or baroque architecture, but because the words John and Smith in the address make him feel at home.

It's Annabel I see first, though. She's crouched on the floor in a silver grey trouser suit, papers scattered everywhere, a tableau that's strangely, jarringly familiar. I'm about to head over and help, when I see she's already got a second pair of hands: a nice-looking young bloke, with a sharp suit and brown-framed glasses.

'I'm so sorry,' he's saying, scooping the papers up. 'I didn't look where I was going.'

'Don't worry about it,' Annabel replies. 'Hey, don't I know you? Aren't you from the Home Office . . .'

Another lamb. I smile to myself and head over to find Gareth.

He's sat at a small table in the corner, rises when he sees me. He's looking good. I may be wrong, but I think he's bought a new suit now he's in government, a suit that's deep, dark conservative blue. The tie, I'm glad to see, is still red.

'Hello, stranger,' he says, shaking my hand firmly. 'It's good to see you.'

'You too,' I say. 'How's government?'

'Getting better. How else can things go?'

I queue up to get some food: salmon with some sort of herb sauce, Italian salad, roast potatoes. Gareth, I couldn't help noticing, has gone for the stew, a stew that's gone by the time I get back, and he's onto the half bottle of red that he's pouring me a glass of.

'So how was Japan?' he asks.

'Mind-blowing,' I say. 'Hot, humid, traditional, futuristic, hi-tech, beautiful, weird, wonderful, extraordinary.'

'Not quite Rochdale then?'

'Not quite, I don't think.'

'And your girlfriend?'

'She's not quite Rochdale either.'

Gareth chuckles at this. 'I still can't quite believe it. One hundred and seventy fucking nine. We stuffed them.'

'It was a bit of a turkey shoot.'

'All my Christmases rolled into one.' Gareth pulls out his wallet, shows me a picture of Michael Portillo on election night, his face frozen as the count was announced.

'You should be careful,' I say. 'That's how rumours start.'

'He's given me a lot of joy,' Gareth says. 'Every time I feel a bit down, I just have to look at that picture.'

'That's interesting. I've got a picture of Winona Ryder that has pretty much the same effect.'

'Yes, well.' Gareth puts his wallet away. 'Anyway. I expect you know what I'm about to say.'

I did. But I suspected Gareth didn't know what I was going to reply.

'I'd like to offer you a job,' Gareth says. 'A proper job. A government job.'

'I'm not going to take it,' I say quietly.

Gareth blinks in surprise. 'You're not going to— Oh, I get it. It's Annabel, isn't it? She's fucking gazumped me, hasn't she?'

'No, she hasn't,' I say. 'I haven't heard from Annabel at all. I'm just not going to take the job.'

'But you don't even know what it is yet.' Gareth is confused.

'It doesn't matter.'

'It doesn't matter?' Gareth's voice is rising. 'We're in government, Ben. Everything we've worked for over the year or so has been achieved. It's time to put it all into practice. It's time to get down to work.'

'I can't do it,' I say. 'You'll probably think I'm mad, but I can't do it.'

'Why not?'

'When I was in Japan,' I explain, 'I went to Hiroshima, to the Peace Park. It is the most extraordinary place, Gareth. The exhibition hall with its skeleton dome against the sky, the museum, everything. I don't think I've ever been anywhere that has had such a profound effect on me. I tried then, and I've tried since, but I still can't get my head round it, just what happened when the atomic bomb was dropped, just how many deaths, how much pain and suffering went on, how many families were destroyed. It's just beyond my comprehension.'

'What are you saying?' Gareth asks. 'You've become a peacenik?'

'Sort of,' I say. 'But that's not really what this is about. Going to Hiroshima has really made me think about things. I mean, I've been campaigning with you for what, nine months or so, but not once have I felt as angry or as passionate about stuff as I did in that Peace Park. That's the key. And the more I've thought about it since, the more important that seems. I want my life to be full of things that I'm passionate about. I don't want to do something because it seems like the best of a bad lot or a practical compromise or anything like that. I want to be involved in things that I believe in.

'And the truth is, Gareth, I don't believe in New Labour. I want the Tories out, sure. I want everything that we've campaigned for: the windfall tax, the New Deal, Scottish devolution, a ban on fox hunting, but as a package it's not enough for me. I think we *should* be putting up taxes to pump money into the NHS, and I don't think we should be ashamed of saying so. It worries me that we're probably going to go ahead with the Dome—'

'I thought you said that was a good idea.'

'Not any more,' I say. 'Think what you could do with that money. I think we should renationalise the railways. I think we should abolish the House of Lords. I think we should have proportional representation. All these are things that matter to me, and we're not doing any of them. Even though we've got a big stonking majority, we're still too worried about upsetting Middle England and the *Daily Mail*. There are big problems to sort out, and all we're going to do is tinker around the edges. And it's not like I don't understand why we're doing this, how important it was to win after being out of power for so long, but it's not enough for me. I don't want to be part of it. I'm glad we got the Tories out, I'm glad I played my part in it, but it's time for me to move on.'

Gareth is silent. He's silent for a long time. He's silent for so long that I ask, 'Gareth?' before he replies.

'So who are you going to work for?' he asks.

'I don't know,' I say. 'Like I say, it's got to be something I believe in. Maybe something to do with nuclear arms, maybe something environmental. But whoever it is, I'm going to work hard and harry the government and give you grief if your policies don't add up.' I smile. 'This is a big realisation for me. It's not just politics, it's everything. Second best isn't going to be enough any more.'

Gareth nods, chuckles to himself. 'Do you know who you sound like?'

I shake my head.

'Me. You sound like I did when I was your age.' Gareth drains his wine. 'I've been there, Ben. I know exactly where you're coming from.'

'So why are you working for New Labour?'

'I'm not. It says the Labour Party on the ballot paper and it's the Labour Party I'm working for. New Labour's just the spin, the sell, and it's not one that I'm buying.' He sighs. 'But I couldn't leave, Ben, even if I wanted to. It's in my blood. And the New Labourites may be edging the battle at the moment, but I'm buggered if I'm going to walk away and let them win without a fight. I'm going to tackle them every step of the way. I want the same things as you, Ben, but I've always worked from within to get them. And you should work from within, too.'

'It'd eat away at me,' I say. 'Doesn't it eat away at you too?'

'Sometimes,' Gareth says. 'Sometimes,' he echoes, a little sadly. 'It won't be easy, you know,' he continues. 'I'm not trying to put you off, but single issue campaigning can be deeply frustrating.'

'I'll take my chances,' I say. 'I'm sorry if you feel I'm letting you down. Especially after everything you've done for me.'

'You've done plenty for us too.'

'I'm talking about you,' I say. 'You've taught me a lot, Gareth.'

'Yeah,' Gareth laughs. It's a warm laugh. 'Seems I've taught you just that little bit too much.'

When I get back to the flat, I call out to see if Bex is there, to see if she's OK, but there's no answer. I go into the kitchen to make myself a cup of tea, and it's there, on the table, that I see it.

Crumpled and creased, smeared with pizza, curry and tea stains, Sellotaped together is Si's letter. I blink, pause, and smile: a smile for Si, but also for me, for maybe, just maybe, I have a chance. I know I shouldn't, but there's no one around and I skim the letter as I wait for the kettle to boil. You go, Si, I think as I read. Who'd have thought he had it in him? You deserve a shot after writing that.

As I make my tea and take it into the sitting room, I smile again. For there on the coffee table is a large, open jar of Marmite. And next to the Marmite, a plate piled high with one, two, three, four Marmite sandwiches, the top one with a large Si-sized bite out of it. You go, Bex, I think, as I count the five, six, seven, eight Marmite crusts lining the side. You know how much Si hates Marmite, and you're making him eat them. I lift up the corner of the half-eaten Marmite sandwich. I shake my head in sympathy for Si: that Marmite is thick.

I hear Bex's door open, a patter of feet and the bathroom door slamming shut. Bex *is* in. I hear the toilet flush, the sound of the shower coming on, and then Bex's door creak open again, the sound of a thicker, heavier pair of feet sauntering down the stairs. And there, dressed almost obscenely in Bex's short white dressing gown, wearing nothing else but a big soppy grin on his face, is Si.

'Ben.' He winks holding his hand out.

'Si.' I shake his hand back firmly. 'Welcome to Greenwich, Marmite breath.'

'Four fucking sandwiches she made me eat.' Si shakes his head. 'I thought she was going to make me eat the fucking lot.'

'I guess the letter must have worked,' I say. 'She threw it away, you know.'

'So I saw.' Si nods. 'I don't know what you said to her, mate, but it did the trick.'

'You're not the only one with a way with words,' I say. 'So what happened?'

'She rang me up,' Si says. 'Said she wanted to see me, that we should talk. I got the next train down. She was a bit frosty at first, said she was cross with me, with the way I'd behaved. She also said how hard it has been, living with you going out with Sarah, with your relationship working when ours hadn't. And the conclusion she came to as the year went on was that she wanted something like that, something worth fighting for, something strong. And going out with Michael just confirmed what she still felt for me, that that was what she should be fighting for. And there was something there so fundamental, so important, that it was worth giving it a second chance. She said that we're not a long-distance relationship sort of couple:

we need to be close to each other for it to work. And if I was prepared to move to London, to move in with her and give it a go, then she'd take me back.'

'And?'

'And I said yes.' Si smiles. 'I'm going to have to do some rejigging with jobs – I was meant to be training in New York for three months – but I don't mind. I'm happy to put Bex first and banking second.'

'You're not just saying that?'

'You know, that's exactly what Bex said. No, I'm not just saying that.'

'And then you went upstairs?' I ask.

'No,' Si says. 'Then she made me eat her Marmite fucking sandwiches.'

'How were they?'

'Absolutely fucking disgusting. But worth it. If I ever get into a Juanita situation again, all I have to think is Marmite, and I'll be all right.' Si shakes his head. 'I've brushed my teeth twice and I still want a cup of strong coffee to take the taste away. Do you want one?'

'I'm OK,' I say, pointing to the cup of tea on the table.

'Indeed,' Si says. 'Indeed.' He reaches into the dressing-gown pocket, pulls out a piece of paper. 'I think this is for you,' he says, handing it over.

My spirit soars as I unfold it. Mika's address.

'Thanks,' I say.

'Pleasure,' Si says. 'Now it's all down to you.'

Dearest M,

I can barely believe that I am writing this letter to you. It is no small exaggeration on my behalf to say that my hands are almost trembling as I write.

The reason I can barely believe I am writing to you is because I've been carrying my thoughts about you for so long that I can scarcely dare to believe they are true. Seeing them here, out of my mind and onto the page, fixes them in reality. It means I can no longer deny them. It means that I am unable to carry on as though nothing has happened.

Mika, I wasn't meaning for this to happen. I wasn't searching for it – not consciously at least. I haven't encouraged it or facilitated it. And yet, despite everything, the single, simple, complicated truth is that I am unable to stop myself from falling, tumbling, cascading into love with you. You've taken me over and I've gone gloriously under, enveloped in a heady rush of exhilaration and intoxication. Like a skydiver, I'm up here amongst the clouds, spinning and speeding my dizzy descent. And like gravity dragging the skydiver down, so love draws me to you. It's like a law of nature, a given. I can't escape the pull.

I have never known a passion like this. It's a loud, noisy, high-maintenance sort of emotion; insistent and unpredictable, expectant of me to drop it all at a click of its fingers. It is recalcitrant; rubbing against my world as and when it chooses. Frankly, my dear, it doesn't give a damn. It teases me and toys with me, takes advantage to play me off against myself. It can do all this because it is far bigger than I will ever be. I'm enthralled by its powerful beauty, in thrall to its beautiful power. My capitulation is complete.

I have never known a love like this. Or maybe the truth is that I have never known love. Have I been getting it wrong all this time? Has my limited experience of life limited me, making me think things are love when they are not? I've always laughed at love at first sight, dismissed people dying for others as ridiculous: these acts are the stuff of fictions and fantasies. When people say 'you just know', I've always rolled my eyes. This is 1997, for fuck's sake. Surely science and reason and rationality have shown up fairy-tale romance for the fairy tale it is. Now though, I'm not sure. Now, I think I'm beginning to know different.

I don't think I've ever met anybody like you. Every single thing you do, however small, be it pushing a hair off your face, a flicker of an eyelid, a drag of a cigarette, they all capture me, captivate me in a way that I would never have thought possible. And as I sit here and replay these images in my mind, their beauty doesn't diminish, the grace that goes with everything you do is immediately apparent.

I'm in awe of your sensuality. I can't get over your grasp of sensations, your knowledge of the sweetest smells, the most delicate of touches, the saddest of sounds, how these are fundamental to who you are, the core of your being. I'm stunned by your beauty: your hair, your figure, your skin, your eyes – I cannot even begin to put into words your delicacy, your delights. How I want to touch you, to kiss you, to stroke you. What I would give to feel your skin next to mine.

I would change my life for you. I would upend it, turn it over, upside down, inside out, whatever it took if it meant we could be together. I know I'm engaged, but if I had the choice, if I knew that you felt for me with the same intensity I do for you, well, believe me, everything would be different.

I've learnt so much in the past few months, Mika. And what I've realised most of all is that I don't want to settle for second best any more. I don't want to do anything that my heart isn't in 100 per cent. It's true with work, and if you gave me the chance, it could be true with love.

Contact me, Mika. Write to me, phone me, meet me. If you feel anything for me like I feel for you, then please, we've got to consider giving this a chance.

I think I love you.

B x

PS The white origami bird enclosed I made in the Hiroshima Peace Park. I'm sure you know what it means. It's not much, I know, but I wanted you to have it.

24

Nothing. I wait, I loiter, I linger for the post to arrive, but the reply doesn't come. It's funny, I remember feeling like this when Sarah first left for Japan, that I'd risk being late for work in the hope of catching the delivery. Where did that go? When I hear the letter box snap shut, the gentle thump of letter on doormat, I crash down the stairs in hope, but all there is – all there is – is a letter from Sarah.

It's not as if I even know she's got the letter. This silence, this cold, unrelenting, suffocating silence is unreadable. I can't get a sense of it, a handle. Is it a no? Or a don't know? In the early 1990s, the government changed the law about the right to silence: whereas once no comment to a policeman meant no comment, now a judge and jury could infer guilt from the fact that someone didn't want to speak. Should I do that too? Should I infer a meaning from this non-response? I don't want to, but the longer the silence goes on, the more I think I should. If it wasn't for my faith, my belief in what I'm feeling, I'd give up the ghost. I'd give it up if I didn't know how much it's going to haunt me.

On the fourth day after I sent the letter, Si knocks on my bedroom door to tell me I've got a phone call. But it's not Mika as I'd hoped. It's Gareth.

'I've got you a leaving present,' he says. 'Be outside Millbank, two o'clock sharp tomorrow. Enjoy it.'

And so, on a crisp June afternoon, I find myself standing outside Millbank Tower, staring out across the road, across the Thames to the buildings opposite. It's strange how quickly you can move on, I think. I came here every day for nine intense months, and now it seems as cold and alien and strange as the day I first arrived. I don't belong here any more, I think. Or maybe I never did.

As I'm standing there, looking at my watch, checking the time, I notice a white limousine, a white limousine that's indicating left and pulling to a halt by the kerbside. And then, to my double amazement, I watch as one of the blacked-out windows slides open, and a young bloke's face looks out, at me, and asks if I'm Ben.

'Er, yeah,' I say, taken aback.

'Come on then.' The bloke indicates for me to get in, opens the door. 'We haven't got all day, mate.'

This is bizarre. I walk a little dazed towards the limousine. What the *fuck* is going on? Who are these people? What has Gareth arranged? I feel slightly hesitant, I have to say, about getting into a car with a group of strangers. But the bloke who peered out the window is out of the car now, and I notice his Boo Radleys T-shirt and jeans, and his hand is out and welcoming me, and he's introducing himself as Andy from Creation Records. I shake his hand, I'm still confused, but I get in nonetheless. I've never been in a limousine before, but I've seen them so many times on TV and films that the squeaky black leather has the air of surreal familiarity to it. There's three blokes who I don't recognise, all young and in trendy designer gear, sitting on the back seat, so I nod and take a seat facing them, my back to the driver.

'Great,' says Andy, slamming the door shut, rapping twice on the blacked-out glass partition for the driver to set off. 'I think that's everybody. OK, guys, this is Ben, he's involved in youth projects for the Labour Party. Ben, this is Dan, music journalist, Chris, he's a record buyer for the supermarkets, Stu, he works for independent radio . . .'

We nod and wave and mouth hi to each other as the limousine pulls out, heads towards Parliament.

'And this is the reason we're all here.' Andy reaches down into a bag and pulls out a CD. On the plain white front, written in thick black letters, are the words 'Oasis' and 'single'.

'Oh my God,' I say. 'Is that the new single?'

This is beginning to make sense. And I'm beginning to get excited.

'Certainly is,' says Andy. 'And when you hear it, you're going to appreciate just how big this is, and why we're not letting it out of our sight. We're doing it this way so the bootleggers can't get hold of it.'

'So what's it like?' I ask. 'What's it called?'

'It's called "D'You Know What I Mean?"' Andy says. 'And you'd better put your seat belt on, because this is going to blow you away. I tell you, when we first heard this back at the office, there was just a stunned silence. It's that good.'

As Andy's rapping on the glass screen again, and the driver's winding it down and taking the CD to put in the

stereo, as the limousine is filled with the nervous anticipation of four grown men reduced to excited teenagers,
my mind is racing with thoughts, of Blur versus Oasis, of
Knebworth, of Sarah. For the first time in months, I feel a
surge of togetherness, of belonging, of us. Oasis is our
band, our tunes, and all of a sudden I feel the aching guilt
of everything about Mika, of wanting Sarah to be here
now and share this moment with me. For the first time in
weeks, I can see a glimmer of things as they were, before
Knebworth, before she went away. I haven't listened to
Oasis for months. It's been all Nick Drake on my stereo.

It's a flicker, but it's there. Maybe I'm wrong about
Mika. She hasn't replied to my letter, has she? Maybe
Sarah and I stand a chance, after all. And maybe Noel and
Liam and Guigsy and Whitey and Bonehead can bring us
back together. And as I'm sitting there, as the glass screen
slides up again, as I wait for the CD to start, part of me is
wanting it to be great: a sign for Sarah and me to share,
to pull us out of this mess and confusion and uncertainty.
I want the song to be 'Live Forever' and 'Slide Away' and
'Wonderwall' and 'Cast No Shadow' all rolled into one,
the killer number in the soundtrack of our lives.

It starts with the sound of an aeroplane. The speakers
in the limousine are so loud that it's as if the plane is in
here. It's comfortable and familiar: it echoes the helicop-
ters at the beginning of 'Morning Glory'. Then the plane
is joined by a whipping-up of white noise: squalls of guitar
feedback, something being dot, dot, dot, dash, dash dashed
out in Morse code, a crash on the drums, the strum of a
guitar, backwards vocals that almost sound as if they're
singing 'fuck', and suddenly we're into the song, its

rhythm loping arrogantly along, a strutting mix of strummed chords and high-pitched guitar notes that echo and hang in the background. And there's Liam, the best voice in Britain, sending the hairs on the back of my neck up as he starts to sing.

The song's called 'D'You Know What I Mean?' but as usual with Noel's lyrics, the answer is no I don't. There's the usual quota of suns and skies and storms, the full complement of namechecks, *Blood on the Tracks*, 'Fool on the Hill' and 'I Feel Fine', by the end of the first verse. But the lyrics aren't what Oasis are about, are they? It's about the feel. And as the first verse segues into the second, the bridge into the chorus, as the Morse code and the feedback and the backwards guitars flit in and out, as the strings appear and push the song towards the chorus, I'm starting to get the nagging feeling that something is askew. It's big and it's noisy and it's blustery, but it's not soaring, it's not slicing through the air like the plane at the start of the song.

I glance round the limo. Everyone else is loving it. The guy from the supermarkets is nodding his head along to the music. The radio guy is playing air drums. The music journalist catches my eye and purses his lips together as if to say, 'Sweet'. I want to be like them too. I want to be loving this single. But as the song goes on, the harder I listen, the more I can't help feeling disappointed. I don't know if it's me, I don't know if it's Oasis, but for whatever reason, the spell has been broken. This isn't capturing me any more. The magic's gone. However much I want it to, this isn't going to put me and Sarah back together again. I look out of the window, at Regent

Street flipping past, at the people on the pavement peering in, trying to get a glimpse of who is in the limo, and I just want the CD to stop.

'That's going to be mega,' the supermarkets man is saying. 'Definite number one.'

'Tell you what,' the journalist says. 'That's the one that's going to do America. That's the breakthrough song.'

'Just brilliant,' the radio bloke agrees. 'It's fucking huge.'

'Ben?' Andy asks.

'Yeah,' I hear myself saying. Then I stop myself. 'Actually, no. I'm sorry, I'm going to get out here. Can you let me out?' I knock on the glass screen for the driver to stop.

'I don't get you,' Andy says, as the limousine draws to a halt. 'Are you saying you *don't* like the single?'

I shrug. 'I don't know. It's different. It's good. It's . . .' I look round the limousine. I'm out on a limb on this one, I think. 'Hey, what do I know?' I open the door. 'You're the experts, not me.'

And then I get my reply.

It's Saturday morning in the flat. Si, Bex and I are in the sitting room, reading the morning papers, one eye on the cricket on the television, devouring a toast rack full of toast, a teapot full of tea. I'm skimming through the television guide, making mental notes of the films on for the week ahead, when Si points the article out.

'Ben, did you see this story about the journalist?' Si is

sprawled across the sofa, using Bex's legs as some sort of headrest.

'What story?'

'This one.' Si waves the main newspaper, folded into quarters. 'This journalist, right, has fallen out with his editor and decided to quit and work for another news-paper instead. On his last day he's writing the leader column, a not very exciting piece about the state of the economy. But unknown to them, he used the first letter of each sentence to spell out a goodbye message. F.u.c.k.y.o.u.R.u.p.e.r.t. By the time they found out what he'd done, it was too late. The paper had been printed.' Si turns the paper over. 'Brilliant.'

'Maybe I should have tried that sort of stunt before I left the Labour party.'

'I thought you'd done that with the manifesto. I thought you'd spelt out, fuck you, Britain?'

'Very funny,' I say. 'Was that Marmite you wanted on your toast, Si?'

A ripple of applause rises from the television as an English batsman hits the ball for four.

Si returns to his newspaper. I watch the replay, the cover drive, the umpire waggling his finger from right to left to right to indicate the boundary, when I have the idea. It something Mika said, on Hampstead Heath, when I thought she was waving me away. 'It's different in England to Japan,' she'd said. 'When you think I'm push-ing you away, I'm wanting you to come closer.'

She hasn't, has she?

'Hey, where are you going?' Si calls out after me as I run upstairs to my bedroom, open my jumper drawer, feel around at the back until I find it, pull out Mika's Rizla packet, the packet in which I've kept all her mysterious messages. I pull the bedroom door to, sit on the bed, my heart beating, pick out the top Rizla paper. It's the St James's Park one, and my mind fleetingly remembers the sweet smell, the squirrel. *Tuesday. AZ1486D30. You smell. Stop Expecting Christmas, You.* Stop Expecting Christmas, You. S. E. C. Y. Nothing. I sigh. Maybe I was wrong after all. But then I'm about to pack the Rizlas away, when I have another thought. What if, rather than Christmas, I used the abbreviation Xmas? Then, I can feel my heart beating once more, then the letters would be S, E, X and Y.

I pull out another Rizla. It's the first one. *I'll absolutely never turn you on. Understand?* I.A.N.T.Y.O.U. But what if I change I'll to I will? I gasp. Then it becomes I.W.A.N.T. Y.O.U. I pick another. *I want a no trouble time, OK? Friendship's everything. Entertaining love, you'd only ultimately regret this. Only unhappiness could happen.* I.W.A.N.T. T.O.F.E.E.L.Y.O.U.R.T.O.U.C.H. I try another. *Typical Englishman, privately thinking Mika's excited.* T.E.M.P.T. M.E. And another. *Give over: romantic gestures – exaggerated or, understated – soon backfire on you.* G.O.R.G.E.O.U.S. B.O.Y.

The Rizla packet is empty, but there's still one message left, the message on the inside of the packet itself. With trepidation, I'm so hyper my hands are almost shaking with the tension, I read and translate. *Mouthing, entwining, embracing, touching . . . magically exciting, obviously not nice. I can't keep denying reality: all kisses end sometime. Ben, I realise this hurts – despite apologising – yet, Ben, your heart is*

Sarah's. Good relationships are very exceptional. Maybe I don't dare aggravate yours. x

M.E.E.T.M.E.O.N.N.I.C.K.D.R.A.K.E.S.B.I.R.T.H.D.A.Y.
B.Y.H.I.S.G.R.A.V.E.
M.I.D.D.A.Y.

I gasp again. I reread the note, check that I'm not going mad, not making this all up. But no, there it all is. Oh my God. My first thought is, This is for real. This is for fucking real. Everything I've thought and felt has been one hundred per cent copper-bottomed blue. Mika feels for me too. Then I have my second thought.

'Bex!' I open the bedroom door, crash downstairs again. 'Bex, when's Nick Drake's birthday?'

Si and Bex both look at me as though I've gone mad.

'Nick Drake's birthday?' she asks. 'Why do you want to know that?'

'I, er, that doesn't matter now. The important thing is, when is it?'

'Off the top of my head, I've no idea.' Bex shrugs.

Please God may I not be too be late. I stare at Si for help: from the way he's looking at me, he's understanding something. He's not sure how or why, but he's nodding slowly and putting Nick Drake and Mika together.

'Where might you find out?' Si asks. 'Have you got a book or something it might be in?'

'Don't think so.' Bex is looking really confused now. 'Oh wait, I've got that book about folk music. It might be in that.'

'Is it in your bedroom? Can I go get it?' I ask.

'I guess,' Bex says. 'It's a bit of a tip, but . . .'

I don't hear the end of the sentence because I'm up the stairs again, turning the other way this time into Bex's bedroom, and she's right, it is a bit of a tip, but at least her books are together, and there, there on the shelf, is a big fat beginner's guide to folk. I pull it down, open it to the index at the back, follow my finger up to D, to Drake, Nick, then flick forward to the relevant page. I pause, read, and smile. *Nick Drake*, the book reads, *Born 19 June 1948. Died 25 November 1974.* The date today's, what? The fifth? Fantastic, I think. Fan-fucking-tastic. I've made it. I've made it with a fortnight to spare.

Where once there was lethargy, suddenly I'm imbued with spirit and energy. Where once life seemed bad and bland and boring, suddenly it's fresh and reinvigorating. I stop skulking and start doing. I apply for a stack of jobs – campaign groups against the arms trade, Third World debt, homelessness. I feel good about myself. Everything I said to Gareth was right: I only want to do things now that I believe in. I don't believe in New Labour. I do believe in these jobs.

For a week the honeymoon lasts. I'm enjoying life, enjoying London: going out, seeing people, having fun. I don't think I've felt so fulfilled, so happy all year. I feel bad about Sarah, sure, but somehow that feels as if that's a decision for the future. All I'm thinking about now is seeing Mika. Once I see what happens there, then I can start thinking about decisions.

Nick Drake's grave is in a small Warwickshire village,

just south of Birmingham, just off the M42. I buy a road atlas, and have to stop myself from checking and double-checking the route. Likewise cleaning and polishing my car, filling up its oil, water, everything. Bex thinks I've gone mad: I'm the least car-interested person she knows, and suddenly I can't keep myself out from under the bonnet. She thinks I've gone mad, and she's right. In a mild way, I guess I probably have.

But then, three days before Nick Drake's birthday, I come back late from an evening in town with an old school friend, come back to find a note from Bex on the kitchen table. *Sarah rang*, it says. *Check yr email. IMPORTANT*. Bex has underlined the last word in case I miss the point. I head to my room, switch my PC on, log in and wire up. As the computer makes its scratchy little noises as it tries to connect, I try to think what could possibly have happened. I can't think. After an age, the computer verifies my user name and password, downloads my emails. And there's the one from Sarah. I gulp as I see the subject heading. *Not Good*.

From: Cardiagan Girl
To: Ben (Home)
Date: 13 June 1997
Subject: Not Good

Dear Ben,

Where are you? I keep on ringing but I can never get hold of you when I want to. I've got some really, really bad news: Granny has died. I got a call from Dad last night. You know she's been having chest pains for a while? Yesterday morning, when her carer went round to see her, she found her in bed. We think, we hope, she must have died in her sleep. I'm really, really upset as you might imagine, especially being stuck out here, away from my family, from you, from everyone. I can't deal with this on my own. Which is why I'm going to take some time off and come back to Britain for a few days.

This is the important bit. The earliest flight I can get is on the morning of the funeral, which is going to be on 19 June. Mum, Dad and Jeb are all staying up at Granny's bungalow, sorting things out and getting the service and reception worked out, so I'm going to need you to meet me at Heathrow and then we can drive up to Leicester together. The flight number is JAL153 and it arrives at Terminal Two at 07.45, so there should be plenty of time to get up to the funeral, even if the flight's delayed. I'm sure I'll speak to you before, but I thought I'd better give you the details now, just in case we don't catch each other.

You have got a black suit, haven't you? Can you borrow one if not?

Sarah xxx

25

The last time I was at Heathrow to meet Sarah, I really wished that her family weren't there. This time, I really wish they were.

If Sarah's family were here, then her mother and father and brother would take over and I'd be left looking on, the concerned bystander, as they hugged and kissed Sarah and asked her how she was and I'd be waving from behind, trying to grasp her attention. This time, the attention's all on me. As is all the tension. And as I know only too well, I'm not much of an actor. The last time I tried it on with Sarah was the day after Knebworth, when I pretended I had a hangover so I could skip lunch with her aunt to write her letter. I was transparent then and I can't help worrying I'm going to be transparent now: especially as this time the pretending is the other way round.

In one way, I'm not surprised that Sarah's returning on Nick Drake's birthday. Not in any female intuition sense, just that life has a habit of bunching like this. I guess there must be people whose lives and big decisions are all neatly spread out. For me, though, that cliché about things happening when you're making other plans is closer to the truth. Trouble, it is said, comes in threes, and it's true. I don't think I've ever known as much trouble as me, Sarah and Mika.

I lean heavily on the rail and glance up at the clock. Eight ten. I wonder if Sarah's grandmother, wherever she is, I wonder if she knows she's saved her granddaughter's relationship. It's funny how things work out, I think, the see-saw between life and death, how one end is somehow the beginning of something else. All relationships have good patches and bad patches, and that's what this is: a bad patch. But the next time I'm here, in a couple of months when Sarah returns from Japan for good, that'll be the start of something different. With Sarah here, we can begin again. We have a chance to put this year behind us, to sit down and really work at our relationship. This year's been too long, too far apart, it's too much for any relationship to take. Look at Si and Bex: they've had their ups and downs, but they've made it through, and they're all the better for it. Maybe the same can happen for me and Sarah.

I adjust my black tie and look up again at the time. Eight twenty. Three hours and forty minutes. Stop it, I chide. I've got to stop thinking about that. I can't keep torturing myself. Mika's not going to happen. I've simply got to forget about it and move on. I'm doing the right thing by being here, I tell myself. Today's not about me; it's about Sarah, it's about being there for Sarah. Sarah who has travelled halfway across the world to say goodbye to her grandmother, who is going to be tired and upset and need all the support I can give her. And when I think about that, and I think about Mika, I can't help but feel like an absolute cunt, and I'm sorry for the language but it's true, that's exactly what I feel like. Mika may be there, like a tiny shard of glass embedded in my skin that I can't get out, but I've got to forget about her, forget about the pain, and start focusing on Sarah.

'Ben!'

I come to, and there, standing right in front of me, is Sarah. She looks pale, not a beautiful white, but sad and exhausted, her eyes are red from tears or tiredness, I don't know which. Her black suit, the one I last saw her wear when she went for her job interview to go to Japan, is crumpled and creased.

'Sorry,' I say. 'I was miles away.' I lean forward to hug her but Sarah stiffens and pulls back.

'Not here,' she says. 'It'll set me off.'

It's just after we've pulled off the M25 and onto the M1 that Sarah starts to cry.

I don't notice at first because I'm concentrating on driving, trying to get past the green Ford Mondeo who's sitting in the middle lane doing sixty-five miles an hour and won't budge for love or money. I don't notice at first because Sarah's sat in the passenger seat, looking away from me, staring out of her window. I don't notice at first because Sarah's turned the stereo on, ejected my Nick Drake tape ('Uh-oh! Hippy alert!') and put on *Parklife* by Blur in a take-your-mind-off-things kind of a way, which is fine until 'To the End' comes on and even above the music, the noise of the engine, even I'm hearing her muffled sobs, can see her body shaking out of the corner of my eye.

'Hey,' I say, reaching a hand across, rubbing her back. 'Hey.'

Sarah doesn't look round, but her hand reaches round for mine. Then just as her fingers are touching mine I withdraw as I squeeze the brakes on, change down a gear as the green Mondeo cuts me up again.

'She'd be really glad you're here,' I say, clicking the music off. 'It'd mean a lot to her.'

Sarah nods, continues to stare out of the window.

'She was a wonderful woman,' I continue. 'I only met her half a dozen times, but she was bright and clever and funny. I know it's sad, but she was what, ninety-five, ninety-six? She's had a remarkable innings. And I think, I know, that today will be as much a celebration as a commemoration of her life.'

'Oh, Ben.' Sarah turns round to look at me. I dart a look across, see the trickles of mascara running down her cheeks.

'I'm sorry,' I say. 'If you want me to shut up about your gran, just say so. I'm probably talking crap to the dozen.'

'It's not about my gran,' Sarah says. 'It's about us.'

Sarah says this as I'm changing back up to fifth and for a split second my foot slips off the clutch and there's a horrendous screeching sound before I slam it back on and get into gear.

'Us?' I ask. I look in my wing mirror and pull into the slow lane. Shit, I think. She knows, she knows, she knows.

'I wasn't going to tell you until tomorrow,' Sarah is talking really quickly now and not looking at me, looking straight ahead. 'But I wasn't able to sleep on the plane from worrying and I can't get through today without telling you even though I don't know how to tell you.'

'Tell me what?' I ask.

'I'm not coming back,' Sarah says. 'I want to stay in Japan.'

There's a silence as I'm taking this in.

'For how long?' I ask.

'Another year,' Sarah says. 'I know we had an agreement, that I was only going to be away for the year, but the thing is, I love it out there. It's changed me, it really has, I've got independence and responsibility and respect and I really, really like it. I think it's brought me out of myself. And I know it's hard on us and that you've been waiting patiently for me all this time, and I know we should sit down and talk about it, but I know that my mind's made up, it's what I want to do and I'd hate myself, hate you, if you made me come back right now.'

I drive on. There's a juggernaut ahead and I should pull out to overtake it but I haven't being focusing and the middle lane is full and I can't get in and I slow down as I'm stuck behind it.

'It doesn't mean I feel any differently about you,' Sarah says. 'It's like you wanting to work for the Labour Party. That changed our plans, that meant we spent the year apart. I didn't have any choice in that. And I guess that what I'm asking you to do now is the same for me: to support me while I put my job first for a year.'

I'm getting hassled by not being able to overtake the

juggernaut. I watch as another lorry drives up behind, then barges out into the middle lane and overtakes me.

'So you'd what?' I ask. 'Stay out for another year?'

'Probably,' Sarah says. 'OK, well, I've got an option to stay out for another two, but I don't think I'll do that.'

Another year. Another two years? 'Do you know how hard this year has been?' I ask. 'Do you know how difficult it is being the person left behind? Do you know how it's been thinking of you coming back that's kept me going?'

'I know.' Sarah nods. 'But you'll get used to it. I mean, I was pretty cross with you for not coming to Japan, but I calmed down.'

'Yes,' I say. 'But another year, maybe another two. By the time you get back, we'll have spent more time apart than we have together.'

'I know,' Sarah says. 'But the relationship's got to work round what we want to do.'

'Maybe what we do should work around the relationship?'

'You didn't say that when you decided to work for the Labour Party.'

She's right, I think. I'm having it both ways.

'Do, do you think our relationship will survive another year apart?' I ask.

There's a pause. Then Sarah says, 'I hope so. I mean, I think we're going to have to sit down and talk about things. If I'm being honest, I do think we've drifted a little bit. Take your letters, Ben: to begin with they were warm and funny and romantic but as time's gone on, they've become less about you and more about Tony Blair or Chris Evans or whatever's in the news that week, which is great and fine and funny but they're not the same as they were before. For whatever reason, you're writing them from that little bit further away.

'I'm going to say something, Ben,' Sarah continues, 'and I've spent most of the plane journey debating about whether I should or not, but I think it's important to be honest and so I'm going to, and when I say it, I want you to think about it and not fly off the handle. Basically, ever since your trip to Japan, I've been torn between wanting to stay in Japan and coming back to be with you, but the more I've thought about it, the more I've realised that, at the moment, I'm not certain enough about you, about us, to come back. The person I left behind all those months ago has disappeared. He's not writing to me any more. And if I'm to come back to Britain, then I'd want him to come back too.'

'Don't you think that's because we're apart?' I ask.

'I don't,' Sarah says. 'Because up to Christmas, the Ben I loved was writing me these wonderful letters. I want to find a way of getting that Ben back. We need to work out how to rekindle things. And if we do, then it doesn't matter how long we spend apart. After all, we are engaged, aren't we?'

We are, I think. We're engaged like a phone is engaged. Like someone's trying to get through, but they can't.

Sarah,

I'm sorry. I can't explain. I'm sorry.

B x

26

It's almost like the poster says: you shouldn't think and drive. We pull over, to a motorway station because I've got to have a cup of tea. I'd like something stronger, but think driving is bad enough. Sarah and I are talking about other things now – about Japan, about the journey, about the funeral, but my mind is still chewing over what she said in the car, and it continues to chew as we queue up in the cafeteria, turn down the frizzled remains of the fried breakfast, wait patiently as the assistant blasts a shot of steam into two stainless steel teapots.

Sarah doesn't really speak as we drink. And that's not because we haven't got anything to say to each other: it's because we've got too much. Sarah's more relaxed now, you can tell from the way that she's sitting. She's unburdened, unloaded and is feeling all the lighter for it. It's me, just me, who is feeling weighed down.

It's Sarah who gets up first, who leaves to go to the toilet, to freshen up, fix her face, powder her nose. It's me who's left there, on a hard green plastic chair that is nailed to the floor in case you want to steal it, though quite why you would I've absolutely no fucking idea. It's me who's sat there alone in the half-empty cafeteria, looking out of the window and out at the cars speeding away from London, me whose mind is racing just as quickly away.

I think this is the saddest cup of tea I've ever had. Because as I sit there, and the tinny, piped sound of Fleetwood Mac's *Rumours* wafts across the tannoy, as the music slips from 'Don't Stop' to 'Go Your Own Way', I'm quickly coming to the unerring conclusion that that's exactly what I should do.

Sarah's right. We have drifted apart. She doesn't know why – or maybe she does and she's just not saying it – but her instinct is spot on. We've drifted apart because I've fallen in love with Mika. Did I fall in love with Mika because Sarah was away? No, I think. I fell in love with Mika because I fell in love with Mika. Sarah not being there made it easier, but it wouldn't have mattered if she was round the corner or on the other side of the world. The feelings I have for Mika are simply unstoppable. And if it hadn't been Mika, then at some stage, it would have happened with someone else. And the reason for this, I realise, is not that Sarah was abroad or that long-distance relationships can't work. It's more fundamental than that. It's because I don't love Sarah. I thought I did at the time, but that's because I didn't know. Until I'd met Mika, I'd never properly, really properly, been in love.

The clarity of this thought hits me with a rush. It's Mika I love. And though Sarah's offering me a second chance to sort things out and put things right, I don't want to take it. There's only one place I want to be right now and that's Nick Drake's grave, because that's where Mika, I hope, is waiting for me. There's no point in sitting down and thinking things through with Sarah, or working

330

at our relationship, because that's not, I realise, what relationships should be about. There's no thinking involved: there's just instinct and connection and you can work as hard as you like but there's no point because there's nothing you can do: it's either there, or it's not.

I open the road atlas on the table in front of me, the one I'm meant to be looking at to work out how to get to the funeral. But a deeper, darker thought is emerging that I can't ignore. I look up the village in the index, flick the atlas open to the relevant page. There it is, no more than a speck in the countryside, just off a junction on the M42. I look at my watch. Ten forty-five. I'm never going to make it, I think. I'm going to have to bomb left up the M6, and then double back round Birmingham: a good couple of hours' driving at least. And I can't leave Sarah here, can I? I can't leave Sarah here to phone her family and get someone to pick her up for the funeral.

I can. I can write Sarah a note on the back of a napkin. *Sarah, I'm sorry. I can't explain. I'm sorry. B x.* I can get up from the table, turn round and walk away. I'm shocked at myself, at the sheer brutality of these feelings, a love that puts Mika first and everyone else second. I'm going to be late, I think, as I slip outside, start jogging across the car park for the car. I'm going to be late but I'm going to give it a go. I'm prepared to throw everything away for a chance of seeing Mika, and all I can think is that if I've got a feeling this strong then that's got, *got*, to be worth something.

It's horrible what I'm doing to Sarah. I can't pretend that it isn't. But there isn't time for niceties, for discussions, for delays. Sarah's put herself first by deciding to stay in Japan and now I'm doing the same. She deserves an explanation, and maybe sometime I'll give her one, but that's not for today. Today is Nick Drake's birthday, and I want to find Mika.

I nearly kill myself driving to Birmingham. I'm no Michael Schumacher and I'm not used to driving at 80, 90, 100 miles an hour. I can see the speed cameras flash in my rear-view mirror and in one journey I may have done enough to lose my licence but I don't care. It doesn't help that I'm nervy, jumpy, excited. I'm swerving and screeching and doing everything my limited driving ability can to get to Mika, to get to Nick Drake's grave before it's too late.

My mind alternates between counting down the junctions and counting up the minutes. Midday comes and goes and I'm still miles away. The lead story on the news is how the government have given the go-ahead for the Millennium Dome. On another day, I'd have been furious. Today, I don't give a shit. Come on, I sit up someone's bumper in the fast lane. I blast my horn and make hand signals for him to get out of the way. If he puts the brakes on, I'm dead, I think. But it doesn't make me slow down.

The roads build up round Birmingham and I bob and weave as much as I can between lanes, but I can't help thinking I'm losing precious time. Finally, I lose the traffic, hit the M42, hit junction 4, 300 metres, 200 metres, 100 metres, and I'm off the motorway, skidding down onto the Warwickshire country lanes, the village getting closer and closer. Suddenly the only grey left is the sky, overcast and threatening to rain. Everything else is green. Hedgerows, trees, fields, gentle rolling hills and dales, everything is quiet and picturesque and magically Nick Drake English. Daisies sprinkle the fields with white. A swallow, a house martin, I'm not sure, swoops down in front of me and effortlessly up again. Finally, finally, I see a signpost for the village, indicate left and scream on.

It's ten past one by the time I arrive. The village is pretty and as English as a village can be. I pull the car up in the high street, a thin strip of whitewashed houses; the customary pub and post office to the left. In the middle of the street, the fork between two roads, sits the village green, complete with First World War Memorial. Behind it, tall and grey except for the golden weathervane on top of the steeple, sits the Parish Church of St Mary Magdalene.

There's no one around. I get out, slam the car door shut and run, down the road and in through the churchyard, through a pair of old wooden gates and turn. I make my way down the left-hand side of the church along a gravel path, crunching under my feet like the stones on Brighton Beach, glancing at the gravestones. But these are big thick slabs of rock, like the ten commandments stuck in the ground, graves whose names have been washed off by the years. Nick Drake died only twenty-odd years ago; his grave is going to be among the more modern ones.

The graveyard opens up at the back end of the church, but as I make my way among them, they're all too old. And then, sheltered by trees, I spy a second field to my right, the stones looking down a gentle slope away from the village, towards the Warwickshire countryside beyond. And as I approach, I spy the occasional speckled grey of modern granite. Nick Drake's grave is going to be here, I'm sure.

There's scores of stones and I'm wondering how long it's going to take me to find the grave when I spot it, almost immediately. Underneath a huge oak tree, just by the path that heads out to the countryside, sits a simple brown-grey stone, straight sides and a smooth, semi-circular top. And I can't read the engravings from this angle but what makes me notice it, what makes me think it might be Nick's, is the small cluster of daisies that someone has placed on top. And as I move round, my instinct is right. In simple capital letters, carved into the stone, it reads

NICK DRAKE
1948–1974
REMEMBERED WITH LOVE
RODNEY DRAKE
1908–1988
MOLLY DRAKE
1915–1933

The grave is covered with flowers: some fresh, some old. In front of the grave, just by the tree trunk, is a potted plant, and embedded into the soil, in a circle round the outside, are a collection of bright, different-coloured plectrums. But as touching as these are, they're not what captures my interest. Because to the left of the grave sits a small, stone vase, in which rests a single fresh red rose. And there, stuck on a thorn, is a small white paper crane.

Mika. I crouch down and pick it off. It's got to be Mika. I look round the graveyard, listen to the silence save for the shrill of birdsong and the shush of the motorway traffic in the distance. Nothing. I look at the crane, my crane. She got my note, I think. She got my note and turned up and waited, and I didn't come, and now she's gone and left my origami crane behind. I stop crouching and sink to my knees. Fuck. I'm too exhausted to feel angry. I took the chance, I knew what was at stake, it didn't come off. I look at Nick Drake's grave, at the flowers there for him. I hope he knows that they're here, I think. I hope he knows that there are people who still care for him, all these years on. I wonder if he knows that his music is all I have left, all I have to remind me of Mika. How I know her intimately, by sight, smell, sound, taste and touch. How that's as close as I'm going to get.

I half expect it to rain, for the heavens to open up and piss on my love parade one final time. But no, I can't even get that right and the clouds just sit there, cold, grey, brooding, ignoring me. I struggle to my feet, make a half-hearted attempt to wipe the mud off my trousers. There's no hurry. Where once there was urgency, now the tension has gone, the elasticity has snapped. I take one last look at Nick's grave, at his view out down the slope, down the path to the wooden gate and the countryside beyond. At least he's ended up in the right place, I think.

I take the rose as well as the crane. I don't know if I should, if that's there for me or for Nick, I don't even know if it's from Mika or someone else, but I want something, even now I'm thinking I want something to remind me of her, even though I'm sure that my thoughts and memories of her aren't going to fade, aren't going to fade away. And maybe sometime I'll be able to sit down and put it all into perspective but right now all I am is as short-sighted as is myopically possible; through the glistening of tears I can't see a thing. Is this what people mean when they say that love is blind?

I hear a whistle, and look up to see a house martin to my left, swooping and climbing, flittering and twittering across from left to right. Its movement reminds me of something, nags at me until I remember. Knebworth. That condom, punched across the crowd. God, that seems an age ago now. I watch as the bird banks and dives away from me, smaller and smaller until it's no more than a black speck against the clouds.

As I'm watching, it reminds me of the little white dot, the little white dot that used to appear on television screens after midnight, together with a high-pitched whine, to tell viewers that the day's programming was over. I think about this as I watch the house martin slowly slip away from view. The colours may be reversed, the high-pitched whine might be absent, the dot may be in the sky not the screen, but its presence, I feel, is demarcating exactly the same.

I stumble back up through the graveyard, along the gravel path, back along the side of the church, clutching my rose, my crane. And then, just as I'm about to turn right, through the gates, back to the car, back to my life, I pause, pause and look left, at the entrance to the church, the thick wooden door inside the porch. And suddenly I'm tired and want to sit down on the stone bench inside, to pause, pause and think. And so I sit, place the rose to one side and cradle the paper crane in my hands. The crane I made in Hiroshima all those weeks ago, the paper crane that has flown halfway across the world, has travelled from me to Mika and back again. The crane that represents how I missed my chance by the smallest of margins.

And it's then that I notice. As I look at the crane, I realise with a start that this isn't it. This isn't my crane. It's too precise, too well crafted, too well made to be mine. Mika, Mika made this. Far from giving me my crane back, Mika has made another for me. And as I'm looking at it, admiring it, making sense of it all, on the inside of its left wing, at the very point of where the paper is folded over and disappears from view, I see a small black squiggle. Nothing much, but enough to suggest more, to suggest it might be part of a letter, a number, a note.

I kill the crane. I flatten it where Mika's breath had blown it into life, unpick its head and tail, fold down the wings and flaps until it is no more than it was before, a single sheet of white paper. And my heart skips, because there, there in the middle of the paper, corrugated along the folds, runs a message. *B, please God you find this. Ring me, M x.* And there, underneath is a mobile phone number.

I gasp. I laugh. I clasp the piece of paper against my chest, can feel my heart thumping beneath. A phone, I've got to find a phone. I spring up, glance around the village green, but there's no phone box to be seen. I thought every village had a phone box. I glance right and notice the pub. They must have a phone, I think, and I'm

337

sprinting inside, into the dark, empty oak interior, into a pub that's empty save for an old woman sitting and staring stoically ahead, her chin resting on her walking stick, a youngish man behind the bar polishing a pint glass. He points at where the phone is, and I follow his instructions round to the back, round by the toilets. I'm so hyped that when I reach into my pocket for some money, I spill my change all over the floor. I scoop it up, grab a fifty- and a twenty-pence piece and punch the numbers in. It seems to take for ever to ring, and even when it does, the ringing seems to be endless. And just as it seems that nothing's going to happen, that all the phone can do is ring and ring and ring, suddenly there's the faintest of clicks and there, there is Mika, Mika saying, 'Hello?' and I'm pushing the fifty-pence piece into the slot and hearing it drop with a clunk against the other coins, and finally I've got through. Finally, *finally*, we're connected.

TOM BROMLEY

Crazy Little Thing Called Love

PAN BOOKS

If music be the food of love, plug in . . .

When Will Harding is offered the job of bass player in Brighton band Double Top, he finds it all but impossible to resist. Especially as the band's photographer is the sexy, sassy and ever so slightly kooky Lauren Miles. Lauren rocks his world, and Will is soon desperate for a role in hers. There's just one complication: Rich Young. Double Top's lead singer; Lauren's boyfriend.

Well hung and well connected, Rich has slept with more women at once than Will has had in his entire life. He oozes charm, confidence and sex appeal from every pore. As Double Top's quest for a record deal continues, Will's stairway to heaven is fast becoming his road to nowhere. But then comes along a crazy little thing called love to change his world completely.

'Perfect for those long days on the beach'
B Magazine

CHRIS BINCHY

The Very Man

PAN BOOKS

After Rory has returned to Dublin to bury his mother, he decides that New York, with the flash job, fast money and high tech apartment is just not for him any more, and it's time to be home again. But where is home and who is Rory now?

His friends try to persuade him he's the same guy they said goodbye to when they finished university, but Rory knows different. Out to screw everyone and everything in Dublin, Rory's life spirals out of control. But having hit the bottom, he finds a saviour in the most unlikely of guises.

The Very Man is the carefully nuanced story of a man who feels he has nothing to lose, but discovers that his life is unravelling before him. It is, also, a brilliant portrait of contemporary Dublin.